Copyright N

All the characters and event work of fiction. Any resemblances to real persons living or dead (or any events that may resemble true stories) are purely coincidental.

First published and copyrighted by the author of this book Joseph Roy Wright in 2019. The author retains sole copyright to his or her contributions to this book. The author has asserted his moral rights.

Amazon Kindle Direct Publishing (KDP) provided layout designs and graphic elements which are copyright of Amazon.com. This book was created using the KDP creative publishing service. The book author retains sole copyright to his or her contributions to this book.

Joseph Roy Wright's
PARANORMAL
HOMICIDE
THE SKINNERS INCIDENT

Introduction:

<u>IMPORTANT NOTICE</u>
THESE NEW DOCUMENTS ARE NOT TO BE SHARED WITH ANY PERSONS OF THE BRITISH PUBLIC, BY OPENING THESE DOCUMENTS YOU AGREE TO THE FOLLOWING TERMS AND CONDITIONS:

1.
The following enclosed documents are subject to controversy in the north west of England. In this following *new* document, witness reports and stories of The Supernatural are to be strictly contained by *order* of The Great British Government. They are to be locked away and hidden inside of underground vaults below Hallington Palace, only a select few members of Parliament are allowed to view these said Documents. You and a small number *of* very important people have been pre-selected to view this said document. IF YOU MENTION **ANY OF THE EVENTS OR CONSPIRACIES** IN THIS FOLLOWING DOCUMENT TO ANY PERSONS WHO ARE NOT A PART OF THE SELECT FEW, YOU COULD BE FACED WITH A **POSSIBLE LIFE SENTENCE** IN SOLITUDE AT *ALEXANDRIA* STATION, IF NOT THAT, YOU COULD BE SENTENCED TO **DEATH** OR SUBJECT TO **LOBOTOMY**.

2.
Documents must be returned to their proper stationary vault positions once reading sessions have finished. You cannot request extra time once sessions are complete; however, you can return to sessions anytime when they are being held if further study is needed. ***IT IS IMPORTANT*** THAT YOU DO NOT MISPLACE OR FAIL *TO* RETURN ANY OF THE SAID DOCUMENTS IN THE TIME PROVIDED as this could lead to non-members of THE SELECT FEW obtaining these enclosed documents. It is of **UTMOST IMPORTANCE** that these files do not fall into the wrong hands for

reasons that will be explained in section 3 of this enclosure, failing to return files may result in the following punishments as stated at the bottom of section 1.

3.

This document holds TOP SECRET reports of Supernatural occurrences related to THE SKINNERS INCIDENT that took place approximately 16 years and 9 months ago (of this date the 21st of April 2018) in the Northern Town of Runcorn. These events will be detailed within this enclosed documentation for YOU and THE SELECT FEW to read **ONLY**. We have evidence provided that the following statements inside these enclosed documents are true and from the real people Interviewed and Interrogated during the events of the now Infamous Incident that shook residents of Northern Britain. For years people have speculated *the existence of Ghosts and Supernatural Entities*, but no concrete evidence has been provided to the public, in these documents enclosed within this envelope are the secrets to understanding and possibly controlling Extra-Terrestrial dimensions beyond this plane of existence. For these reasons alone it is of **VITAL IMPORTANCE** that these Enclosed documents **MUST NOT UNDER ANY CIRCUMSTANCES EVER LEAVE HALLINGTON PALACE.**

BY SIGNING THE DECLARATION BELOW, YOU ACCEPT THE TERMS AND CONDITIONS ABOVE:

G.cartwright

Prologue:

```
12th of August 1984:
```
Sarah White lay on top of the chaise lounge as the Psychiatrist, Peter King, sat beside her on his black leather office chair. Sarah White looked around the inside of the room from where she lay, the ceiling was painted in white, a turned off light bulb hung from the ceiling with a dark green lamp shade around it. The walls were covered in red maroon wall paper and just in front of her there was a closed window revealing the busy streets of Liverpool outside. It was raining heavily that day; rain drops were causing loud splashes against the glass. The room she was inside of was a rather small square shaped room with a pine wooden door behind Peter King. The carpet in the room was patterned in beige and brown polka dots and the Psychiatrist's desk stood nearby behind him with a computer on top of it next to a bunch of files.

'Sarah, tell me more about the bad man with the blackened eyes...' Peter King smiled, patronizingly at Sarah White. Sarah was just six years old at the time wearing a plain bright green sweater and pink tracksuit bottoms with white sneakers. Her hair was curly and dark; it contrasted nicely against her pale, white face. Peter King however was middle aged with blonde hair that was greying at the sides. He wore a dark green striped suit and a pair of reading glasses. His smile was wide and wrinkles would appear around the corners of his mouth every time he made that expression.

'He comes at night... mostly.' Sarah White answered.

'Every time I try to go to sleep at night he'll show. Mummy says that I'm just imagining these things, that I've been watching too many scary movies, but... I don't watch naughty things like that...' Sarah whimpered. Peter sighed silently in his head but managed to hide it through his forced smile. *Another kid with a wild imagination, this is going to be a pain...* Peter King thought.

'Well, sometimes we all fear the dark sweetie, I've watched plenty of scary movies and we all imagine strange monsters before bedtime, but what you've got to remember is that none of those monsters are real, Sarah. All you have to do is shout "stay away!" and they will go home and leave you alone.' Peter King's smile widened. Peter's attempt at comforting her fell flat as Sarah's worried face turned into a look of frustration.

'I tried that Pete, but The Black-eyed Man, he hurt me!' Sarah cried as she pulled up the right sleeve of her green sweater revealing several large scars on her small delicate forearm. Peter was shocked; his wide comforting smile slumped down into a frown of concern. He thought Sarah was a victim of abuse.

'Sarah, tell me now... who did this to you?' Peter's patronizing tone vanished, now he was speaking to her more like a Detective rather than a Children's Psychiatrist.

'I told you Pete, it was the man with the black eyes...' Sarah's cries grew louder. Peter was about to approach her, to give her some comfort, but before he could do so, something strange caught his attention. Peter heard a scratching sound coming from the window to his right. He looked over to the window and saw nothing, but scratch marks were beginning to form on the outside of the window.

'He's watching us, from outside!' Sarah pointed at the window, but Peter couldn't see anyone standing outside, then a loud thud hit the window, cracking it slightly. Peter jumped back in his seat in shock.

'Make him stop, make him stop!' Sarah began to shake her head violently; her long dark hair shook around as she did this. Peter was dumbfounded; in all his years, he had never witnessed something so bizarre. So, he just sat there, too afraid to scream, too afraid to move. Eventually the window smashed open and the once ambient sounds

of street life and heavy rain exploded into the room with a loud gust of wind. Sarah then sat up straight on the chaise lounge and screamed 'Stay away!' And soon enough the chaos subdued, the wind settled and Peter & Sarah were left alone in the small empty room.
'I guess your advice was right, Pete...' Sarah smiled at him through her tears. Peter King, still shaking and covered in sweat from what had just happened turned around in his chair to face her. He looked at her then chuckled nervously.

Shortly after, Peter King led Sarah White outside of the room and into the building's hallway. Her father, Cody White, was sitting on a chair next to other clients outside The Psychiatrist Office. The wallpaper outside of Peter King's office was olive in colour and there was a long row of other doors leading into different office rooms along the endless looking hallway. The floor was made of marble and although it was black, the glossy texture shined slightly against the ceiling's lights. Cody stood up abruptly with a look of shock on his face.
'What happened, peter?' Cody asked Peter King. Sarah White bowed her head down and walked over to her father, she wrapped her small arms around his legs as she stood. Cody looked down and stroked his daughter's hair as Peter King began to speak.
'Your daughter... I can't help her.' Peter King sighed.
'What do you mean, you can't help her?' Cody growled. The other clients sitting behind him gave Cody a weird look, but he didn't care to notice.
'What your daughter has is something... I have never seen before, she is mentally sound my friend. But something else is haunting her.' Peter King explained.
'What- What's haunting her?' Cody asked half puzzled, half annoyed.
'See for yourself...' Peter King said as he opened the door to his office behind him.

Once Cody, Sarah and Peter were inside, Cody's jaw dropped as he saw the smashed window inside of the office room. Peter frowned once he saw Cody's reaction.

'As I was explaining to your daughter here, that her *Monster* does not exist, something strange happened... She told me The Black-eyed Man was there.' Peter pointed at the broken window.

'She said; he was trying to get in from the outside. Now I have never been a believer of the Supernatural, Mister White. But after what I have witnessed today, I now know that something... Sinister is watching your daughter.' Peter King said with concern in his voice.

'Get lost!' Cody yelled, his Daughter cried as he shouted, he instantly regretted it, but he couldn't help it. This was the third time a Psychiatrist had said something "Supernatural" was haunting his daughter and now he finally lost his patience and snapped.

'Look what you've made me do; your idiotic claims have disturbed my daughter. I thought Psychiatrists were supposed to help the mentally ill, not harm them!' Cody yelled.

'I'm sorry, Mister White... but, your daughter seriously needs to see a Priest or... something...' Peter king tried to persuade him, but Cody refused to see the truth.

'No, I won't let you poison my daughter's mind anymore... come on sweetie, we're leaving!' Cody snarled as he snatched his daughter's hand and pulled her along with him as he stormed off towards the exit with her struggling to keep up behind. Just before Sarah was dragged out of the building by her father, she looked behind her and noticed Peter King still standing there, his shoulders slumped forward in defeat, he smiled weakly with sadness in his eyes, as she and her father approached the exit.

Part 1
The Disappearance of Kyle Cross

Chapter 1:
Your Son is Missing

August 12th, 2001:

Erin Cross was in the living room alone, she lay on the brown sofa watching her favourite TV show, Secrets of Cornwall. It was a soap opera about the town of Cornwall where everyone in town had a dark secret, sometimes there would be a murder mystery, other times there was an affair going on, just typical made for TV drama scenarios. Although she loved this show, her teenage son, Kyle Cross, despised the show, he thought it was cliché and dumb. In a way the forty two year old was glad that her eighteen year old son was out partying that night, she was beyond sick of his hormonal mood swings and the loud pop music he played in his bedroom. As she lay down on her sofa watching the TV she looked over to the clock on top of the fireplace and noticed that the time was 1:00am, usually her son would have at least given her a call to say that he was alright but so far, he had not called once. A small amount of concern clouded over her and the character's voices on the TV began to fade from her mind as she began to worry about her son. Maybe he was just busy having a good time she thought, maybe he's lost his phone but other than that he's ok she thought. But then concern took over her, what if he's been mugged, has he blacked out from drinking too much? Maybe he's been spiked, or even stabbed! She picked up her phone and punched in Kyle's numbers with her finger. The phone rang. No one picked up. She tried again. No one picked up. She breathed deeply then lay her phone down.

'I'm sure he's alright, his friends will look after him.' she reassured herself. The stress had caused her to sweat so she sat up and removed her green dressing gown revealing her rather slim yet slightly wrinkled body; she wore a pink tank top underneath. For *her* age she still had her looks, although slightly aged, she had a pretty face and only a few grey hairs inside her rather short red hair. Precise to say, if you saw Erin Cross, you'd think she was only thirty five.

Two hours passed and still, Kyle Cross had not called, by this point she had turned off the TV and wandered into the kitchen. She had pulled up a chair beside the kitchen counter and poured herself a glass of red wine to calm her nerves, it was now 3:00am and she could see from just outside her kitchen window that the sun outside was beginning to rise. She had spent the whole night trying to call her son, but he wouldn't pick up, she even tried calling her divorced husband who was a taxi driver that worked near The Runcorn Old Town where Kyle was drinking that night. She asked him if he had seen Kyle around town and unfortunately, he replied with a worried sounding "No..." She only had two more options left; she could call his friend that was out that night, Joshua Riley. Or call the Police and tell them her son was missing. But of course, she remembered on Secrets of Cornwall that you can't file a Missing Person Report until said person has been missing for at least 24 hours and besides, Kyle was eighteen years old, he wasn't a "missing child" So, in reality, Erin only had one choice. She picked up her phone from the kitchen counter (that was placed right next to the half empty bottle of wine she had been drinking from) and called Josh Riley. The phone rang several times before he answered, when he picked up a loud sound of drunken yells and distorted pop music blasted through the speakers.
'Hello!' Josh drunkenly shouted down the phone to her, his voice too loud for comfort.
'Josh... where is Kyle!?' She yelled into her phone.
'Kyle he... we left him on the dancefloor, inside The Dungeons nightclub, last time we saw him he was grinding up against some fit

bird!' Josh laughed down the phone, Erin was annoyed but she realized that he didn't understand that Kyle hadn't called.
'Where are you now, can you go inside the nightclub? He hasn't called.' She replied.
'Ok... I'll go look for him; we're in the beer garden so he shouldn't be too far. I'll call you back, yeah?' Josh said, this time his tone had changed and there was concern in his voice.
'Thanks...' Erin said as she hung up. Before she lay her phone down on the kitchen counter, she checked out the time on her phone, it was 3:20am. *The Dungeons will close soon and maybe then, Kyle will call.* She thought as she lay her phone down.

After several minutes which felt more like hours to her, the phone rang, she picked it up immediately. It was Josh.
'Erin... I can't find him anywhere; we've been looking all over The Old Town for him... but he's nowhere to be seen. We've looked in all the bars and restaurants around the area too, even asked a few strangers if they had seen him, but most were too drunk to respond and the others said they hadn't seen him.' Josh breathed heavily, like he had been running.
'Josh... what are you saying?' Erin held her breath waiting for a reply.
'... I'm sorry Erin, but I think... your son is missing...' Josh near enough cried over the phone as he said that. Erin just hung up right there and then and dropped her phone from her ear and it fell on to the ground. She then bowed her head into her hands.
'Oh God, Kyle... where are you?'

Chapter 2:
The Interview

```
11:30am, Saturday,
The 13th of August 2001.
1 day after Kyle's disappearance.
```

Lindsay Evans sat outside waiting for her bus to arrive near Castlefields; she had been waiting at the bus stop for what felt like hours. Lindsay was a fairly young girl, she was eighteen years old and she had long blonde hair that was straightened nicely and she wore a full mask of makeup. Her lips were coated in glossy red lip stick and she wore a clean pair of black skinny jeans and a black leather jacket over her white buttoned up shirt, she wore black high heels too. Normally she would never dress this smart but today she had a very important job interview at the McRoonies fast food restaurant near The Runcorn Shopping City. She knew the job sucked, but her mother was in debt, so she needed the job. It was either this or become homeless, so now here she was, waiting for the bus, dressed up like a super model and on her way to work at a shitty fast food restaurant, well only if she passed the interview of course, but she was naive enough to think her CV was strong enough to get the job. As she sat there at the bus stop, checking the roads to see if there was a bus approaching. She suddenly felt hot wearing her leather jacket due to the unusually hot weather. The sun was shining immensely that day and there were very few clouds in the sky, the time was 11:30am and her interview was at 12:20pm. She removed her leather jacket shortly after as she didn't want to sweat and smell bad for her interview. After she removed her jacket, she heard someone whistle, she looked over and was disgusted to see a man dressed in tracksuit bottoms and a sports hoodie with a black cap on smiling at her. When she looked at him, he pouted his lips and winked, then he laughed. He looked dirty and his voice, it was as just filthy as his appearance. She looked away in the hopes that he wouldn't pursue her any further, but he stood there for a couple of uncomfortable seconds before walking off in the opposite direction. Lindsay let out a sigh of relief once he was out of sight.

'Fucking asshole...' She said to herself. Suddenly her phone rang, she groaned then searched for it frantically in her hand bag, eventually see found it, but as she picked it up, it slipped out of her hand and fell onto the pavement, she groaned again then leant over to pick it up.

'Hello!' She snarled down the phone out of annoyance.

'Lindsay... it's Erin Cross, Kyle's mum. Have you seen Kyle around lately? He's gone missing.' Erin sniffed on the other end, like she had been crying.

'Err... no, last time I saw him was last week. What happened to him? Where has he gone?' Lindsay asked with concern in her voice.

'I'm... I don't know!' Erin began to whimper through the phone, it saddened Lindsay.

'Look I'm sorry. I haven't seen him, but...' Lindsay paused as she heard a vehicle approaching the bus stop, as it got closer she could see that it was her bus.

'I'm sorry, I've got to go now, I'll call you later!'

Lindsay had to hang up and hail her bus, as it stopped the door slid open, then she entered the bus, paid the bus driver and sat down at the back with her handbag. She leant her head against the window and felt the vibrations of the moving bus as it travelled through Castlefields towards The Runcorn Shopping City.

She got off near the Library and walked through the busy shopping city until she exited the building and reached Tyrant Park, from there she took a right and walked through the car park, crossed the busy road then walked up the stair well, she then took another right under the busway bridge and just in front of her she seen the giant red M sign for McRoonies. She sighed to herself again as she really didn't want to work at such a shitty fast food "restaurant" but she had no choice, so she walked over to the building. As she approached the entrance, the automatic doors slid open and a loud collection of busy staff members ordering each other around, children crying and un-fit parents shouting at said children came into ear shot, there was a busy line full of impatient customers leading up to the front counter. Lindsay cut passed the line and caught the attention of one of the not so busy staff members.

'Hey!' She called over to him. The boy turned and looked at her.

'Wait your turn!' He pointed at the line.

'No, I'm Lindsay Evans. I'm here for the Job Interview...'

'Oh... sorry about telling you off there, come around the back, I'll let you in.' the boy walked over to the doors near the toilets. Lindsay walked over to the area where he was, and then he led her through the busy kitchen. The Staff were too busy to stop and say hi. He led her to the Manager's Office; she opened the door and was greeted by a rather large man who appeared to be in his late thirties. He sat behind a computer desk and in front of her there was a plastic chair.

'Sit down...' The Manager asked her, pointing at the chair in front of his desk. Lindsay closed the door behind her, as it closed the sounds of busy staff members faded out to silence, now she sat in a silent room with the Manager of McRoonies. The room's silence made her feel uncomfortable in his presence. The Manager had a bald head and a stern look in his eyes, Lindsay was a fairly confident girl, but this man freaked her out slightly.

'Let's have a read of your CV then...' He asked rather casually. Lindsay just nodded then she opened her handbag and handed her qualifications over to him, he looked through them. He found her qualifications to be lacking, she had never been to college, all of her GCSEs were mostly C and she had no experience at all when it came to kitchen work. He was about to send her away, but then he looked at her again. She sat there all stiff and uncomfortable, but he couldn't help but notice how clear her blue eyes were, her figure was slim and she had a pretty face to go with it. Lindsay could feel the creep's eyes on her, she was frozen in fear. She knew it was incredibly unlikely that the Manager was actually going to hurt her, but her fears got the better of her. The Manager chuckled breaking the silence and Lindsay awkwardly chuckled unsure whether or not that was a good move. 'So, tell me... what made you want to work here?' The Manager asked her.

'Oh, I've always had an interest for kitchen work, I like to cook at home and I'm real polite to people... my father used to own a shop and sometimes I would help out, serving customers and stocking shelves.' Lindsay forced a smile. The Manager thought it was cute. He knew she was lying and he also knew she would be terrible at this job, he should have sent her away right there and then but he took a liking to this girl, he knew she was only eighteen but he didn't care. 'Well then... if you're really interested in working here, I'll give you a shot. Come back tomorrow at 7:30 and we'll sort you out a uniform and see how well you do.' The Manager finished, he then held his hand out to shake Lindsay's hand, she almost hesitated but she shook it and forced another smile. She then got up and exited the Manager's Office.

Chapter 3:
Guilty Conscience

```
2:43 am, Sunday,
The 14th of August 2001.
2 days since Kyle's disappearance.
```

The next night after Kyle's disappearance, Josh Riley sat on his bed staring outside of his window. He could see The Silver Jubilee Bridge and the rest of the town that was lit up from there. He lived in The Old Town near The Docks and he lived on the top floor of one of those tall apartment buildings. He was only twenty years old, but he had scored it lucky as he had won £28,000 on a scratch card a couple of years ago when he was eighteen. He moved out of his parents' house two years ago when he had the money to move out. He was a Bachelor, but he had the looks to pull a girl, he just chose not to since he preferred being single. Last night he went out with Kyle Cross and they were having a blast, he knew Kyle through college and although he was a little younger than him, they were pretty close and had a lot in common. That night he, Kyle and two other friends, Steven and Jordan were all out drinking. They all started off in The Kings Bar which was the go to place on a night out in Runcorn. After that bar closed, they all went to the nearest pizza place, Mikes Kebabs, after that they went to the main attraction, The Dungeons night club. Everybody went there after The Kings Bar closed and when they all got there Kyle ended up dancing with this down right gorgeous looking girl. She wore a red silky dress that sparkled against the strobe lights and she had long dark hair with brown eyes that any man would fall in love with. Josh and his friends decided to leave him to it and go to the beer garden, that's when Kyle's mother called. Josh went back in to look for him, but he was gone. The three of them left The Dungeons nightclub and searched all over The Old Town for Kyle, but he was nowhere to be found.

Josh replayed the night over and over again in his head, he hated himself for just leaving Kyle in there, he imagined what would have happened if he had just stayed with him all night, Kyle would have gone home and he would still be around but now, nearly 23 hours later, he's still missing. Kyle's mother called Josh a few hours ago to explain that Police were going to be visiting her house; she said that they wanted a description of Kyle and they also wanted to speak to Josh about the night Kyle disappeared. She told Josh that he had to come over to her house at 5:00am. She also told him that Steven and Jordan were coming too as the Police wanted to talk to all of the people that were with him that night. Josh didn't argue, he wanted to help the Police and solve this mystery just as much as Erin Cross. He told her that he would be there and she thanked him. Josh thought about what he was going to say to the Police, he didn't want to slip up and make himself look guilty or mislead them in anyway. He was also terrified that they might put him in custody or even blame him for Kyle's disappearance, but even if they did point the finger at him, he would accept the punishment. If it meant finding Kyle he'd do anything they told him to. His alarm clock rang, awakening him from his deep thoughts. He sat up and turned the alarm off, and then he dressed up in a green jumper and blue jeans. On the way out, he noticed his hair was sticking up at the back, so he slicked it back with a wet comb and headed out the door and off to Erin's house in a hurry.

Chapter 4:
Missing Person Report

```
3:00am, Sunday,
14th of August 2001.
2 days since Kyle's disappearance.
```

Sarah White lay asleep on her bed, the curtains were closed and the room was dark. She slept alone on the queen sized bed, she kept her windows open at night, so the whistling of owls and birds could be heard from outside. Suddenly her phone buzzed with a melody and the screen glowed, awakening her. She opened her eyes slowly and the brightness from the screen stung her eyes.

'Who the fuck is calling me now?' She groaned as she rolled over and picked up her phone from the drawer next to her bed and answered. 'Hello...' She yawned.

'White, it's me, your Chief Officer, Mark Spencer. You were supposed to start today at 2:00am! Somebody has gone missing and we need you to question their family members and friends. I'll tell you more about it when you reach the Police Station. We told them you'll be there by 5:00am and its 3:00am right now, so I suggest you get down here ASAP!' Spencer ordered down the phone. Sarah panicked, she forgot to set the alarm, or perhaps her phone had forgotten to ring, or maybe she just overslept, whatever the case, The Chief of Police was pissed.

'Yes sir, I'll head over now.' Sarah agreed.

'Excellent Miss White, see you there. We have a new recruit joining us tonight; you're going to have to teach him the ropes. But I'll introduce him to you once you get here, understood?' Chief Spencer replied.

'Yes sir, I understand completely. Anything else I should know?'

'Yes... but I'll tell you more about it when you get here, over and out.'

The Chief then hung up. Sarah climbed out of bed and switched on the bedroom light, her bedroom was small, the bed it's self near enough took up the whole space of the room and at the right side of her bed there was a window and a drawer. On her left there was a wardrobe where she kept her Police uniform and next to that was the door leaving the room. She only had enough room left to stand up, get dressed and leave. Once outside of her bedroom, there was a small living room connected to the kitchen and a bathroom nearby. She lived in a dirt cheap apartment and although she could've afforded a better place, she lived here by choice since the rent was so cheap. She did however keep the place spotless and the furniture was expensive. She walked into the bathroom and saw herself in her underwear; she looked rough and covered in sweat from the heat. She got a quick shower then brushed her teeth and walked back into her bedroom to put on her Police uniform. Now she was all fresh and ready for work, by now it was 3:10am so she didn't have time to make herself a quick cup of tea or a round of toast, so she headed out the door in a hurry. As she walked down the stairs, a rather young looking dark haired man dressed in a green jumper and blue jeans ran right passed her in a hurry nearly knocking her over. He already ran out of sight before she could tell him to "Watch it!" So, she just groaned and continued to walk down the stairs. She exited the apartment building where she lived and got inside her red car, she turned the ignition on and the engine started.

She drove passed The Docks and took a right turn driving towards The Kings Bar, from there she waited until the road was clear and then she drove towards the Police Station near The Runcorn Shopping City. By the time she arrived it was nearly 3:25am so she parked her car frantically, exiting the vehicle and entering the station. Inside, The Chief of Police, Mark Spencer, waited for her with his arms crossed. A new recruit stood idly by with an awkward smile on his face.

'About time you got here, Miss White...' The Chief moaned. His bald head shined against the ceiling's lights.

'Sorry Sir, there was traffic.' Sarah lied.

'Whatever the case... it doesn't matter now. This here is Michael Carr; he'll be your new partner. Now we've had a report of two missing people, they disappeared last night around 3:00am near The Old Town. A teenager named Kyle Cross and the other is a female named Tiffany Wright, the girl has brown hair and was last seen in a red dress, while the boy was dressed in a polo shirt and he also has brown hair. We've told the mother of Kyle Cross that two Police Officers will be visiting her house at 5:00am, don't worry about Tiffany's family, I've got Inspector Miranda Carlton to send out another patrol to talk to her family at that house. Anyway, it will be 5:00am soon, so you two better get going. Kyle's Mother lives in Stenhills, so you better hurry. I'll send you the address through the Police Radio. Sarah lead Michael to your Police cruiser, you're driving.' Chief Spencer ordered her as he threw her the keys and she caught them.

'Yes sir!' Sarah White nodded before leaving the Police Station with Michael Carr.

Chapter 5:
Clues

Erin Cross sat in her living room with Steve and Jordan. Jordan was twenty one years old, the oldest in Kyle's group and he had a ginger goatee and longish hair that reached his shoulders. He wore a black t-shirt with a rock band named The Roland printed on it. Steve was the same age as Kyle, eighteen years old. He was a bit of a Chav, he had a number two haircut and he wore a checkered baseball cap with a Liverpool football shirt. They both sat on the sofa next to her as they waited for the Police and Josh to come in. She served them each a cup of tea, they all drank together and conversed.

'We're so sorry about losing Kyle, Erin.' Steve said in a rather strong scouse accent.

'Hey it's alright... it wasn't your fault love.' Erin smiled weakly.

'Ah cheers, he's a sound lad your son. We've been through a lot together and he always comes out just fine. I'm sure he'll be ok.' Steve reassured her.

'I hope so kid...' Erin took a deep breath and then there was silence. The only audible sound in the room came from the clock that kept ticking on top of the fire place next to a school picture of her son, she looked at the photo and his smile and wide eyes reminded her of the times she had spent with him as a child, she remembered holding him in her arms for the very first time, the way he stopped crying and stared into her eyes with pure love when he was just a baby. Tears began to form in her eyes and as they fell, she could feel the cold drips slide down her cheeks, Jordan put his hand on her shoulder for comfort. A loud knock on the door broke the silence and everyone looked over, Erin wiped the tears from her eyes and approached the front door. She then pulled the handle down and pulled the door open, Josh Riley stood outside.

'Everything ok?' He asked her.

'Yes Josh, come on in, the Police aren't here yet.' Erin said as she waved him on in. Josh entered Erin's house and wiped his shoes against the mat inside before walking into the living room, Erin closed the door behind her, entering behind Josh. He sat down on a sofa opposite to the one that Jordan and Steve were sitting on; Erin sat in the same spot between Steve and Jordan.

They mostly sat in silence as they waited for the cops to show up. They waited for what must have been twenty minutes or so before they heard a vehicle drive towards the house from outside with a rapid collection of blue flashes. The vehicle then stopped outside her house and as they heard the engine cut, the flash lights shut off and then the Police car outside made a clicking noise before the door opened and two Police Officers emerged from the vehicle, one male, the other female. Erin approached the front door and opened it before they could knock, she was greeted by the female Officer who had her long black hair tied up into a pony tail, she had a fairly young pretty face, her uniform looked professional and clean. Behind her stood a younger looking man who must've been about 19-20 years old. He had black hair and a couple of small zits on his face, Erin thought he looked a little too young to be a Police Man.

'I'm Officer White and this is Officer Carr, we're here to ask you a few questions regarding the disappearance of your son, Kyle Cross. Are Steven, Jordan and Joshua here Ma'am?' Officer White asked.

'Yes, they're in the back. Come right in Officers.' Erin replied.

'Thank you, Ma'am.' Officer White nodded her head at Erin as she and Officer Carr entered the house. They walked into the living room and saw the three young lads sitting around on sofas; they all looked over to her in unison with a bit of fear in their eyes.

'Don't worry lads; we're only here to ask you a few questions.' Officer

Carr announced. Erin Cross soon sat down next to Steven and Jordan again. Officer White sat down beside Josh and Officer Carr stood still with his hands held in front of him near the fire place watching them.
'First of all, we're going to need a description, what does Kyle look like, what was he wearing the night he went missing?' Officer White asked them all.
'My son, he's only eighteen years old. He has short brown hair and blue eyes; he's slim and quite short. He has a thin long nose and small lips.' Erin Cross explained. Officer White looked over to Carr.
'You writing this down?' She asked him.
'Oh right, yes of course.' Officer Carr picked up his note pad and started writing down Kyle's features. After that, White then looked back at Erin Cross.
'That's very good Miss Cross, what was he wearing the night he disappeared?' Officer White asked.
'Kyle? He was wearing... I... I can't remember!' Erin gasped.
'It's ok, boys can any of you remember?' She asked the lads, they all looked unsure.
'Come on guys, anything could be helpful to The Investigation.' Officer White pleaded.
'Err... I remember he wore a new shirt that night, a black polo shirt with purple rings around the collar.' Jordan finally spoke. Officer White looked behind her to see if Carr was writing this down, he was and she turned back to face Jordan.
'Can you remember anything else?' She asked him.
'Yes he wore his old jacket, a black bomber jacket with silver zips on it... other than that, I can't remember, I wasn't really looking at his downstairs.' Jordan explained, Steve chuckled slightly. It was a serious moment but Jordan saying, "I wasn't really looking at his downstairs" was admittedly a weird choice of words, nobody blamed Steve for chuckling.

'Hmm... thanks for the information, Jordan.' Even White found it difficult not to smirk.

'But seriously lads, is there anything else you can remember?' Officer White asked again. There was a short silence.

'I'm afraid that's all we can remember, Officer.' Erin sighed.

'That's ok, thank you all for your co-operation. The information you have given will aid us greatly in the search for Kyle Cross... just before I go though, I'd just like to ask one more question. Did any of you see a young woman with brown hair and brown eyes wearing a red dress the night Kyle went missing?' Officer White asked the group.

'Yes, the girl Kyle was with wore a red dress and she had brown hair!' Josh gasped rather loudly.

'Ok relax, what can you tell us about the girl?' Officer White asked Josh.

'She was all over Kyle, they were kissing and cuddling up to each other in The Dungeons nightclub on the dancefloor, so we all went into the beer garden to give him some time alone with her. But when we came back, he was gone, I don't know what happened, but I bet he went with her. Do you know where she is?!' Josh asked with excitement.

'I'm afraid not, she's missing too, Josh. But now that we know that they were together. We'll have a better chance at finding them both...' Officer White said as she got to her feet.

'Thank you all for your co-operation, we'll show ourselves out now.' Officer White announced as she and Officer Carr approached the house's exit. Once outside, Erin Cross closed the door behind them and the two Police Officers got inside their car.

'What do you think, White?' Officer Carr asked.
'You write down all the clues?' Officer White asked.

'Yes, everything is all on this note pad. Kyle has brown hair, blue eyes, a thin nose and he's pretty short with small lips. He was wearing a black bomber jacket with silver zips and a black polo shirt with purple rings around the collar. Most importantly he was seen with Tiffany Wright, the girl in the red dress the night of the disappearance.' Officer Carr explained.

'That's good Michael... I think Kyle and Tiffany met in The Old Town last night and they ran off somewhere together. Question is, where did they run off to and why haven't they come home or at least gotten in contact with their parents?' Officer White asked.

'I think the next place we should go to is The Dungeons nightclub, Josh said that's where they were last seen. Perhaps a bartender may have seen them exit the bar.' Michael replied.

'I think you're right, Michael. The nightclub should still be open by now, they close it off to the public by 5:00am, but the staff will still be cleaning up the mess that the drunks leave behind. We better hurry!' Officer White said as she started the car's engine and drove towards The Old Town.

Chapter 6:
The Woman in The Red Dress

Officer Carr and Officer White arrived outside of The Dungeons nightclub at 5:35am in their Police cruiser. They killed the engine as they approached the building's entrance and the car stopped immediately, then they opened the car's doors and proceeded to enter the now empty nightclub. The doormen outside let them in without any hassle. Inside the nightclub, no music played and all the regular lights were turned on without the flashing strobe lights so the bar staff could see what they were cleaning. some were wiping the tables, others were brushing the floor, a couple of them stopped and stared at the two Police Officers as they approached the bar counter to question one of the staff members. Officer White and Carr approached a young woman with blonde hair who was busy cleaning out some wine glasses with a white cloth; she stopped and stared at them with a worried smile on her face as the two Officers walked over to her.
'Hello there, how may I help you two?' The Barmaid asked them.
'We're investigating a Missing Person Report, a man and a woman went missing last night... they were last seen in this nightclub, the woman was seen wearing a red dress the night of the disappearance, she also has brown hair and brown eyes. The man however was seen wearing a black bomber jacket with silver zips and a black polo shirt with purple rings around the collar. He also has short brown hair and blue eyes; he's also known to be pretty short.' Officer White explained to the Barmaid.
'Oh yes... that would be Kyle Cross, the boy of course. He was seen in here last night with a woman in a red dress with brown hair, they were dancing on the dancefloor behind you for what must have been ten minutes or so before they kissed each other and headed back

outside towards the exit. But that was the last I saw the two of them. You're better off asking one of the doormen outside, you'll meet Harry outside, he's the bouncer with the circle beard. He was on last night, so he'll know where they went.' The Barmaid smiled.

'Thank you for the help, Miss...?'

'Kimberly Campbell.' The Barmaid finished Officer White's sentence.

'Alright, thanks Kimberly we'll go see that bouncer. But before we go, I'd just like to ask you one more question...' Officer White said.

'Shoot!' Kimberly smiled.

'How do you know Kyle Cross if he's just a customer here?' Officer White asked.

'Oh Kyle... we've had to deal with him on a number of occasions; he's a bit of a... *sex pest* when he gets drunk you see. Always putting his hands where they shouldn't be, starting fights with other guys over girls, stuff like that... it's always the men who start the trouble isn't it?' Kimberly winked at Officer White.

'Hey don't you think you're being a little sexist there?' Officer Carr butted in, anger grew in his voice.

'Michael... oh dearly me I didn't recognize you in all that uniform... I would just love to tell your partner here how many times we've had to kick you out due to your *bad behavior*.' Kimberley smirked at Officer Carr; Officer White gave him a funny look. Carr looked away in embarrassment.

'Anyway as I was saying...' Kimberly continued.

'We've had to deal with Kyle Cross on a number of occasions because he always comes in here looking for a hook up, but nine times out of ten he's too drunk to impress any of the ladies. I guess last night he finally got lucky and left with the woman in the red dress. We only know his name because his friends are usually sober enough to tell us who he is. His friends are actually alright, and you should get in contact with them. Their names are Josh Riley, Jordan Cress and Steve

Matthews. I actually dated Josh once; I've got his mobile number if you're interested?' Kimberly asked.

'No, that's fine thank you, we've already questioned his friends. Again, thank you for the information; it could be vital to our investigation. We'll talk to Harry on our way out.' Officer White nodded at Kimberly before leaving the building with Michael Carr. Outside they met the bouncer with the circle beard; he greeted the two Officers with a smile.

'What's happening?' He asked them.

'Harry, I presume?' Officer White asked.

'Yeah that's me, how may I help you Officers?' He asked.

'We are looking for two people, a woman in a red dress and the infamous Kyle Cross. We've been told that you were here last night on guard. Can you remember where they went?' Officer Carr asked.

'Yes Officer, Kyle is always coming here, but the girl he was with... I've never seen her before, she must be new in town or she's just turned eighteen. They walked off together; they took a right from here. I heard the girl say, that she was going to take him somewhere *private*... my best guess, they were probably going to the canal near The Binder Art Gallery.' Harry explained.

'Ok thanks for the information, we'll see you later.' Officer Carr thanked the bouncer as they shook hands. Officer White and Officer Carr then walked down the nightclub's stairs and entered their Police car; Michael sat in the driver's seat.

'Not much to go on...' Sarah sighed.

'Yeah I know right, all we know now is that Kyle and Tiffany were last seen leaving the nightclub together.' Michael sighed too.

'We better get going, tell Chief Spencer what we know, I'm sure the other patrol has some interesting clues we could go on.' Sarah suggested.

'Sounds like a good idea...' Michael said as he turned the ignition on and began to drive the car through town.

On the ride, Sarah White noticed something strange outside of the car window. Outside there stood a woman in a red dress watching them from a far on top of the canal bridge next to The Binder Art Gallery.
'Stop the car!' Sarah yelled abruptly. Michael braked and the car skidded harshly making a loud screeching sound.
'What!' He yelled in a panic.
'Look!' Sarah pointed at the woman in the red dress on top of the canal bridge. Michael Carr looked over to where Sarah was pointing, but he couldn't see a thing.
'What...? I don't see anything.' Michael gave her a weird look.
'Can't you see her? There she is, Tiffany Wright! The woman in the red dress...' Sarah explained.
'No... I don't see her...' Michael told her. At first Sarah had no idea why her partner couldn't see the woman. But on closer inspection she soon realized that Tiffany's eyes were completely black, just like the man nobody else could see when she was a child. Tiffany Wright was now watching Sarah from the canal bridge, invisible to the rest of mankind.
'She's gone now, but follow me I seen her walk passed us.' Sarah lied, Michael bought it. The two Police Officers exited the car and Sarah led Michael towards the canal bridge, before they could walk up the spiral stairs, Tiffany Wright jumped off the bridge and into the canal's water creating a huge splash.
'What the fuck!' Michael jumped back in fright. He saw the splash but not the woman, Sarah smirked. Tiffany Wright suddenly emerged from the water and she began to swim downstream, Sarah seen this, but all Michael could see were ripples forming in the water where Tiffany swam. Sarah followed Tiffany along the canal's walkway and Michael followed behind Sarah out of confusion. Eventually Tiffany

stopped swimming; she turned around and faced Sarah before diving into the water below her. Sarah realized that Tiffany was trying to tell her something. Sarah held her breath and began to climb into the canal below her.

'Sarah, get out of there. The water is filthy!' Officer Carr yelled at her. Sarah just ignored him as she searched the ground underneath the water where Tiffany dived, soon enough Sarah felt something fleshly underneath the surface. She lifted the creature up from off the ground and onto the canal's walkway, both Michael and Sarah gasped when they saw what it was. It was a dead woman in a red dress, with brown hair and brown eyes; it was the dead body of Tiffany Wright.

Chapter 7:
The Accident

At 11:48am a woman drove her car down Runcorn's heath road, with her current boyfriend, Jacob Kennedy. She was a fairly young woman with short brunette hair and blue eyes, she was gorgeous. But unfortunately, her boyfriend was not the admiring type; he made her feel worthless as he always disrespected her. Nobody knew why Jessica put up with him, he was the worst fit imaginable, he was on the dole, poor and at the age of twenty five he still lived with his parents. Jessica however, she was rather successful, she had a nice car, a four seater that was an automatic and although she also lived with her parents, she was saving up for a new apartment and she was currently working a steady job and all at the age of twenty one too. Jacob sat back in his seat beside her without his seat belt on; he wiped his hands against his grey sweat pants after eating a McRoonies Ham Burger. He then threw the wrapper it came in out of Jessica's car window.

'Jacob!' She snapped at him.

'What bitch?' He grinned, showing his crooked teeth.

'Don't throw that out there...' She mumbled.

'Who cares, nobodies around...' He winked.

'Yeah, but what if a Copper was about? They might fine us, you tit!' She growled.

'Don't call me an idiot, Jessica...' Jacob stared at her, menacingly.

Although Jacob Kennedy was poor (and on the dole) he worked out every day, and in all honesty, Jessica only got with him solely based on his good looks. He was a "tough guy" always acting hard and he never took shit from anyone. His attitude intrigued her at first, but as time went on, the more abusive he got. He never hit Jessica or anything like that, but he would often threaten her from time to time.

She had enough, enough of his bullshit, of him treating her like dirt. She had tolerated his presence for far too long, but she also feared to speak up herself. He scared her, but she didn't care anymore, this shit had to stop. So, she held her breath.

'Oh fuck off, Jay' she let her anger out and immediately regretted it, as Jacob sat there in silence with fury rising in his face.

'Excuse me?' He growled, slamming his fist against the car's dashboard.

'I'm... getting sick of your shit, Jacob. You're a fucking loser, I only got with you because you were fit, but underneath all that muscle... you ain't nothing but a fucking loser, a worthless Yob... a waste of space...' She bit her bottom lip in fear of what he might say or do next. Jacob just laughed. His laughter sent chills down her spine, the cheek of it, she was angry and he was laughing like it was just some kind of joke. Jessica snarled as she revved the engine higher, the vehicle began to speed down the road and Jacob's laughter soon faded as he realized how fast they were going.

'Hey stop, we're going too fast!' He demanded, a look of panic on his face, sweat falling from his forehead.

'You want me to stop, Jacob! Now you're scared ain't yer? How about this... I'll just keep going faster then, huh?' She grinned as she stepped down on the accelerator harder.

'Look I'm sorry, Jessica! Stop already, we're nearing the roundabout, we're going to crash for fucks sake!' He screamed at her, squirming back into his seat and covering his face with his hands like a scared child. She thought it was funny at first, but then as she tried to slow down, her brakes locked. The vehicle kept speeding down the road and the brakes only made her steering loose. She struggled to keep her vehicle straight as it drifted, uncontrollably, onto the opposite side of the road. A large truck sped up the road on the opposite side as her vehicle approached that side of the road. The truck driver braked harshly but it was no use. Before Jacob and Jessica could even react, they crashed straight into the truck's front bumper and the windshield's glass on Jessica's car smashed open as Jacob flew outside of the window, blood splattered from his head as it exploded against the truck's grill. His now dead body fell back inside of Jessica's car and it lay directly on top of her, luckily she wore her seatbelt so she did not suffer the same fate as Jacob. Jacob's blood covered the entirety of the car's interior and his blood ran down Jessica's face like water. The smell, the horror, and the realization that he was now dead, crept up on her. She sat there in silence, shaking uncontrollably, unable to scream with his blood, gore and body parts all over herself. The other driver exited his truck immediately and walked over to confront Jessica, but when he saw her with Jacob's dead body and the blood all over her, his jaw dropped. Her tear filled eyes looked at the truck driver standing nearby; she mumbled a few words that were unintelligible before clearing her throat.

'Call 999...' She cried and gurgled through her tears and Jacob's blood. The blood dripped out of her mouth like vomit and there were even big chunks of his brain coming out too. The man nodded his head in silence then pulled out his phone, he then dialed 999 into his mobile and an operator picked up immediately.

'Hello, what's the emergency?' The Operator asked through the phone.

'Hi, my name is Richard Page. I think we're going to need an ambulance; I'm at Heath Road roundabout... there's been an accident.'

Chapter 8:
The Crime Scene

```
The time is 12:43pm,
Sunday the 14th of August 2001.

I've just arrived in Halton Lea and now I'm heading
down to The Runcorn Old Town. The body of Tiffany
Wright has been found by two Police Officers,
Officer White and Officer Carr. They were looking
for clues around the canal near The Binder Art
Gallery at approximately 6:05 this morning. They
followed the water down stream and Officer White
found the body under water. The two Officers called
the local Police Department immediately after
finding her body, however The Police in town, they
have no idea how she died. According to these
reports there have been no signs of blunt force or
any self-inflicted wounds of any kind. They believe
that she may have drowned, but they are not
entirely sure, so that's where I come in. I've been
sent down here from Liverpool to this small run
down town in order to help the local Police solve
this case. Scotland Yard wants me to investigate
this crime scene. Hopefully it's not too difficult
and we can wrap this up sometime soon. I will be
writing a second update later, letting you all know
what's going on in the town of Runcorn. This is
Detective John Prescott, signing off.
```
John Prescott then pressed the save button on his personal laptop, he then folded the machine away and lay it on top of the passenger seat beside him. He then proceeded to drive towards the crime scene in his black car.

When he arrived, Police were all over The Crime Scene and a large group of civilians stood nearby taking pictures on their phones and cameras. John sighed; he hated the Press, always interfering with Police Business. John parked his car near The Binder Art Gallery and exited his car, he then walked over to the crowd of people and skirted passed them to the front of the line. Police tape guarded the crime scene and a Police Officer stood behind the tape pushing people away, he looked at John as he approached the area.

'I'm sorry sir, but this is Police Business, go away!' He yelled at John unprofessionally. John pulled out his Detective badge from the inside of his black blazer, the Police Officer looked embarrassed.

'You better watch your tongue, Officer. I'm Detective John Prescott. I've been sent here all the way from Liverpool to help solve this investigation. May I come in?' John asked the Officer, sarcastically.

'I'm sorry... I had no idea, come on in...' The Officer lifted up the tape and John knelt down and walked underneath it and into the Crime Scene. Two Police Officers and an Inspector walked up and down the canal, searching the area for clues, and the dead body of Tiffany Wright lay just in front of him. John called over the two Police Officers; they were both male, one shorter than the other.

'My name is John Prescott; I'm a Homicide Detective from Liverpool. I've come here to investigate the death of Tiffany Wright' He showed them his badge.

'What have you found out so far?' He asked them both.

'Oh, so you're John Prescott? Inspector Miranda Carlton has been meaning to speak with you. We've been here for hours searching the area for more evidence, but we've had no such luck. All we've found is the body and there are no signs of assault on her or anything like that. The Inspector knows more, speak to her.' The shorter Officer shook John's hand before leading him to Inspector Miranda Carlton. The Inspector turned to face Detective John; she was slightly chubby with short brown hair and green eyes. She noticed that John was wearing a black suit with a red and blue striped tie, his short blonde, combed over hair and his professional mannerisms were dead giveaways that he was indeed the Detective, John Prescott.

'Hello Detective...' Miranda greeted John with a slight smile. John smirked, the way she spoke sounded a little flirtatious.

'Hello Miss.' He nodded his head at her.

'So, tell me what you know so far?' He asked her as he pulled out a note pad and a pen to write with.

'Well, Detective... Officer White and Carr were here earlier this morning and they found the body in the canal behind me. Afterwards we arrived and they headed back to the station. We've investigated the area; it appears as though any clues leading up to her death have been washed away in the water, her body is spotless. But we haven't done an autopsy or anything yet so maybe the answers... are inside of her... but, maybe you'll find something we haven't.' Miranda sighed. 'It's such a shame too, young girl like that... after you've finished investigating the area, report back to me and I'll call the Coroner and tell her to take Tiffany to an autopsy room.' She smiled weakly and walked passed John Prescott. John walked over to the dead body of Tiffany Wright, she lay face up on the ground, her red dress covering her body like a thin blanket. The heat and the sun on her body burnt her dead skin slightly, the Police should have placed her body under the shade, but it was too late for that now. John Prescott kneeled down beside her and put on some plastic gloves, he then rotated Tiffany's wrists with his hands, looking for any cuts or bruises, but there were none. So, he opened her hands to see if there were any cuts or bruises there too, but there were none. He checked her legs for anything, but nothing called out to him, so he inspected the girl's head, but there were no signs of assault anywhere on her body. John was about to turn back but then he noticed something; her bottom lip had a small, barely noticeable cut in the center of it. John opened her mouth to inspect further. Inside her mouth, John could see several small cuts that were scarred into her tongue and down the insides of her throat, they appeared to be scratched into her like something had clawed its way inside of her, or possibly outside of her. In all of his years investigating, John Prescott had seen a lot of weird stuff, but this, this was something he had never seen before.

Chapter 9:
Familiar Faces

The time was 2:45pm, on a Monday the 14th of August and Lindsay Evans was working her first shift at the McRoonies fast food restaurant, struggling to keep up with the older staff members. Lucas Miller, the Assistant Manager (who was a young man with black hair), ordered Lindsay Evans to go into the dining area to clean the tables surfaces. She didn't like Lucas Miller very much, from the first moment she had met him, he told her to "Wait your turn!" when he thought she was just a customer the day she had her interview. Ever since then she's grown to despise the dickhead even more as he's ordered her around countless times in that same old cocky manner. She's reluctantly accepted his orders though as she doesn't want to lose her job, not because the job is fun, but because she needs it to help her mother pay rent. Lucas Miller handed her a cleaning spray and cloth to clean the tables before opening the door for her to go into the dining area, she wanted to snap at him, tell him, "I can open the door myself!" but she knew it was wise not to, so she just nodded her head and began cleaning tables inside the dining area. A small group of young men stared at her from the right side of the restaurant, they were dressed in track suits and one of the men, she recognized. He was the same guy that whistled at her at the bus stop, was he following her? Unlikely, Runcorn is a small town, and everybody eats at McRoonies. But whatever the case, that guy creeped her out. So, she walked over to the left hand side of the restaurant in order to avoid them. As she walked over to the left, she soon noticed another familiar face; it was Steve, a friend of Kyle Cross. He was sitting down by the window on a four seater booth watching the traffic outside with a double cheeseburger in his hands. She approached him with a smile; Steve looked up at her and chuckled slightly.

'Hey there, I didn't know you worked here!' Steve smiled.

'Hi Steve... what brings you to McRoonies, you waiting for someone?' Lindsay asked with a wide smile, as she leaned her hands against the table Steve was sitting behind.

'No, I'm not waiting for anybody... I just needed sometime away from home, I've been thinking about Kyle, looking for him too. Hoping I'll see him around Runcorn, but I've had no luck. I fancied a McRoonies Cheese Burger, so here I am.' Steve chuckled quietly as he took another bite out of his burger.

'Kyle Cross... what happened that night, the night he disappeared?' Lindsay asked out of curiosity.

'He... look I'm sorry Lindsay, but I really don't want to talk about it. The Police have already asked me too much and I just want to relax for the time being, you know? Anyway, it's nice to see you, when did you start working here?' Steve changed the subject.

'This is my first day, I've only been here for two hours and already I want to go home. But I got four more hours to go... it really drags...' Lindsay looked over to her right; Steve looked over to where she was looking. The same men in tracksuits were still staring at her with sinister smiles upon their faces.

'I think that guy has been following me. The one with the skin head, I seen him at my bus stop yesterday, he was staring at me then too. His friends creep me out as well.' Lindsay told Steve.

'I'm sure it's just a coincidence, this place gets real busy Lindsay. I think everyone in town has been in McRoonies at least once. You'll probably never see him again.' Steven reassured her.

'Yeah, I hope so...' Lindsay sighed.

'Anyway, I better crack on before Mister Miller kicks off again, I'll see you around, Ste.' Lindsay winked at him as she stood up and began to spray the next table beside him. As Lindsay wiped the table down

another familiar face walked into the restaurant, the Main Manager, Graham McDonald, the bald guy who interviewed her yesterday. He walked towards Lindsay and smiled, she smiled awkwardly at him.
'Hello Lindsay, nice to see you again. I need to speak to you in my Office...' Graham said and Lindsay had a worrisome look on her face. 'Don't worry, you're not in trouble. I just like to get to know my staff members better, walk with me.' Graham chuckled as he led her through the dining area, into the kitchen and into his unsettlingly quiet office.

He sat down behind his desk and Lindsay sat in the same plastic chair in front of it. Graham opened one of the draws from his metal desk; he took out a huge bundle of money. He lay the money out on his desk in front of her, she looked on in fascination, Graham grinned.
'How would you like to make £21,000...' he smiled.
'£21,000?' Lindsay asked again in disbelief, confused about what she had just heard.
'Yes Lindsay, how does that sound?' Graham's smile turned creepy as he tilted his head to one side.
'That sounds great, but why would you give me that much money?' She asked cautiously.
'Well, I want you to do me a little favour...' Graham Chuckled.
'...And what is that?' Lindsay asked, but she didn't like where this was going.
'This Wednesday, I want you to come over to my place, I will give you the address and I want you to be there by 10:30pm. There I want you to do something a little... different for me...' Graham paused as he seen the shock and horror develop upon Lindsay Evans face.
'Mister McDonald, *are you trying to seduce me*?' Lindsay gasped and Graham grinned again.
'I suppose so... if you do as I say, when I say, I will give you the

£20,000 after we're done... here is £1,000 to keep this arrangement between us. You can have the rest of the day off. You *could* tell the Police about what I said but then you won't get the other £20,000 and they won't pay you *anything* for bringing me in. Think about it Lindsay, you do this for me and you'll have more money than all of the guys in here combined and enough money to rent your own place.' Graham then lifted the £1,000 off the table and handed it to her; she then grabbed the money off him and immediately exited the building, on her way home she thought about his offer.

If I just do this one little thing, if I just pull through this and do what he says quickly, I will have enough money to pay my mother's debt, enough to move out, maybe I'll move to another country or city. I could buy a car, a nice car and I wouldn't have to work for a while either... She hated herself for even thinking this but, maybe sleeping with her boss was worth the price.

Chapter 10:
Waking up

Jessica's eyes opened slowly, her vision unclear and blurry. She blinked several times readjusting her eyes to the brightness of the hospital room. She lay on top of a hospital bed in a patient's gown and a male doctor stood over her smiling.

'Good morning Jessica, my name is Samuel Davidson and you're in Runcorn Hospital. We've had to do surgery on you after your car accident near Heath Road. Fortunately, your injuries aren't too severe and you can go home soon, the time is 3:45pm and your parents will be here to pick you up by 4:30.' The Handsome Doctor explained. 'Now we've got some spare clothes here if you want to get changed and out of that hospital gown... don't you worry I'll close the curtain surrounding your bed and wait outside while you get changed.' The Doctor then handed her some spare clothes and proceeded to close the curtains in front of him so that he couldn't see her as she got changed. Jessica removed her hospital gown and laid it on top of the bed; she then stood up beside the bed fully naked. She felt a little embarrassed even though the Doctor couldn't see her she still felt awkward standing there naked in a hospital room. She soon noticed that she now had a couple of small scars around her belly button that had been stitched up after her surgery. She then picked up the white and pink polka dot knickers The Doctor had given her and she then proceeded to put them on, she then strapped the purple bra on, struggling slightly hooking them on at the back. She then put on the black skinny jeans, the black trainers and red tank top. She looked down at herself and smiled as she was now fully dressed and ready to go home at last. As Jessica opened the curtains the young Doctor (who looked a lot shorter now that she was standing up next to him) turned around and smiled at her.

'Hey, that suits you.' Doctor Samuel smiled.

'Thanks, Doc...' Jessica blushed.

'You're welcome, Jessica. You can sit down on the bed or the chair beside it while you wait for your parents to arrive if you like? A Nurse will be here shortly with your breakfast, are you feeling hungry at all?' Doctor Samuel asked.

'Not really Sam lad, but I do have a lot of questions that need answering...' Jessica replied.

'Oh ok, that's fine, what would you like to know?' Samuel asked with a smile on his face.

'Where's Jacob... he alright?' Jessica asked. Samuel paused, his smile diminished into a look of regret.

'...I was going to tell you this later on, but... unfortunately Jacob didn't make it... we tried all night, Jessica. But we couldn't bring him back, I'm so sorry for your loss...' Samuel told her. Jessica paused, tears flooded in her eyes as she thought about what she had done, Jacob drove her crazy but now that she knew he was gone, she began to remember the things she actually liked about him. Jessica sat down on the end of her bed and she buried her head into her hands and cried quietly. Samuel Davidson hated that part of the job, telling patients bad news like that always killed him inside. He gently lay his right hand on top of Jessica's right shoulder.

'You'll be ok, Jess... I can leave the room and wait outside if you like?' Samuel said to her.

'No... it's fine, stay with me. Please...' Jessica said through her sobs.

'Ok Jess, if that's what you'd like, I'll stay here with you.' Jessica could feel the Doctor's grip on her shoulder tighten slightly as he said that, it was strange, but Jessica found his presence somewhat comforting and nice. Eventually Jessica calmed down enough to wipe the tears away from her eyes and stand up. She faced the Doctor with a weak smile, her eyes now watered up and red from crying.

'Thank you, Sam, for staying with me... I really appreciate your company.' Jessica told him.

'Don't worry about it, Jess, that's what I'm here for.' Samuel smiled. Jessica studied the Doctor's features, he had a square jaw and terrific cheekbones that looked great next to his blue eyes, his dark wavy hair and 5 o'clock shadow looked great too. It was strange, even though Jacob was now dead, she couldn't help but feel an intense infatuation for Doctor Samuel Davidson. He was handsome, a Doctor and gentle, a real gentleman that would really look after her if they were together. She wondered what it would be like to be with Samuel and she couldn't help but love the idea, even though it was really inappropriate considering that he was her Doctor and that her boyfriend had only recently just died a couple of hours ago. Doctor Samuel checked his watch; the time was now 4:15pm.

'Oh look at the time, your parents will be here soon, I better head over to the waiting area to greet them and lead them here. Don't worry, a Nurse will be here soon with your breakfast, just wait here and I'll be back in fifteen minutes.' The Doctor smiled.

'Yeah ok, see you in a bit.' Jessica smiled back.

'See you in a bit.' Samuel smiled and waved his hand just before leaving the room. Jessica then smiled to herself as she thought about the Doctor. She then sat down on the chair beside her bed and looked around the hospital room. The walls were painted white and the floor was covered in black and light blue tiles, towards her left there was a window showing the world outside. Jessica looked at the window and noticed something rather strange imprinted on the outside of the window. On the window someone had written the words "I'll get you for this..." with their finger. Jessica's smile faded as she felt someone breathe on the back of her neck, she turned around quickly but nobody else was in the room. She then turned to face the window yet again, but this time the message had gone.

'I must be imagining things...' She told herself. But as soon as she said that, a cold breeze entered the room from the doorway and the door creaked open slightly without anyone there to push it, she then felt like someone was watching her, but nobody else was around.

Chapter 11:
The Suspicious Detective

```
2:43pm, Monday,
15th of August 2001.
3 days since Kyle's disappearance.
```

'Officer White, Officer Carr... a Detective by the name of John Prescott wants to speak to you both at the Runcorn Police Station ASAP. He wants to ask you a few questions regarding the circumstances for Tiffany Wright's death and the disappearance of Kyle Cross.' Inspector Miranda Carlton spoke through the Police Radio.
Officer Carr picked up the radio's mic from its holder and held down the answer button.
'Understood Ma'am, we will head on over to the Police Station now.' Officer Carr spoke down the mic before letting go of the answer button.
'Roger that, see you at the Station...' Miranda Responded through the radio. Officer Carr put the mic back into its holder and nodded at Officer White who was driving the Police Cruiser in the driver's seat next him.

Soon enough the two Police Officers arrived at the Runcorn Police Station, they parked in the staff parking lot and exited their Police Cruiser. They exited the vehicle and entered the Police Station. Chief Spencer stood inside the building waiting for them with a frown on his face.
'Good you're here. At least you're not late this time... follow me. I'll lead you two, to Detective John Prescott.' The Chief told them as he made his way over to the back of the Police Department. The three of them walked passed the rather busy Police men and women working

behind desks. Spencer led the two Officers to a small closed off office room and he opened the door to the office, inside a man in a black suit with a red tie and blonde hair sat against a desk awaiting them. Chief Spencer let the two Officers enter first and he closed the door behind him as the sounds of Police Staff, typing and phones ringing faded into the background. Inside the office; The Chief stood by the door and Officer White & Carr stood in front of the man in the black suit.

'My Name is John William Prescott, I am a Detective sent down here from Liverpool. I understand that it was you two that discovered the body of Tiffany Wright at the Runcorn Canal at 6:05am yesterday. Is that correct?' John Prescott asked.

'Yes, that's right we found her body yesterday.' Officer White answered.

'Interesting... what led you to her body?' John asked.

'One of the bouncers at The Dungeons nightclub gave us a lead, he told us that he seen Kyle Cross and Tiffany Wright walk over towards the canal near The Binder Art Gallery. So, we walked over to the canal and investigated the area. We found traces of footsteps leading up to the area where we found her body; I... decided to... go into the water and... see if there was anything else in the water that might give us something to go on. Unfortunately, we found her body under the water.' Officer White lied, she couldn't tell John Prescott she was Psychic and that see seen the Ghost of Tiffany Wright. It would sound like a joke and she'll lose her job and nobody would take her seriously. John Prescott raised his eye brows suspiciously.

'We couldn't find any traces of footsteps leading into the canal, Sarah... are you holding back on information, information that could be vital to The Investigation?' John Prescott asked with a snarky tone.

'No Detective, that's honestly what happened.' Sarah gulped.

'Is that what really happened?' John Prescott asked, looking at Carr.

Officer Carr paused. He looked at Sarah and thought about what she said, how she was seeing Apparitions of the now dead Tiffany Wright and how it would sound ridiculous to the Detective.
'Hello...?' John Prescott waved his hands in front of Michael.
'It's true Detective. We just had a hunch that something would be in there, honest.' Carr answered.
'Lucky hunch, huh?' John smiled, smugly.
Yes sir...' Carr gulped.
'Come on John... they found her body in the canal, they are not suspects, they are my Police Officers and they are on our side, stop interrogating them!' Chief Spencer stepped in.
'Fine Mark... you're right they aren't suspects, but I just find it hard to believe that they just found her body in the canal by a hunch. But I guess they just got lucky.' John said to Spencer.
'Anyway, I think you two have given me enough information for today, if anything else pops up I may need to ask you two a few more questions... but for now I've got to speak to the Coroner. Mark can you lead the way?' John Prescott asked the Chief politely.
'Sure John... White and Carr, you're back on patrol, we'll call you in again if we need your help answering anymore questions.' The Chief told them.
'Understood sir.' The two Officers spoke in unison, and then they exited the office room.

As Carr and White exited the Police Station, Michael had a lot of questions.
'So, are we ever going to talk about yesterday... where you supposedly saw the Ghost of Tiffany Wright?' Carr asked as they walked over to their Police Cruiser.
'Yes Michael. You deserve to know the truth; we'll go somewhere quiet to talk about it. I don't want anybody else to know about this.'

White replied as they entered their car.

'Ok Sarah, I understand....' Carr nodded at her from his passenger seat.

'Thanks, for understanding.' she smiled sincerely.

Chapter 12:
The Post Mortem

"The Coroner's surgery room is just down this corridor, John. Follow me.' Chief Spencer said to Detective John Prescott as he led him through the Police Station. Eventually they arrived at the Coroner's surgery room; Spencer opened the door for John Prescott to enter. Once John entered the room, the Chief closed the door behind them. Inside; the Coroner stood next to a surgery table with the dead body of Tiffany Wright on top of it. Tiffany's body was covered up with a white plastic blanket. The Coroner was a fairly young, slim woman with ginger hair; she wore a surgical mask and a white pair of Scrubs. She removed her mask and approached Detective John Prescott.
'Hello there, you must be the Detective from Liverpool, John Prescott?' The young woman asked with confidence.
'Yes that's right... is this the body of Tiffany Wright?' John asked as he pointed at the dead body on top of the surgical table.
'Yes, that's Tiffany... let me show you what we found, Detective.' The Coroner said as she lifted the white blanket off of Tiffany Wright's body. Tiffany's body had been cut open prior to John Prescott's arrival, her chest was open, revealing her insides and there was a small opening on her neck. Chief Spencer cringed at the sight of her, the Coroner rolled her eyes and John Prescott frowned, he found their reactions disrespectful.
'As you can see here, Detective...' The Coroner pointed at the opening on Tiffany's neck.
'Her lungs have small scratches along them from the inside; she drowned in her own blood as something... we don't know what... crawled its way inside of her... or outside of her.' The Coroner explained to the Detective.
'I've never seen anything like this before... any ideas what this... *Thing*

may be?' The Detective asked.

'Honestly we have no idea... it's like some sort of creature jumped inside her mouth and its claws cut her lungs open, causing her to bleed and drown in her own blood, it could be a spider or some kind of rat... or something else entirely. But it gets even weirder!" The Coroner then pointed at Tiffany's chest.

'As you can see here, her heart has been crushed slightly, like something has squeezed it. By following the cuts along her lungs, we discovered that whatever crushed her heart also caused the cuts inside her lungs. On closer examination you can see dents on her heart and even cuts that are similar to the ones on her lungs.' The Coroner explained.

'Do you think her death was murder or accidental?' John Prescott asked.

'It is hard to say... but it is certainly more likely that her death was caused by somebody else. My two cents... the Killer used some sort of creature to kill her by forcing it down her throat. It sounds like a stretch but it's either that or this mysterious creature landed in her throat when she opened her mouth and crawled its way inside her, killing her on its way. Also, it seems strange that two teenagers went missing that night instead of one, perhaps Kyle Cross isn't really missing... maybe he's hiding.' The Coroner raised her eye brows.

'You suspect that Kyle Cross is behind her murder?' John asked.

'I don't know for sure John, but it sure does sound suspicious, doesn't it, Chief?' The Coroner raised her eyebrow again, this time at Spencer who was standing by the door.

'Thank you, Miss...'

'Stacy Evans, my name is.' The Coroner finished John's sentence.

'Ah yes... Stacy Evans. Thank you for this information.' John smiled at her before exiting her surgery room.

As John exited the Coroner's surgery room, Chief Spencer followed behind him.

'Mark... I need to speak to you in your office, we need to talk about this Kyle Cross fellow. He may be behind this murder and if he's not... well I'm sure he'll have some interesting information to share with us *when* we find him.' John Prescott said to Spencer.

'I understand, Detective. Follow me; I'll lead you to my private office.' The Chief then led the way towards his office. Once inside, Spencer sat down behind his office desk. His desk had a silver name card on top of it saying, "Chief of Runcorn Police, Mark Spencer." There were also a bunch of files that were laid upon the top of his desk in a tidy manner. John sat down on one the chairs in front of Mark's desk.

'So, about this Kyle Cross... does he have any friends, relatives or any acquaintances that live nearby?' John asked.

'Yes John, he has a mother named Erin Cross who lives in Stenhills, his father lives in Beechwood as they are divorced. The father's name is Kevin Cross. Kyle has a large number of friends, but his closest friends are Josh Riley, Steve Matthews and Jordan Cress. They were with him the night of the disappearance, but we've already talked to his friends about the night he disappeared, John.' The Chief explained.

'Oh no, Mark... I don't want to ask them questions about the night Kyle disappeared. I just want to ask them questions about Kyle Cross himself. What he liked, what he disliked and whether or not he owned some sort venomous spider or some sort of small creature like that. You know, like something the Killer may have used...' John smiled and leant his head back against the chair.

'So, you suspect Kyle may be the Killer? Okay, since you are a Scotland Yard Detective from Liverpool... I will allow you to visit Kyle's friends and family for questioning. Let me write down all the addresses you'll need for your investigation.' Chief Spencer said as he opened the top draw on his desk, he then picked up a note pad from within and proceeded to write down the addresses Detective John Prescott needed for his investigation.

Chapter 13:
Sarah's Secret

Officer White and Carr arrived at Runcorn's local Cronton Arms Pub near Castlefields. The time was 5:45 pm and they knew driving to a small pub for a quick chat like this was against their duty as Police Officers, but the two of them needed the privacy as Sarah White was about to reveal her secrets to Michael. They sat down outside on one of the booths towards the back of the beer garden, they ordered a cola each at the bar as they did not want to break the law by drinking any alcohol on duty, the staff and customers looked at the two Police Officers in curiosity as they sat down. Eventually Sarah and Michael were the only two patrons in the beer garden and with their new found privacy; Sarah held her breath before speaking.

'...So, you're probably wondering why I'm seeing Apparitions and Ghosts...' Sarah puffed.

'Yeah... are you some kind of... Psychic?' Michael asked.

'Pretty much, I've seen them for as long as I can remember. When I see them, they are shown wearing the clothes they died in and the fatal wounds that killed them still remain upon their bodies even in death. Some of the Ghosts died peacefully, meaning that they still look like regular human beings except with blackened eyes. However, the ones that didn't die peacefully... they are just like walking, talking corpses. I have seen some so badly burnt that their skeleton can be seen underneath; protruding from their damaged, fleshy pink skin with blood still pouring out endlessly from their wounds. Others have been brutalized beyond belief. I have seen a young boy carry his own body with his only right arm. His left arm and the two of his legs had been sawed off completely. I could go on, there have been thousands of unfortunate souls like this but, I'm sure you get the picture...' Sarah looked down at her drink and played with rim of the glass before picking it up and taking a small sip of her cola.

'I'm sorry Sarah... it must be rough having to go through all of that.' Michaels' worries sounded genuine. Sarah smiled slightly, her eyes looking sad but at the same time a look of thanks caught her eyes.

'It's okay Michael. It's a curse that's for sure... but at the same time, I guess it can also be a somewhat strange gift at times too...' Sarah smiled a little more. Michael looked at her suspiciously.

'For years I fought against these... visions, trying to ignore them, act as if they weren't there but it was no use. Hundreds of them would all come around haunting me every week and at first, I thought my life was a living nightmare, but then I realized something... these Ghosts weren't just sent here, to me, in order to scare me... they wanted me to help them redeem themselves. Do you know why Ghosts linger in this realm of existence, Michael?' Sarah asked him. Michael paused.

'I have no idea...' He admitted.

'Ghosts linger on this earth because they have unfinished business. They have the option to go to heaven if they so choose, but not everyone wants to leave our realm as they don't feel satisfied with the way things ended. They want to tell their loved ones they loved them, sometimes they want revenge. Some Ghosts stick around because they want to see their daughters or sons grow up, I still talk to my own grandmother at times, which is really nice. I've told her she can go if she wants but she doesn't want to, she's told me that I have a gift and that I should use my power to help lost souls find their purpose. So, I became a Police Officer and you know what? I've helped the Police solve so many cases with this curse. I've found killers and I've solved mysteries. That is why it is also a strange sort of gift as well as a curse.' Sarah explained. Michael had a look of curiosity and fear upon his face.

'What's wrong?' Sarah asked.

'Is she here... now?' Michael asked.

'Who? My Grandmother?' Sarah chuckled.

'Ye-Yeah...' Michael stuttered. Sarah smiled and then her glass filled with cola began to move by itself, it moved towards Michael slowly and he squirmed back slightly in his chair, eventually the glass stopped.

'Damn...' Michael breathed in disbelief.

'Does that answer your question for ya?' Sarah's smile widened.

'What about hell... does that exist?' Michael asked shyly, keeping his voice down. Sarah's smile dimed.

'Yes that place still exists... but Ghosts who have done evil deeds... they are not allowed to linger, if you're an evil man, Michael, you will go to hell, no questions asked, no second chances... however, sometimes a soul can escape that realm. After a long time, damned souls begin to change. Their once human bodies become twisted and hideous beyond comprehension. Their skin sours red due to the impossible heat and their eyes become yellowish in colour. The ones that have been there the longest, their skin has soured so much it's entirely black, so black in fact that it can be almost hypnotizing. Their yellow looking cat eyes stand out against their incredibly dark skin. We call these escaped residents of hell Demons... and they can take on physical form and have even been known to possess certain individuals, blending in with society, living life in their victims' body like as if they had never even died at all. If the victim is strong enough, they can come through just long enough to gain control again but ultimately and unfortunately the Demon always wins. I have met so many serial killers that were once normal living and peaceful before they were possessed by Demons... unfortunately, not everyone is Psychic like I am, so even if these victims could regain full control of their body, they will forever be seen as a monster that kills for fun.' Sarah's smile turned into a look of sadness as she explained this to Michael. There was a short pause between the two of them.

'Do you think it was a Demon that killed Tiffany Wright?' Michael asked her.

'Honestly... I have no idea. But I sense that something Supernatural is happening in Runcorn and I fear... for everyone's safety.' Sarah breathed heavily before finishing off her drink. She gently slammed the drink down onto the table in front of her and Michael downed the rest of his too. They both stood up and walked back to their Police Cruiser in order to continue their patrol.

Chapter 14:
The Cat

```
7:45am, Tuesday,
16th of August 2001.
4 days since Kyle's disappearance.
```

Sarah White was off duty, she had to go back to the Station in her uniform to meet up with the Chief and John Prescott. They were all to go over the case files investigating the disappearance of Kyle Cross later today at 4:00pm. In the meantime, she kept herself busy by playing golf at Runcorn's Golf Society on Clifton Road. A secondary school stood nearby the golf club which was named Clifton High - Secondary and Sixth form. The school kids would walk passed the golf club every time she went to the golf club in the morning. Sometimes, they were a nice presence at the start of the day, other times they were a nuisance that she couldn't stand. Going to the golf club before work was daunting and made her work life all the more tiresome and stressful. Some days she wouldn't even bother going to the golf club, but she needed to do this because it gave her a break from the constant Police work that kept her mind occupied. It was a form of socializing too as the golf club always had a large cast of interesting members. Sarah White drove her car towards the entrance of The Runcorn Golf Society, it was clear that morning as it had been all week. The boiling hot weather was a nice change from the usual rain, cold and depressing weather that normally haunted the cloudy skies of Runcorn. She had her windows rolled down to stop the car from getting too hot inside and the morning breeze of the air woke her up too. As Sarah made her way into The Runcorn Golf Society entrance, a young school boy jumped in front of her car laughing and

pulling a face, she damn near ran the soft lad over and after he got out of the way he joined up with a bunch of his mates. Some of his friends were boys but they were mostly all girls he was hanging out with. The boy was obviously trying to impress his lady friends, and it instantly put Sarah White in a bit of a shitty mood.
'Fucking bastard...' She sighed under her breath. Once the entry way was clear she entered the car park, parked her car up and exited the vehicle. She was already dressed in casual clothes, her Police uniform had been packed neatly into a gym bag that she kept in the boot of her car, she intended on changing clothes after golfing. She walked into the golf building and was greeted with a reception area. Sarah approached the woman behind the reception desk.
'Hello Sarah, nice to see you again. You weren't here last week, how come?' The receptionist smiled cutely. Sarah sighed.
'...Police work, it's a lot of trouble, let me tell you...' Sarah smiled weakly.
'I can imagine.' The receptionist smiled, she had green eyes and tanned skin that had been burnt by sun beds. Her blonde hair was tied back into a pony tail.
'Anyway, Sarah, I'll just sign you in for the day...' The receptionist said as she picked up a piece of paper from a draw in her desk, she lay it down on top of the desk's surface and began to sign Sarah in.

Sarah collected her golfing equipment from the room where they kept all of the golf sticks and golf balls, she exited the room and entered the large outside golf course.
'Hello Sarah, it's been a while!' A fellow golf member said to her as she approached. It was David Presley, a man older than she was, he had grey hair and as far as Sarah knew, he came here almost every day.
'Hey Dave, how're you doing, you been here long today?' Sarah

smiled.

'Nope, not really... only just got here with my wife about...' Dave checked his watch; it was a sliver one that must have cost a pretty penny.

'... An hour, damn, time sure does fly! Well... you're free to join us if you like? It's up to you, I understand that an Officer needs their time alone so it's not a problem if you can't. Anyway, we're over there...' David pointed towards his wife in the far distance.

'Anyway, I'll see you around the course, I have some... urgent matters to attend to.' David raised his eyebrows and hurried passed Sarah and into the men's toilets behind her. Sarah chuckled, *good old Dave...* She smiled to herself. Sarah joined up with David's wife, Claire. Considering David's age, you'd expect his wife to be old too, but Claire appeared to be younger than Dave. She had short dark brown hair that was styled into a pixie cut, and she had a slim figure, (although, she did seem to be significantly older than Sarah, by at least 10 or maybe 15 years.)

'Nice shot!' Claire yelled as Sarah finished her swing, Sarah's ball went flying across the golf course.

'Thanks' Sarah smiled. Suddenly Sarah heard a "Hiss" sound from in front of her and behind Claire. Claire looked at Sarah suspiciously as Sarah looked passed her, Claire turned around, but nothing was there.

'Why is there a black cat out here?' Sarah asked, but she wasn't asking Claire, she was just thinking out loud. Claire was confused, *what cat?* There was no cat, at least, not one that Claire could see; it was only when Sarah studied the cat's features more closely that she discovered that the cat had red eyes, *red eyes?* Sarah thought, it confused her, she had seen hundreds, if not thousands of dead victims with blackened eyes, but never ones with red eyes and a cat none the less? This was strange, but Sarah had a feeling this had something to do with the case, as crazy as that may sound. She knew it was the truth. The cat walked towards the golf building but stopped shortly after to turn its head. It looked at Sarah and meowed, beckoning her to follow, and she followed.

'Sarah, where are you going?' Claire asked.

'Oh, I'm sorry, Claire... I just remembered something, tell Dave I said goodbye.' Sarah smiled, before following that invisible cat again.

'Ok...' Claire raised her eyebrows as Sarah trailed off, following some invisible force.

'Jesus Christ... Sarah is fucking crazy...' Claire whispered to herself. Sarah followed the cat outside of The Runcorn Golf Society and across the road, and down the path towards Clifton High. The cat approached the front gate to the school and turned to look at her, it meowed and turned it's head back towards the gate, then back at her.

'Through here?' Sarah asked the cat. The cat nodded it's head, then it began to spasm, it shook violently, it's legs kicking out at its side, then it fell over. Sarah approached the cat and laid a hand on it, stroking the cat's fur, but to anyone else who walked passed, Sarah appeared to be stroking thin air. Eventually the cat came back to life; it jumped up quickly and stared motionlessly at Sarah for a few seconds, its eyes now black like all the others. It hissed and ran off quickly, in fright. Sarah watched as the cat ran away, it's body disappearing into thin air as it ran, *the poor thing doesn't even know it's dead...* Sarah thought.

Sarah returned to The Runcorn Golf Society and put her golfing equipment back into the equipment room, she then left the premises and entered her red car. She knew it would look strange if she entered the school without her uniform and the Chief would be asking questions about her. No, she would have to investigate this lead tomorrow, on patrol with Michael Carr.

Chapter 15:
The Haunting of Daniel Harriot

```
1:30pm, Tuesday,
16th of August 2001.
4 days since Kyle's disappearance.
```

Daniel Harriot was sat at home, watching TV on his sofa, in his living room. Daniel lived in a somewhat decent one bedroomed flat. It had a small kitchen area, a bedroom, a bathroom and living room. Daniel had an unkempt beard and longish hair that hadn't been brushed that day at all; in fact, Daniel hadn't even bothered to shower that day. It was his day off work and he could not be bothered doing anything, all he wanted to do was sit around all day and watch TV, occasionally check his phone for texts and order a takeaway later that afternoon. Daniel sighed as there was nothing particularly interesting on TV, but he just kept it on because at the very least, it was more bearable than the silence of his empty apartment. He was mid-way through watching a rather boring episode of a British sitcom he didn't even know the name of when he heard something in his kitchen fall. Daniel picked up the remote from the coffee table in front of him and muted the television. Silence hung in the air and Daniel listened carefully, there it was again, the sound of something moving in his kitchen. Daniel put the TV remote down onto the coffee table and stood up to investigate. Daniel slowly opened the door to his kitchen, the door shrieked loudly as he did so, the only sound in the room. But inside the kitchen, nothing was there. He shut the door behind him and searched the kitchen area, looking through draws and cupboard doors. He looked towards the sink to see if anything was in there, and he looked inside the bin, but nothing was there either. *I must be*

imagining things... Daniel shrugged. Daniel then opened the door to his living room and walked in, but something wasn't right.
Right there in front of him, stood a man covered in blood, his eyes a colour so dark that Daniel could have sworn they were completely black, like looking into the deep unknown, space or the deep abyss of the ocean. But that wasn't even the worst part, this man's face had been slashed open with blood still pouring out, its nose had a large chunk taken out of it and a large scar remained open across the man's right cheek, revealing all of his bloodied teeth that had been chipped into various sharp points. His tracksuit had been ripped open, huge burns scared his chest and his right hand was missing three fingers, the wounds were still wet and grotesque. The man's tongue licked the long row of teeth on his right side, blood washed off them and onto his tongue. It smiled then limped towards Daniel slowly, Daniel walked backwards, slowly, in absolute terror.
'Hel-Hello... Da-Danie... el.' The Creature struggled to speak. Daniel just stood there in silence, too confused and terrified to even speak.
'I wa-want... you t-to do me a fa-favour.' The thing kept stuttering on its own loose jaw.
'...You can't be... real!' Daniel finally spoke. The thing's smile widened even more, blood leaked from it's mouth as it's skin ripped open.
'Oh, but I am real, Daniel.' The thing spoke more clearly now.
'What do you want?!' Daniel screamed, his hands shaking at his sides and sweat falling from his forehead, his pupils expanding with absolute horror.
'A favour...' It smiled.
'There is this woman, her name is Jessica McKenzie and she is the one... that has done this to me.' The thing's smile turned into a hideous snarl.
'Who... are you?' Daniel asked, half terrified and curious for the answer. The thing looked at Daniel, deep into his eyes and smirked.

'Jacob Kennedy was my name. Before I was killed that is...' The thing chuckled quietly.

'Jessica was the one that murdered me, and left me like this...' The thing smirked again, it's voice was rasp and distant like as if the monster was shouting from a far, deep inside the dark abyss that was it's eyes. It was another entity from a different dimension making contact with Daniel through an empty vessel.

'Well, what do you want me to do about it...?' Daniel asked. Terrified yet again of what the answer may be.

'I want to see her suffer, the way she ruined me... I want her to experience the pain she caused me in my last few breaths.' The thing spoke more seriously now, and it sent shivers down Daniel's spine.

'No...' Daniel shook his head. The thing stood over Daniel and it grabbed his neck, tight with it's right hand, Daniel could feel the wetness of the thing's finger wounds on his neck and the feeling made him want to puke, but things only got worse for poor old Daniel. Daniel was squeezing his eyes shut and The Beast wanted Daniel to see what Jessica had done to him, so with it's left hand; The Monster dug his sharp fingers under Daniel's eye lids and forced them open, so Daniel had no choice but to stare right into the eyes of the hideous beast that was once Jacob Kennedy.

'You will do as I say, kill Jessica McKenzie and make sure the bitch fucking suffers!' Jacob's Ghost roared, a horrible stench of death crept its way into Daniel's nostrils' (it was enough to make Daniel physically sick.) He hurled up his breakfast and it went all over himself, the sick just went through Jacob as he wasn't really there, only a spiritual entity that only Daniel could see. To everyone else, this scene would have looked like Daniel was just having a heart attack or stroke, but in reality, or at least in Daniel's reality, a living breathing corpse stood over him, torturing him endlessly.

'Please... Stop! PLEASE FOR THE LOVE OF GOD, STOP!' Daniel

begged, pleading for his life and the monster smiled.

'If you kill Jessica, this will all be over. You may get caught, thrown in the slammer, but at the very least, you'll be rid of me... what do you say?' The monster laughed, and what a disgusting laugh it was, it's voice gurgled as blood spat all over Daniel's puke covered face. Blood, sick, sweat and tears blurred Daniel's vision and he could feel lumps of sick and the monster's gore under his eyelids. He could taste rotten flesh as parts of the monster's face fell apart and flew directly into his mouth, he even swallowed parts of it as he tried to breath, he coughed up pieces of the monster too as they would block his windpipe. Of course, if somebody else was in the room, they wouldn't even see the blood or gore go down Daniel's throat, to them it would appear as if he was choking on something, but to Daniel the gore, the monster that was once Jacob and the hideous smell that was coming from it, it was all **too real**.

'I won't stop until you agree to kill Jessica! I can do this all day; I've got nothing else to live for... hell I ain't even alive no more!' the monster joked and laughed wickedly.

Chapter 16:
Lindsay's Night

```
10:01pm, Wednesday,
17th of August 2001.
5 days since Kyle's disappearance.
```

It was the night Graham McDonald planned on, for a lack of a better word, screwing Lindsay Evans. He had been thinking about her that morning, the way she looked at him so shyly and how nervous she appeared on The Interview. He liked that, he had this kink for shy girls and how innocent they were. Of course, Graham felt like no girl would ever want to touch him (at least not without payment) and saddest fact of all was that he's never had anything even close to a relationship with a girl, he has been overweight since childhood and the only girls that ever dated him, only did that out of a dare or cruel joke. He was a laughing stock by women and he knew it, but with that came a strange hatred towards them. Deep down inside he always wanted to humiliate them, to put them through as much, or even more shame than the girls in school and college used to put him through. He laughed to himself, he knew £21,000 was a lot of money, but he knew it would never be enough to rid the horrid memories that would almost definitely haunt Lindsay Evans for years to come. He marveled in the fact that this girl, who was only eighteen, so sweet and innocent, would later tonight feel ashamed and used, after the "plans" that he had in mind. *Maybe I could even get my money back...* He smirked to himself. Graham McDonald surely was a pathetic, sad and cruel man indeed.

Lindsay Evans looked at the clock in her living room, the time said 10:05pm and she was dreading her night with The Beast, The Monster that was her boss, Graham McDonald. She almost bailed completely, the idea of kissing that foul man and letting him do what he wanted disturbed her somewhat. It made her feel sick just to think about it, but she was so desperate to leave town. To start a new life somewhere else, to escape this small, empty, run down town and enter a paradise of huge proportions, perhaps a place full of happy people and rich opportunities. She would pay her mother's debts then move away somewhere abroad, possibly Spain or Australia, maybe even America. Hell, she would have enough money to move anywhere she wanted, that is if Graham McDonald held up his part of the deal of course. She hated the fact that she was even thinking about doing this, but she really wanted to get out of here as fast as possible. *Look I'll just go in there and let the fat fuck do whatever he wants, then he'll pay me the £20,000 and I'll have enough money to do what I want, surely that fucker won't take too long...* She told herself one last time, before biting the bullet and picking up her handbag, putting on her coat and heading out of the door, she didn't even bother to tell her mother she was going out. Confronting her would only make things worse anyway.

After waiting for her bus in the middle of the night, standing around in the dark, freezing cold (despite the fact that it was summer) and then getting on the bus only to be greeted by a bunch of smack heads at the back and a couple of old women who looked miserable, a bearded old man that smelt and appeared to be homeless, an uncomfortable bus ride and a few un-nerving stares from the smack heads later; she finally arrived in Beechwood, where Graham McDonald lived. She was pleasantly surprised to see that this area of Runcorn was actually kind of nice. Lindsay Evans walked around Beechwood aimlessly, looking for Graham MacDonald's address and after a while, she finally found it. Lindsay looked at his house, it was a tall two-story building with a fancy looking convertible that was parked outside on his driveway. Next to his driveway stood a small front lawn and the house was painted in white, his roof was tiled nicely, and Lindsay thought his place looked pretty decent, with fashioned windows and all that jazz. She still felt un-nerved by it all though, even though it was a nice looking house it still stood threateningly tall in the darkness and a feeling of uneasiness and dread filled her bones as she approached the front door (and she wasn't even sure if she even had the right address!) a part of her almost hoped that it wouldn't be his house, so she wouldn't have to commit to his sick desires. But she knocked on the door and waited, with what felt like a huge lump in her throat.

Graham heard a small knock on his door, even from the way it sounded, he could tell that it was Lindsay Evans who was knocking. His smile widened as he struggled to get up from his couch and walk over to his front door, his huge body bounced slightly as he made his way over.

The door in front of Lindsay opened slowly and she was horrified to see that she had indeed found the right house, because there he was, that sloth of a man, Graham McDonald. He stood staring at her with his big, green, bulgy, huge and ugly eyes and a huge smug smile on his face.
'Hello Lindsay, such a... pleasure to see you... thanks for coming...' Graham giggled, but it didn't sound cute.
'Come right in...' He laughed again in that creepy, unsettling voice.
Lindsay didn't want to, she felt uneasy, almost faint as he walked into his house with the door open. Graham was inviting her in, inviting her into his den, like a spider inviting a fly into its web only to be met a with a devastating, tortuous end. Or to be met with a fate worse than death, and perhaps that was exactly what Graham McDonald

had in mind, she wasn't entirely sure what Graham wanted, or if he even had the £20,000 in the first place. But ignoring her better judgement, Lindsay Evans took a deep, long breath and entered the household. Graham McDonald led her upstairs into his bedroom, the room was dark, the moonlight shone the room in a dark blue, the window's blinds shadowed the bed and the room with stripes. Lindsay felt incredibly uneasy now and when Graham slowly closed the door behind himself, leaving the two of them alone in the cold room, she felt like crying, but she didn't dare show it, not to Graham, she hardly knew the guy, but she had this sick feeling that somehow, he would find her suffering erotic. He walked around her, staring at her up and down like a hungry beast, waiting to strike, she held her head up high and tried so hard not show any fear, but a single tear dropped from her right eye and it was enough to show Graham just how much she feared him and that fear only escalated as he began to undress her, unbuttoning her coat and slipping it off her small and slender body. He then proceeded to untuck her shirt and lift it up, she hesitatingly lifted her arms up in the air and allowed him to continue. He removed the shirt and threw it on the floor beside her, she now stood there in front of him, feeling cold as the air in the room touched her skin. She felt so small standing there in front of him wearing nothing but a pair of dark blue skinny jeans and a pink bra. Still terrified she stood still, unable to move, too afraid of what may happen if she did, but at the same she didn't want this to continue, she felt violated, humiliated and depressed all at once. *Screw the money, this isn't worth it!*

'That's enough!' She demanded, her voice croaked as she said that, she wanted this to stop, but at the same she was fucking terrified and didn't want Graham to hit her. Her worse fears came true and something even more horrific began to happen, as he grabbed her neck tightly with his right hand, he spun her around and threw her onto his bed, she fell back onto the bed, her head hit the back wall, and just like a small child, she began to cry hysterically with a jolt of pain. But that didn't stop Graham McDonald from climbing on top of her and strangling her with a wicked, unsettling smile upon his face.

Chapter 17:
Sarah's Dream

Sarah White awoke from her slumber, with a cold sweat dripping down her forehead. She searched with her right arm for her alarm clock that was supposed to be on the floor to the right of her bed, but the clock was nowhere to be found, so she threw the blanket off of her body, the cold air in the room sent a chill down her exposed legs, arms and stomach as all she was wearing was her underwear. She climbed out of bed and looked inside her wardrobe for some clothes. She put on a pair of pink sweat pants and a black t-shirt that had the words "The Roland" printed on it in gothic font, she smiled to herself as she remembered seeing them live at a concert in Manchester that one time. After that she walked over to her bedroom wall in order to find the light switch, but when she flipped the switch on, the lights only flickered for a split second and then the room was dark again. All it took was for that one small second of light to make Sarah realize that she was no longer in her flat in Runcorn Old Town, the walls were painted in a bright pink and posters of girl bands from the 1990s were plastered all over the walls, in fact she remembered now that her "The Rolland" t-shirt got lost years ago back in 1998 when she stayed over at her now ex-boyfriends house that one time back in her college days.

'Sarah, do you know what time in the FUCKING MORNING IT IS?!' It was her father's voice, *what is he doing here? My father doesn't live...* then Sarah remembered, this wasn't her flat anymore. Somehow, she had travelled back in time and was re-living her past, where her father, Cody White, Screamed and shouted all day long about how she wasn't haunted and that she needed to grow up and stop imagining silly things like Ghosts and Ghouls. Sarah winced as she heard her father approach her old bedroom door, the door snatched open, but Cody wasn't there. Sarah looked out towards the landing and noticed that the landing she was now looking at looked nothing like the one she remembered from when she was a child, no, the room she was standing in was her old bedroom but the next room in front of her had nothing to do with her past, it was a part of another household, one that she had never seen before. Sarah took a deep breath and entered the landing in front of her, immediately she noticed that there was a mirror beside her, when she looked at the mirror, she was both equally shocked and pleasantly surprised to see a younger, eight teen year old version of herself, with a slimmer waist and younger skin. Her eyes looked cuter and her body was tighter, her hair looked better too as it was shorter, silkier and lighter. It was trippy seeing herself like this, like looking into a mirror and seeing a completely different person standing there mimicking every move you make, but Sarah liked it, she had no idea just how much her looks had faded over the last five years. She still looked great for a 23 year old but damn, did she look beautiful back then. Sarah also felt younger and healthier too, come to think of it. She smiled at herself, that same old smile she always gave herself, but this time there were no wrinkles that formed around her cheeks like there had been yesterday. She pulled a few faces and checked her hair to see if there were any small grey hairs still hiding in there, but there weren't any at all, it felt good to be younger but at the same time, she was terrified that last 5 years of her life had been completely erased. Sarah stepped away from the mirror and continued to walk down the long dark landing that separated her bedroom to the next. To her right, Sarah could see the exit to this bungalow she was inside of, she walked over to the front door and tried to open it, but the handle wouldn't even budge, like as if it was permanently stuck in that one position forever, super glued in place for some strange and bizarre reason. She turned around in defeat and realized that she must have been here for a reason, whatever that reason may be, she wasn't allowed to leave until her mission was complete. There was nothing that stuck out to her in the landing, so she tried opening other doors that led to other rooms inside the bungalow. Just like the handle on the front door, a lot of the doors wouldn't budge open, no matter how much Sarah leaned, pushed or threw herself into them. Eventually though she did find this one door that did open with relative ease, the door felt so light it was almost like the door was pulling her in, like this was the right place that The Dream needed her to be. Once inside, Sarah realized that this was a young teenage boy's bedroom, however you wouldn't really know this if it wasn't for the dark blue walls. There were no posters or any signs of there being a teenager living here, there was no TV or video game consoles anywhere, only a desk with a wheelie office chair behind it with a secondary school math book laid out on top of the desk, on the front cover the words read:

"Clifton High Mathematics: year 7

Student Name: *Andrew Bates*"

Sarah smiled to herself, remembering her old days of being in school, that seemed like such a long time ago now. Shortly after, Sarah began to look around the bedroom again, she noticed that the wardrobe at the back of the room was slightly open, so she walked over towards it to investigate and just before her hands touched the wardrobe's door, she heard someone yell in a whispered tone behind her.

'Don't open the wardrobe!' the small voice squeaked. Sarah spun around and looked behind her in a sudden fright, but there was nothing to be afraid of, it was just a small terrified boy, who was halfway burying his face behind his blanket. Sarah hadn't even noticed the small boy before as he hid himself well under the blankets, perhaps he thought she was the "Monster" under the bed.

'Why what's inside the wardrobe?' Sarah asked in a friendly tone with a surprised smile on her face.

'The... escaped one...' The boy said, shyly.

'The escaped one?' Sarah asked, but before the boy could reply, they both heard a small creak coming from behind her. An entirely black skeletal hand creeped its way around the wardrobe's door, the boy quickly hid his head behind the blanket again and two yellow eyes shone within the darkness of the wardrobe's interior and a hideous, wicked and insidious, yet quiet chuckle came from whatever was inside. Sarah, without much thought, quickly ran into the wardrobe's door and with all her might, she began to push the wardrobe's door back against The Demon's hand. When the door slammed shut, the thing's laughter faded, and the room stood in an eerily silence. After a minute or so, Sarah spoke to the boy.

'There is no need to be afraid, I'm here to help...' She told him, and although she wasn't completely sure why she was here, she knew it had something to do with this kid. The boy slowly turned his blanket down, revealing the confused and frightened eyes that Sarah was all too familiar with when she was a child. Now she knew what it was like to see how things were from an adult's perspective and seeing this kid look so defenseless and small, this only made her memories of Hauntings and Demons seem even more terrifying.

'You're not... one of...' The boy paused, second guessing himself.

'No, no... I was just like you. In fact, I still am, I see them too, you're not alone.' Sarah smiled, reassuringly. The boy smiled back and for the first time since they met, he finally felt at ease around her.

'Do you know what that thing was, why it's been haunting you?' Sarah asked. The boy looked towards the wardrobe and then back up at her, his eyes watered up and then he finally spoke the truth.

'...That thing in the wardrobe. It's been trying to get inside me, but I... I won't allow it to... I don't know where it came from, but it's been here for a while now, toying with me, it doesn't even need me anymore, but it just stays around. I was dreaming one night, I awoke from my bed but... things weren't quite right. I remember walking around the house and I walked into what was supposed to be our toilet, only to find that it led me into a long hall way that sloped downwards. I felt like I was being dragged down by an invisible force and when I reached the bottom, I noticed there was a black door that was opening up, a fiery, red background lay behind the door and as I fell onto it that very same skeletal hand grabbed my arm tight and then... I woke up. I thought it was just a nightmare, but then I kept on seeing the thing, everywhere I went it was always there. It was never in clear sight, only in the distance, hiding somewhere, just out of view and it knew how to hide, but it always made sure that I knew that it was always, always there... eventually, I stopped seeing the thing in the day and for a while I thought it had gone, but now the thing has returned but it only haunts my nightmares, teasing me, maybe even thanking me for allowing it to leave whatever hell hole that thing came from. But whatever the case may be, I don't want any part of it!' The boy explained to her. Sarah stood in silence, unsure of what to say next, she had never heard of anything like this before, but as far as she could tell, whatever this thing was, it now ran free in the town of Runcorn and she feared for everyone's safety.

Chapter 18:
Kyle's Snake

```
11:45am, Thursday,
18th of August 2001.
6 days since Kyle's disappearance.
```

John Prescott drove his car towards The Runcorn Old Town. He was on his way to Josh Riley's apartment in The Docks area of the town. Now John had a lot of questions to ask, not only to Josh, but later on he planned on speaking to Erin Cross at her house in Stenhills. John wanted to investigate both leads thoroughly in order to find clues pointing to the possible whereabouts of Kyle Cross. John approached a car park near The Docks and parked his car up close to Josh's apartment building. He exited his car and approached the building, he pressed his finger against the intercom's number to Josh's room and then a static sound escaped the intercom.
'who is this?' a voice came from the intercom,
'My name is John Prescott, Mister Riley. I am a Homicide Detective from Liverpool, I am here to ask you a few questions regarding the disappearance of your friend, Kyle Cross...' John said to the intercom and then there was a pause.
'But I've already spoken to the Police, two Officers came to Erin's house and I was there answering questions to help them in their investigation...' Josh said through the intercom, there was confusion in his voice.
'Yes, Mister Riley, I am aware that you spoke to those two, but I am here for different reasons. I want to learn more about your friend, so I can understand the way he thinks and what motivates him, etcetera...' John waited for Josh to reply but there was no response through the intercom, so John continued.

'Information like this would really help us in our investigation, Mister Riley. You see, if I can learn as much about him as possible, I could figure out where he may be hiding or where he may have run off to. Even the smallest detail can lead to... pleasing results...' John waited for Josh to reply and then he heard a sighed breath through the intercom.

'Okay... you can come on in, I will try and answer as many questions as possible.' then the intercom's static dropped and a loud click came from the door in front of John Prescott, John then proceeded to open the door in front of him and get into the elevator, he pressed the button to Josh's floor and when he exited the elevator he headed towards the room where Josh Riley lived. The door opened before John even had the chance to knock, inside the room, Josh dressed in a creased t-shirt and dark blue tracksuit bottoms, he stood in the doorway looking at John.

'Hello Josh, nice to meet you finally, I don't have a lot of questions to ask, so this shouldn't take too long, may I come in?' John asked, but Josh sensed that it was a rhetorical question and the Detective was just saying that to come across as polite and professional, when in reality, Josh Riley had no real choice in the matter.

'Sure... come on in, take a seat.' Josh answered, then he turned around and walked towards the living room, John Prescott followed behind him and when they reached the living room, John sat down on the sofa facing the TV while Josh grabbed a chair from his dinner table and he stood it towards the back wall facing John Prescott, so that he could get a good look at him while he asked his questions. When Josh sat down on the chair, John took his note book out of his suit's blazer and then he pulled a pen from out of his pocket, he loosened his collar and then he began to ask Josh Riley a series of questions.

'So, Josh, how long have you known Kyle?' John asked in a polite manner. Josh paused before answering.

'I say... about... six or seven years now. We were friends in Secondary, you see. Since then we've been hanging out almost every weekend.' After Josh said this, John wrote down a bunch of words that Josh could not see on one of the pages inside the note book. After that, he smiled at Josh and asked another question.

'That long, huh? he must mean a lot to you?' John asked.

'Yes... he's one of my closest friends.' Josh replied with sorrow in his voice and a look of empathy spread across John's face.

'I understand that this may be hard for you Mister Riley, but out of all of these years... did Kyle ever mention that he had a small pet of any kind-'

'*What* does that have to do with anything?' Josh interrupted the Detective as the question seemed oddly strange and off topic. John paused for a second, thinking about what he should say next.

'Mister Riley...' He smiled,

'There are somethings... in this investigation that are, let's say, for a lack of a better word, confidential. I cannot explain to you why this question is important but, believe me… it is. This has been a strange case and I know that some of the questions I may ask you, they may seem odd or random, but believe me, they are important and vital to solving this case... so, Mister Riley, I will ask you again. Did Kyle Cross ever have an interest for small animals, did he ever mention that he may have a small pet of any kind?' John Prescott asked him again, he forced a smile trying to be polite, but Josh could tell that underneath that smile there were signs of impatience and an anger that was boiling deep inside. Josh didn't know what to think, but one thing was for sure, he didn't like this "Detective John Prescott" and his strange questions. So, Josh decided it would be best just to answer his stupid questions as quickly as possible without questioning them himself, *the sooner The Detective gets his answers, the sooner he'll be out of here* Josh thought.

'Okay then, Detective, I will answer your questions... Kyle Cross did have a pet snake, it was only a small one though, it should only be a couple of months old by now, that is if Kyle's mother, Erin Cross, hasn't got rid of the thing. She wasn't a big fan of the animal, it was his idea and she would always joke about how she didn't like the thing to us all when me and our group of friends came over to hang out with him. He also fed the thing small mice too...' Josh answered John's question and the Detective wrote another thing down on his note book, just as Josh predicted.

'That's great information, Mister Riley. Thank you very much.' John smiled, this time with a more genuine smile on his face that didn't look forced.

'Another question....' John smiled again, this one looking a little smug.

'Did Kyle Cross ever carry his pet snake around with him? Outside of the house I mean.' John asked with his pen and notebook ready.

'No... Kyle never took the thing out of it's tank, he always kept it inside as the temperature was different to what was outside. He feared that the snake would get ill or die, due to the cold temperature of his room.' Josh explained and after John nodded and wrote another thing down inside his note book, he looked back up at Josh and asked his final question.

'Alright Mister Riley, the information you have given me has been incredibly useful, but before I go, I have one more question to ask... do you know if Kyle's pet snake is venomous in nature?' John asked, and a look of surprise caught Josh's face.

'I wouldn't think so, Detective... the thing didn't look *venomous* to me, and the way he held it in his hands never gave me the impression that snake was harmful by any means... you're not suggesting that Kyle used it to kill Tiffany Wright, are you?!' Josh stood up from his chair and rose over John Prescott who was still sitting down on the sofa in front of him, with that smug look on his face and that pen and notebook that was still in his hands.

'Everyone is a suspect in this Investigation, Mister Riley.' John said as he stood up from the sofa and looked down on Josh as he stood a good foot or two taller.

'Even you...' John threatened with a serious demeanor. Suddenly Josh felt small and he gulped in fright, this made John smile and then he walked off with his notebook and pen, he put them back inside of his suit as he approached Josh's front door and after he opened the door he left it wide open as he walked down the hall outside, towards the elevator. Once John was out of sight, Josh Riley grabbed the nearest thing that was close to him (which was the TV remote that lay on top of the coffee table) he roared with frustrated anger and then he threw the remote across the room and a part of it smashed against the wall that it crashed onto. After that, Josh fell to his knees and the familiar guilt that taunted him the night Kyle Cross first disappeared suddenly came crawling back and he didn't know what to do.

Once John Prescott left Josh's apartment building in Runcorn Old Town, he decided that now was the time to visit Kyle's mother, Erin Cross. The Detective exited the premises and entered his car, he drove the car through Runcorn Old Town and towards Stenhills. He followed the address that Chief Spencer had sent him, he arrived outside of Erin's house, he parked up on her driveway, then he walked up to her front door and before he could knock, the door already began to open. In the doorway stood Erin Cross, she appeared to be about forty five, she looked tired and her hair looked messy, the roots in her hair were growing grey and it stood out badly against the dark red hair that she had obviously dyed that way. She wore no makeup and John could see a couple of small spots on her face as well as an oily skin complexion, almost like she had been

sweating beforehand, she wore a pair of baggy grey sweat pants and a pink cardigan that covered her body. John smiled,
'Hello, are you Miss Cross? I am Detective John Prescott a Homicide Detecti-' Suddenly Erin broke out into tears and fell to her knees.
'Oh god... no...' she whimpered. That's when John realized what he had just done, when Erin Heard him say "I am a Homicide Detective" she immediately went straight to the conclusion that John was explaining to her that they had found Kyle Cross dead, he laughed to himself silently because of the misunderstanding.
'No, no, Miss Cross I am not here to tell you that we found Kyle's body. He is still missing, I am only here to gather clues, I just need some information that's all. I am here to help.' John explained as he held out his right hand towards Erin Cross. She looked up at him and took his hand, he helped her up, then she turned around and invited him into her house. John Prescott sat down in her living room on top of a sofa facing her TV, photos of Kyle Cross were all over the place, on the window shelves and on top of the fireplace, there were photos of him on the walls and opened photo albums of him on the floor. The whole house seemed to be in a mess and John didn't judge, Erin was obviously struggling being on her own, staying in the house all day thinking about Kyle must've been hell for her. Erin was in the kitchen making herself and John a cup of tea, eventually she came back and handed him a cup, he smiled and apologized for coming unannounced.
'Yes... I could've done with a phone call. You guys should have explained that you were coming around to ask questions. I would have tidied the place up a bit and you could've saved me that moment of distress just then, but I'm glad you're here to be honest... I just feel like the Police haven't been trying hard enough to find my poor Kyle. You coming here gives me more confidence that they are trying harder, what do you need to know Detective? Please ask

away.' Erin sat down on the opposite sofa facing him with her cup of tea, she crossed her legs and a genuine smile grew on her face.

'Well Miss Cross, I would be happy to ask you a few questions, however I am also here to look around. I have come to search Kyle's room for any possible clues that may lead to his whereabouts. I'll need all the clues I can get if I ever hope to find your son. I hope you can understand...' John explained to her, she had a look of concern but reluctantly agreed, nodding her head in response.

'Okay, great. Is Kyle's room upstairs?' John asked as he put his tea down on top of the coffee table in front of him.

'Yes... but, let me come with you! ... I Left his room the way it was when he left and I... I Just need to make sure you don't mess things up, I want things to be perfect for him when or... if... he returns.' Erin whimpered a little. John agreed and they both went upstairs together, Erin showed him to Kyle's room. She opened the door and inside John could see that there was a tank for reptile pets on top of a desk that was inside the room, he walked over to the tank and looked inside of it through the opening on the top of the tank. Here he could see inside that there was fake grass on the bottom of it with wooden logs for the reptiles to sleep and there was a small bowl of water that looked like it had been refilled recently.

'Oh... Kyle sure did love his pets.' Erin smiled as she stood beside John. The two of them looked inside the tank for a while and soon a snake began to crawl its way outside of the log, it hissed at the two humans then it crawled towards the bowl and began to drink out of it. The snake looked strange, it was patterned in both yellow and black stripes.

'May I take a closer look at this snake?' John asked as he began to open the hatch on top of the tank, Erin quickly lay her hands over John in order to stop him.

'Oh no, no, not a good idea Detective... you see this is called a Tiger

Snake, they're extremely poisonous. I never liked Kyle owning one, but he insisted, we had to get a license for it and have a member of the local council to come around to check if things were safe and what not. I used to hate the thing, but... I like the little fella now, it's one of the only things that keep me sane after Kyle's disappearance, I like to care for it, feed it and give it water, you know? It takes my mind off the fact that he's missing and if I can't take care of my son, then at least I've got this snake. Anyway, what I'm trying to say is that this snake only trusts me and Kyle to hold it and touch it, etcetera. If *you* did, you'll... need to go the hospital I'm afraid.' Erin explained to the Detective with a smile on her face, however she frowned when John gave her a menacing stare.

'What's the matter, Detective?' Erin asked with worry in her voice. John Prescott removed a pair of handcuffs from inside of his suit's blazer.

'Miss Erin Cross, you're under arrest for the suspicion of murder! I have reasons to believe that *you* and Kyle Cross may be behind the murder of Tiffany Wright. You have the right to remain silent, anything you do say may harm your defense in court and may be given in evidence.'

Chapter 19:
A Disagreement Between Police

```
11:32am, Friday,
19th of August 2001.
7 days since Kyle's disappearance.
```

Sarah White and Michael Carr were on patrol, driving through Castlefields when their Police Radio began to make a static sound. Sarah slowly pulled over onto a nearby curb and proceeded to answer the call, on the other end was Inspector Miranda Carlton and she had an important message to announce.
'Officers White and Carr, come in.'
'Yes Ma'am, what is the problem?' Sarah asked.
'No problem Sarah... in fact, we have some good news. John Prescott has found a possible suspect that fits the motive behind the murder of Tiffany Wright.' The Inspector announced through the radio, Sarah imagined Miranda having a huge smile on her face as she sounded quite pleased through the radio.
'That's excellent, Ma'am. Who is it that you have taken in?'
'This may come as a shock, Miss White, but Detective John Prescott has reasons to believe that Erin Cross may have been behind the murder.' She told them. Sarah sat motionless, taking in the new information that Miranda had just announced.
'Officer White, are you still there?' The Inspector asked through the radio. Michael nudged Sarah White on the shoulder, she awoke from her day dream, and looked at him in confusion, then she returned to the radio to speak to the Inspector.
'Yes Ma'am, I hear you loud and clear, but... Erin Cross can't be the Killer, she's Kyle's mother and she is clearly in distress. What makes you believe that she may be behind the crime?' Sarah asked, half

infuriated and halfway curious.

'Well Sarah, I would not have guessed so myself, however John Prescott has investigated the situation further and he has discovered a couple of interesting facts about the murder. You see, Tiffany Wright was found with several small cuts around her lips, and when we took her body to the Coroner's office, we found that something had crawled its way inside of her and destroyed her heart. We do not know exactly what it was that killed her, however John Prescott has discovered that Kyle Cross is the owner of an Australian Tiger Snake, Tiger Snakes are known to be incredibly venomous and we have come to the possible conclusion that either Kyle Cross or Erin Cross have used the snake in order to murder Tiffany Wright. My gut instinct is that Kyle had this sick fantasy of killing a victim with his snake and his mother, obviously shocked but afraid for her son's safety created this cover story where Kyle Cross has "presumably" gone missing in order to throw us off from the despicable truth that... her son is really behind The Murder of Tiffany Wright.' There was another long pause before Sarah began to speak back.

'But that can't be possible, Erin Cross is clearly depressed by this whole ordeal. Me and Michael seen her the night after Kyle disappeared, she was crying and... she seemed genuine...'

'I understand that this may be hard a pill to swallow, Sarah, but this kind of thing happens all the time. It's only natural for family members to protect their own and you'll be surprised how well people can act under pressure. There is simply just so much evidence pointing towards her being involved in the murder, that the only possible conclusion we have is that Kyle used the snake to kill Tiffany Wright and he must have returned the snake to his mother in order to remove himself from the scene.' The Inspector explained.

'Detective John Prescott will be at the station at 12:30pm later today, You and Officer Carr are needed there too. We will be going through

all the evidence that we have found in this investigation so far. We'll see you both at the station, as for now, stay on patrol, understood?'
'We understand' Officer White and Carr responded through the Police Radio in unison.
'Very good, I'll see you soon.' Miranda said through the radio one last time before the radio's static fell silent. Sarah White put their Police Cruiser back into ignition, she drove off the curb and was back on patrol, cruising through Castlefields.
'So, what do you think, Sarah? Do you think John and Spencer are right about Erin Cross?' Michael asked her. Sarah paused, concentrating on her driving.
'I... don't think so. I mean it is clear to me that this isn't just some typical murder case, I know for a fact... well I at least suspect that something Supernatural is going on. Why have I been having these dreams of Demons and seeing Ghosts of Tiffany Wright and dead cats? I sound like a fucking lunatic, don't I?!' She asked Michael with a clear look of distress on her face.
'Anyway... John's story just doesn't add up! Why would they keep the snake if it was the reason behind Tiffany's death? It seems ridiculous to think that Erin would just openly keep the murder weapon on display for all to see... you saw her, didn't you? She was clearly distressed about the whole thing and why would she call the Police immediately after his disappearance? If she really wanted to cover this up, wouldn't she have kept things under wraps?' Sarah asked Michael, he paused, thinking about what he should say next.
'Perhaps she doesn't want to look suspicious by not calling the Police after her son disappeared... but at the same time, she kept the god damn murder weapon. I'm not sure to be honest, Sarah.' Michael admitted.
'This sure is one hell of a confusing investigation huh, Michael?' Sarah smiled weakly.

'You're damn right about that' He chuckled.

Officers Michael Carr and Sarah White arrived outside of the Police Station at 12:25pm, five minutes early as not to be late. John's red car and several Police Cruisers were stationary outside of the Police Station with a couple of officers entering and exiting the building. Sarah parked her Police Cruiser next to one of the others and then she left the vehicle with Michael, they both entered the station together. Inside, Chief Spencer, the Coroner Stacy Evans and the Inspector Miranda Carlton were waiting inside (along with a small crowd of other ranking Police Officers who were assigned to the same case) near the entrance for both Officer Carr and White to arrive. Carr and White both joined the crowd as they waited together for the Detective. Eventually when he arrived, Chief Spencer led them all into his private office to discuss the Investigation further, he had a bunch of photos stuck up on a wall in his office, all of which were evidence that the he had gathered. Sarah noticed there were pictures of the Tiger Snake that John had found and images of Tiffany Wright's naked body, zoom-ins of her injuries were clearly displayed in these photos. Towards the bottom of this collage were photographs of witnesses and suspects, she recognized a few like Josh Riley, Kyle Cross and a couple of Kyle's friends.

'I have brought you all here today to discuss our findings, John here has reasons to believe that Erin Cross may be behind the murder, but we cannot jump into conclusions...' Chief Spencer began to point at the first image on the left of the collage, which was a photograph of Tiffany Wright's dead naked body.

'This is the body of Tiffany Wright, the seventeen year old girl who went missing last Friday on the 12th of August this year, exactly 7 days ago. She was underage going to a nightclub, she got in with a fake ID and then this happened to her... according to her family and friends, this was her first night out on the town, such a shame...' The Chief paused, and a small, hardly visible tear rolled down his eye. He then proceeded to point towards the next photograph which was a zoom up of her mouth.

'Here we can see that there are several small cuts or scratches on her bottom and top lips. John investigated this further by looking inside of her mouth, he found that...' The Chief then pointed at the next picture which was a photograph taken from the inside of her mouth.

'...There were small cuts along the insides of her gums and throat, like something had crawled its way inside, or perhaps outside.' The Chief then turned his head to look at his staff.

'Our Coroner, Stacy Evans, took things further by opening Tiffany's chest, inside we found several strange injuries that we have never seen before. Stacy, would you care to explain?' He asked her rhetorically, she was quick to accept, and the Chief joined the other officers as Stacy took the stage, she pointed at the next picture, which showed the inside of Tiffany Wright's chest.

'Here you can see that Tiffany Wright's heart has been squashed or squeezed tightly, on further inspection I have found that her heart is actually full of small cuts and the excess blood that leaked from her heart may have led to the result of her death. I believe that something crawled its way inside of her body and damaged her heart, it sounds crazy, but it is the only reasonable explanation that I can come up with. My suspicions were further confirmed when Detective John Prescott here, found this little critter...' Stacy then pointed at the photograph of the Tiger Snake that John found in Erin's home.

'This here is a Tiger Snake, it is incredibly venomous and was found in the home of Erin Cross.' Stacy then pointed at a photo of Erin at the bottom of the collage.

'This woman; is the mother of Kyle Cross.' she then pointed at Kyle's photo.

'As we all know, Kyle Cross went missing the very same night as Tiffany, where Tiffany Wright was found dead, Kyle Cross was missing... to make matters worse, John found the Tiger Snake in Erin's home, now we believe that this snake may be the reason behind Tiffany's death, however there is one damning piece of evidence that goes against this... there have been no signs of poison inside of Tiffany Wright's body, so we cannot 100% confirm that this snake may have been behind the death of Tiffany. However, given the fact that Kyle has gone missing and there have been no signs of his presence in Runcorn at all, we do have reasons to believe that he may be behind the murder.'

'That's right, Stacy.' Chief Spencer agreed, he then walked over and stood beside her facing the observing officers.

'Although Erin Cross appears to be guilty, we simply cannot prosecute her at this very moment, not until further evidence comes to hand. She will be kept in custody as unfortunately *another* girl has gone missing in this town, in fact she is the younger sister of Stacy here, the girl we are referring to now, is Lindsay Evans...' A collective look of shock grew across the faces of both Michael, Sarah and the other officers as this was the first time that they had heard that another person in town had gone missing. John and Miranda seemed to have blank expressions on their faces however, as they must've already known this beforehand.

'Because of this, we simply cannot take the risk and allow Erin Cross to go free in case she is guilty of The Murder of Tiffany Wright.'

'Honestly, I think we should just prosecute her right now, she and her son are obviously behind the murder!' Detective John Prescott blurted out.

'...I wouldn't jump straight to that conclusion, John...' Carr intervened.

'and why not?' John groaned.

'Well... there may be a lot of evidence pointing towards her being the

Killer, however, Stacy has found no signs of poison inside of Tiffany's body, also why would Erin keep the murder weapon out in the open for all to see, even the dumbest, most rash criminals out there have the common sense to at least try and dispose of their murder weapon. If Erin really was behind such a strange and complicated murder, then she would have surely disposed of the snake and it's tank, wouldn't she?'

'You make a good point...' Stacy agreed.

John's face contorted into a look of disgust.

'I can't say I agree.' He groaned. Chief Spencer chewed his bottom lip then he looked over at Inspector Miranda Carlton.

'Miranda, what's your take on this situation?' The Chief asked.

'Well, I got to agree with John here, it seems like there is a lot of evidence pointing towards Erin and Kyle Cross. You can even argue that the poison in Tiffany's blood stream may have washed away while she was under the water of that canal. Although that does seem to be a bit of a stretch...' Miranda admitted.

The Chief sighed and nodded in agreement.

'Yeah... I admit, it looks bad for the Cross family, but we can't just jump straight into conclusions just yet. There are still certain facts that just don't add up or are simply missing. So, Officers Carr and White...' The Chief looked towards them, Sarah and Michael stood up straight and looked at their Chief intently.

'We'll need you two, to go to Lindsay's mother's place and gather as much information as you can about her.' The Chief ordered, he then looked over at John Prescott, who had a look of frustration on his face.

'John... I'm going to need you to interrogate Erin Cross after this meet up, see if you can get any more information out of her.'

'Don't you worry, I'll get a confession out of her, I'm telling you, I'm right about this one.' The Detective smiled smugly.

'Hopefully you are right, John. But I think it's a good idea to have both Officers White and Carr patrol the streets in case she isn't behind the murder. After all, another person has gone missing and the Killer may still be on the loose.' The Chief explained.

'As for Stacy Evans and Inspector Carlton, you two are free to carry on with your usual duties.'

'Understood.' Both Stacy and Miranda said in unison.

'Excellent, I'm glad we had this discussion. You're now all free to leave and continue your duties. Except for John, I will show you where the Interrogation Room we are keeping Erin Cross is.' After The Chief announced this, Sarah, Michael, Stacy and Miranda left the Chief's office along with all the other officers who were discussing The Investigation openly with each other on the way out. Officers Carr and White sat down in the dining area and had a coffee before leaving. After they had finished their coffee and headed towards the exit, Sarah White overheard Erin Cross crying in the Interrogation Room where John was busy interrogating her, the door was closed but she could hear the Detective yell and Erin Cross cry hysterically through the door as he kept on screaming at her, saying that he knew Kyle was behind the Murder and that she needs to confess. Erin's cries deeply upset and disturbed Sarah as she could tell they were genuine and not an act.

Chapter 20:
The Crying Man

That night Sarah White lay in bed, dreaming again of something strange and unnatural. She awoke only to find herself yet again inside of her old childhood bedroom this time with child friendly cartoon character posters and the same pink wallpaper that was plastered all over her walls, it was clear to her that she was having another one of those strange dreams again. This time however her room seemed taller, her bed was bigger too and she also felt incredibly young and small, on top of that she was also wearing a pair of Little Kitty Pajamas. There were little teddy bears and cuddly characters all over the floor too and when she tried to hit the light switch button, she couldn't reach it and the darkness that clouded her room seemed all the more threatening. She could just about reach the door handle, she then pulled it down and struggled to open the door fully. Sarah exited her old bedroom and was relieved to find herself in the old landing she used to know from her childhood instead of some random landing from elsewhere. She looked to her left and there stood the mirror high on the wall, she could just about see the top of her head in the mirror. A tear of fear rolled down from her right eye as she seen a five or maybe six year old version of herself standing there in the reflection. After the strange occurrence of what appeared to be something more than a Demon in her last dream, she was afraid of what may happen to her in this small and fragile form. Her train of thought was broken when she heard a small whimper (which sounded like it came from a young man in his twenties) creeped its way up the stairs and into her ears, she turned around and looked down the stairs which seemed to go on for miles, she could only see what must have been twenty steps in front of her before the rest faded into darkness. She stared for a while unsure on what to do, then she figured that whatever had brought her here wanted her to go down stairs and see what was what. So, she took a deep breath and hesitated before finally making her first step towards the dark stairway that lay in front of her. As she walked into the darkness that shrouded the stairs, she suddenly heard an echoed yet barely audible chuckle coming from behind, a chuckle that she recognized to be her father's, Cody White. When she turned around, all she could see was the dark silhouette of his body standing unnervingly still at the top of the stairs, however something seemed off about him, he stood a lot taller than she ever remembered and his limbs seemed to be stretched thin like those of spider legs. She gulped and then turned around to head down the stairs the way she was heading, after she done this, she heard her father say,

"That a good girl... you're going the right way..." in that same echoed voice. when she turned around to look at him again, his un-natural silhouette was nowhere to be seen. As Sarah walked downstairs, the sounds of whimpering from the unknown man became louder and louder as she came closer and closer to the bottom of the endless looking stairway. Once she reached the bottom of the stairway the floorboards beneath her crumpled and fell apart, she struggled to stay on top but eventually she fell through. She hit the floor beneath her with a loud thud and when she looked around, she found herself inside of an old abandoned warehouse or garage of some kind, the floor was made of concrete and the wind outside rustled against the metal walls that confined her. In front of her she heard the whimpering and seen a young man with his shoulders slumped over and crying. He stood facing away from her with the walls in front of him shrouded in darkness, as she slowly approached the young man, she could hear a second voice of another man that was unfamiliar to her, this second man's voice seemed to echo like her father's, but this

man seemed to be mispronouncing his words and struggling to speak. When she got close enough to the first crying man, he heard her footsteps and looked behind himself to see what was there, he had a look of distress upon his face and his eyes were red with tears. 'Wha- What are you doing here?' he asked Sarah, even though Sarah knew this was a dream, all she could do was blink back at the man as she felt so vulnerable and defenseless in this toddler body. A slurping laughter escaped from the mysterious stranger that stood in the darkness in front of the crying man, the creature shrouded in darkness revealed itself to her as it stepped into the light that was her peripheral vision. Sarah gasped and took a couple of steps back before tripping and falling over her own legs as she lay her eyes upon the monster that stood in front of her, it wore a tracksuit that had been stained with blood and the man's nose had been sliced off at the base giving him this grotesque pig like nose that had chunks of wet flesh that was still hanging off of it, the monster's right cheek had been sliced open wide, splitting all the veins, bones and cartilage that kept them together so that the jaw hung loosely and drool constantly pooled and drooped from its bottom lip. The creature also limped to one side and it's eyes were as dark as the night itself.
'Wel-Well ain't this-s-s a s-surprise...' The creature struggled to say as it's tongue (that was slit into many haphazard points) wrapped their tentacles around it's cruelly cut and bloodstained teeth.

Sarah White then awoke from her crazed nightmare, she found herself lying in the bed she owned in Runcorn again and back into her adult body, it felt good to feel big and tall again and not a defenseless child, hell thinking of it now, that beast wasn't even the worst she had seen. But it absolutely terrified her in that childish state. she walked over to the curtains and opened them quickly to make sure she really was back in reality and she had never been so relieved to see the empty streets of Runcorn Old Town outside, normally she hated the place, but in all honesty it was great to be back and away from that nightmarish hell hole that she had just awoken from. Sarah had no idea what that dream meant but she immediately picked up a pencil and began to draw the crying man from her dream, she remembered the man looking around twenty four years of age and she remembered him looking a little scruffy with longish brown hair and an unkempt beard, while his clothes also looked a bit tatty and un-clean too. She would go on patrol later today and keep a look out for this mysterious character as he may be the key to proving Erin's innocence and solving this case once and for all.

Chapter 21:
The Body in The Forest

```
2:35pm, Friday,
20th of August 2001.
8 days since Kyle's disappearance.
```

Donald Parker decided to take his Golden Retriever, Georgia, out for a walk around Runcorn's Hallwood Park. He and Georgia lived in Halton Lodge with his wife Sophie and daughter Chloe. He had lived his whole life here and never witnessed a horrid thing, (apart from the foul language of the youthful locals and an occasional threat from some nob head down at The Kings Bar in Runcorn Old Town) his experience with the town had always been a pleasant one at best and at worst, just a minor discomfort. He knew the town wasn't exactly sunshine and rainbows per se. He had heard several horror stories through newspapers about the town in the past, like local muggings, abusive parents, shop robberies and most recently the disappearance of two local teenagers, Kyle Cross and Lindsay Evans with a third person named Tiffany Wright who had been found dead by Police several days ago. But Donald was smart you see, he knew the town well and always stuck around with the right people, I guess you could say it was like he had this strange gift where he could sense whether or not someone was alright or a shady fellow, he didn't suppose it was a Supernatural ability but more perhaps the fact that he supposed that you could tell a lot about a person from the way they dressed, spoke and presented themselves. He always avoided men and women who only wore tracksuits and spoke in a harsh scouse accent with slang. I guess you could say he was a bit of a snobbish character for presuming everyone who looked and spoke like that was some kind of criminal, but by doing this he hadn't encountered anything ugly or unpleasant in the last 15 or so years since his late teens. Donald and Georgia walked down the long alleyway that separated the primary school and chip shop that was connected to another small grocery store. On the way across a bunch of teenage Yobs asked him if he'd go the shop for them to buy some "Ciggies" he looked at them funny, some were boys and others were girls and he wondered if in another 6 or so years if his very own daughter would join them once see turned 13.

'You going to get us one or what?!' one of the teenage boys asked in a snotty tone, Donald just ignored the lot of them and continued to walk his dog down the path. As he passed the playground that stood to his left on the way to the bridge that crossed the motorway beneath, he noticed a piece of paper that was taped to one of the lamp posts near the park. He approached the notice and looked at it. It was a Missing Person poster with a picture of a teenage girl on the front of it saying:

"Seventeen year old Lindsay Evans, has gone missing, last seen near Beechwood. Please call if you have anything that could lead us to her whereabouts, yours thankfully, Mrs. Katie Evans."

Donald gulped, he knew the missing were within their late teens, but he still feared for his daughter's safety and even if this crime was solved, he worried about her future and for the other teens behind him. Suddenly that snotty kid who asked for Cigarettes didn't seem so hostile and threatening anymore, not with a killer possibly on the loose. He pushed the thought out of his mind and proceeded to cross the bridge in front of him, cars zoomed endlessly across the ever-expanding motorway below and he couldn't help but take in the beauty of the sun that shined against the slightly damp roads that had been soaked by the morning rain. He smiled to himself and petted his dog as they walked across to the other end, he then took a left and proceeded to take the next walkway that headed straight towards The Runcorn Shopping City. This walkway was covered in forestry and he always found it relaxing and peaceful hearing the birds and other critters whistle and hum high within the trees just out of sight. Suddenly Georgia began to bark, she jumped high and the strength of the seven year old dog forced Donald to let go the dog's leash, she then began to sprint into the forest beside them.

'Georgia!' Donald screamed as he ran into the forest after her, he ran around aimlessly, looking around for his dog, calling her name for a while before finally coming across her again. Georgia looked at him, she turned her head in the direction behind her and barked, beckoning him to go and take a look.

'Alright Georgia, I'll take a look, just don't run off like that again, ok!?' Donald yelled at his dog just before walking over to a large stack of leaves that appeared to be purposely stacked up against a tree in the forest out of sight. As Donald wandered over to the stack, he smelt something foul and unpleasant and his record of never seeing a truly horrific thing in the town of Runcorn was about to be broken, because within that stack of leaves was a dead man's body. Donald jumped back in fright, then he puked, it would've been bad enough if he just found the body fully clothed and untouched but no, this was far worse. The man's skin had been removed completely, as if skinned by some sicko with a knife. Huge chunks of red flesh were missing and bones stuck out in broken pieces with veins stretched and ripped apart, the man's face had a look of absolute terror that Donald could still see even without the face's skin to express such emotions, as the man's jaw hung wide open as if screaming, the heart, kidneys and other parts of the human body were exposed and on the ground, the leaves around it were stained red with blood that still appeared to be leaking from the exposed flesh of the poor man. After weeping for

what must have been several minutes a woman with brown hair came on to the scene as she heard Donald crying.
'Hey, hey are you okay? what's the mat-' she stood in silence when she saw the skinned body in front of her, after a small pause she finally took out the flip phone that was inside of her purse, she then began to dial 999.

Chapter 22:
Another Found Dead

At 3:01pm that following afternoon, a dispatch came through to Sarah and Michael's Police Cruiser, Sarah parked up on a corner and answered the call.
'Hello, this is Officer White, what appears to be the problem?'
'Sarah... we've found another body in Runcorn...' It was Miranda Carlton on the other line; she sounded tired and emotionally drained.
'...I see, I'm sorry to hear. Have we got a possible ID of the victim?' Sarah asked the Inspector through the radio professionally.
'You see that's the thing... the body has been found... *Skinned*. All we can tell you is that the body appears to be that of a young male. I'm asking you two to go and check it out for me, I do understand that this may be a little out there as I can only imagine that this must be a truly horrific and disturbing sight. I have only heard about this from two civilians who have stumbled across the body, so I really need you two to go up to Hallwood Park and secure the area and let those civilians go, as we have told them to stay in the proximity until Police arrive. Can you guys do that for me?' Inspector Carlton asked through the speakers, Officers Carr and White both looked at each other, then they nodded in agreement.
'No problem Ma'am, we'll make our way over ASAP.' Sarah agreed.
'Glad to hear it, the woman who found the body will be waiting at Hallwood Park, she will lead you to where the body was found.' The Inspector said before cutting off, the radio went to static and then Sarah and Michael were on their way towards the crime scene.

When they finally arrived at Hallwood Park a dark haired woman who appeared to be in her early thirties (who was clearly in a lot of distress), approached their car and Officer White could see the dry

tears that were stained upon her red cheeks, she had stopped crying, but the signs of depression were still evident. White rolled down the window from the inside of her car and nodded at the woman.
'Miss, I am Officer White. I understand that this may be difficult for you, but I am going to need you to remain calm. You're going to have to show us where you found the body, can you do that for us? Once we have the area secured, you're both free to go as we will keep the crime scene on lock down, we just ask that you please keep this incident to yourselves.' Sarah explained to the distressed woman beside her car.
'I... understand. It's this way.' The woman spoke shyly and waited for both Officers White and Carr to park up and exit their Police Cruiser. The woman nodded at them both then began to walk up the pathway towards the hill where the body was found. Before the officers noticed the body, they seen a middle aged man sat down in the fetal position with his head buried into his hands, he appeared to be stressed and deeply upset by the whole ordeal, it was only when they looked up a little further from his position that they saw the reason why. About ten feet behind the man lay the skinned corpse of what appeared to be a young male. Michael choked by the sight of it, but Sarah, (who had been on the Force for a very long time) was used to seeing such distressing sights, she removed a pair of white plastic gloves from her Police Vest and walked over to the corpse to inspect it. she kneeled down beside the body and began to inspect the male's head, she looked at his face, the skin had been peeled off but she could see a look of horror that still remained as his jaw hung wide open and the male's blue eyes had their pupils dilated to an extent that indicated an intense fear and pain that proved that this man must have been alive while this whole ordeal took place. Sarah took a deep breath as the smell from the rotting corpse was revolting, after her gut felt well again, she proceeded to inspect the rest of the victim's body.

The body hadn't been skinned neatly, huge chunks of the male had been removed and grotesque wounds had been left in their place as if this man had been devoured by some hungry beast and then spat up again, it seemed ridiculous, insane even to think of, but she remembered what Andrew Bates had told her in that dream she had. Perhaps something truly horrific was haunting the town of Runcorn after all. Of course, the rest of the Police Force would not believe it, they would believe that some sort of animal took the boy out, like a bear of some kind. But even if that was the case, where would that thing have come from? This wasn't Africa or in the middle of a derelict forest in America somewhere, this was in Runcorn, near the local Shopping City and Hallwood Park for Christ sake, the only creatures around here were birds, squirrels and perhaps the occasional rat. A snapping sound awoke Sarah from her thoughts and she looked up from the body that lay beside her, the sight in front of her took her by surprise, but she had grown to expect such things with being Psychic. A man stood in front of her, inside of some forestry, but this was no regular man, no it was the skinned man's Ghost, his eyes were black and an unnatural presence surrounded the area as it began to speak in echoed/whispered tones.

'Follow me.' The Skinned Ghost spoke in a tone that sounded all too clear and loud within Sarah's ear. She stood up from her position and began to follow the Corpse Ghost but then she felt a sudden yank on her shoulder, she turned around and Michael stood in her direction.

'Where are you going?' He asked sternly, the two civilians had gone by this point as he had gotten their details for questioning and cleared them from the area while Sarah was inspecting the corpse. Sarah smirked sarcastically, to show she didn't take him seriously as a Police Officer, he frowned.

'I'm just going to take a look in the wooded area behind me. You never know, the perpetrator may have left behind a vital piece of evidence in those woods, you stay here and keep a look out.' Sarah ordered him, Michael chuckled slightly.

'You really think a man did this?' he asked half amused.

'Perhaps...' She nodded at him before turning back into the woods, The Skinned Ghost stood patiently waiting for her to follow. The Ghost led her to a pile of leaves that appeared to be blood stained, she pushed the leaves out of her way and underneath she discovered a mobile flip phone that was stained with blood, when she looked up to speak with the Ghost again it had disappeared from the area as if on cue. The phone was black, and the blood stained a bright red against the plastic casing, she opened the phone carefully and pressed the "on" switch, but when the screen lit up, it showed a dead battery icon. She exited the wooded area shortly after and approached Officer Carr who was busy writing notes and inspecting the body from a far.

'Find anything?' he asked her confidently.

'Yes actually, I found this.' Sarah hung the phone out to him with her thumb and index finger holding the top half of the flip phone.

'I'm going to return this to the car and put it inside of a plastic wallet in order to show the Chief back at the station for evidence.' Sarah explained to him.

'Understood, I'll inform Inspector Carlton of our findings.' Michael nodded as he took out his Police Radio Transceiver and began to contact the station. Sarah nodded at him again before heading off towards the car.

Chapter 23:
The Evidence

Later that night at around 5:45pm, Sarah, Michael, Chief Spencer, Detective John Prescott, Inspector Miranda Carlton, the Coroner Stacy Evans and the other ranking Police Officers all gathered round the flip phone that was found near Hallwood Park that following afternoon. They had managed to get their hands on a charger cable that had fit the phone found at the crime scene. The phone charger was hooked up to a plug socket that stood nearby the Chief's desk, the lead stretched just far enough for the phone to lie-down neatly on top of it. The team waited patiently for the phone to charge up enough to be turned on. Eventually, when there was enough battery inside of the phone to be turned on, Chief Spencer took the honors and switched on the power button. The screen flashed blue for a split second then a white logo saying "Sokia Tech" glowed up on the screen against a dark green background for a couple of seconds while a happy go lucky beeping tune played. Afterwards, the phone showed three options; an option to call on the left, in the middle was the main menu and settings stood to the right of the screen.
'Select the main menu, the phone has a camera on it. Surely there will be some photos of the victim on there.' Michael suggested, the Chief nodded and then he used the directional keys on the phone to select the main menu, a high pitched beep rose from the phone and then they were shown the main menu. The first icon Chief Spencer noticed was a missed call logo, he clicked on that first and a bunch of missed calls from a contact simply named "Mum" scrolled down the screen. Chief Spencer scrolled down the page some more and found that a contact named "Josh" and "Ste" had also contacted this number. Chief Spencer backed up and proceeded to check out the text box

from the main menu, there were a bunch of texts from the contact named "Mum" saying:

"Son, you haven't called in a while, is everything ok?"
dated 11th of August, Saturday at 11:32pm.

"Ky, please talk to me, I am very worried love..."
dated 12th of August, Monday at 0:50am.

"ARE YOU STILL OUT WITH JOSH?!"
dated 12th of August, Monday at 1:14am.

"I've spoken to Josh. We don't know where you are, please get back in touch with us love."
dated 12th of August, Monday at 3:45am.

"Kyle...

'...I miss you...' Chief Spencer read the text out loud. Everyone standing around him bowed their heads down and there was a moment of silence, a single tear fell from Stacy's left eye. The text was dated the 15th of August.
'We should go on...' John finally broke the silence. Chief Spencer then backed out of the text menu and proceeded to click on the camera icon, once he clicked on it, they found several low resolution photos of Kyle Cross and his mates out on the town, they appeared to be taken on the night of the disappearance. The latest images showed pictures of Tiffany Wright smiling at the camera, she appeared to be dancing inside of The Dungeons nightclub when they were taken. She was even wearing that same old red dress that Sarah White had found her in on that unfortunate day when they found her body. One

of the photos had a play logo on top of it, Miranda pointed out that this meant this was a video to the Chief, he nodded his head and proceeded to play the video.

On the video the team seen Tiffany Wright dancing beautifully, she had a wide, comforting and welcoming smile that incited life and a joyful youth that only brought tears to Sarah's eyes as she could only imagine what kind of person Tiffany must have been. It was so devastating to see a person so full of life reduced to nothing but a motionless corpse. The video continued and Tiffany laughed cutely over the music and a teenage boy's voice could be heard behind the camera, the camera then swung around revealing the person behind the camera to be none other than that of Kyle Cross himself with the black polo shirt and the purple rings around it's collar, just like his friends had mentioned that night of their questioning.
'Where do you want to go after here?!' Kyle shouted over the music to Tiffany in the nightclub.
'What? Sorry?' Tiffany leaned forwards, she turned her head to one side and pushed the back of her ear towards Kyle's direction, so she could hear him better over the music.
'I said... what do you want to do after here?' Kyle laughed.
'Oh...' she laughed.
'My parents are out of town for the night, why don't you come back mine?' She asked. Then the video cut and the phone returned to the photo menu. Chief Spencer then turned the phone off, he didn't need to investigate any further. This phone clearly belonged to that of Kyle Cross, however another thing became apparent to the team, they were not certain, but they had the feeling that the body Donald Parker had found in Hallwood Park that afternoon was indeed the body of Kyle Cross himself.
'Stacy Evans...' The Chief asked.

'Yes, Chief?' Stacy responded.

'I am going to need you to inspect the body that Donald Parker found this afternoon, find out the body's age, the blood type, anything that can prove the identity of this young man... we're going to need to find out what blood type Erin Cross has, I hope to dear god it isn't her son, but if it isn't... then Kyle may not be the only teenage male who has gone missing in town.' The Chief sighed.

Part Two
Murder in Runcorn

Chapter 24:
Jessica's Night

21st of August 2001,
8:35pm, Saturday night.

Jessica stood in front of the bathroom mirror inside of her parents' house, she had taken the time to recover after her car accident. She has made plans to go on a night out with her friends tonight and they will all be meeting up at The Kings Bar for a few shots and bevvies at 9pm. Jessica preferred going Liverpool on her nights out, but a little night out down the Old Town never hurt anybody, well not exactly, you always had to be careful what you say or do to some people because (not on every night, but on most) there is always a fight. Luckily Jessica never got into one, as she knew to be careful. She didn't want to meet any guys tonight due to the recent trauma she had just been through, but she still wanted to get dolled up for the night out regardless because she still liked to look good in front her friends. Her favourite girl band were playing loudly on her laptop in her bedroom nearby, she had turned it on to get hyped for the night out she was about to embark on. She sang along to the lyrics while she brushed her teeth, applied eye lashes and makeup to her face. She finished her look by applying a thin layer of bright red lip stick and then she went back into her bedroom to straighten her hair. She then put on a dark red short skirt that was made of silk (that cut just above her knees and wrapped tightly around her firm body), then she put on a white short sleeved shirt that had a large v neck that showed off the line between her breasts, after that she put on a brown leather jacket and a pair of red high heels. She walked out of her bedroom and looked in the mirror, she really liked her look, the tight skirt and zipped up leather jacket really showed off how slim and curvy her

body was and even though she wasn't out to pull a lad, she still loved the idea of looking cute. She winked and blew a kiss to herself in the mirror before returning to her bedroom, she then turned off the music on the laptop and picked up her pink mobile flip phone, she blew her hair out of her face and then she began to look at the time on her phone and she was shocked to see that it was already 8:59pm.
'Shit! My friends are probably waiting for me!' she gasped to herself.
'Dad!' she yelled downstairs.
'What!' he yelled back from the living room downstairs.
'We better get going, the girls will be waiting for me!' she screamed. There was a short pause and then she could hear him get up from the couch downstairs and turn off the television, when she heard his footsteps approach the hall downstairs, he yelled back at her saying; 'alright, alright. I'll get the car ready.' he sighed, this must have been the 100th time or maybe more that he had to take his daughter out on a night out and at first she was grateful, but soon enough she took it for granted.

Once in the car and on their way to the Runcorn Old Town, her father Harold, told her she ought to be careful what with all these recent teens that have gone missing in town lately. She told him, she would be careful not to walk around at night on her own or go home with any strange lads, he smiled, feeling confident that she would be safe, but a part of her was only saying that to shut him up.

Soon enough they arrived outside of The Kings Bar, her father rambled a few words that she didn't bother to comprehend and once she left the car, she dismissed him by quickly saying "ok bye", he rolled his eyes lovingly and then proceeded to drive off. Finally, she was alone and ready to meet her friends inside of The Kings Bar that stood beside the 80s bar named Coco Bananas and a couple of take away pizza places and a local shop. She approached the entrance to The Kings Bar, there were a few drunks sitting outside of the bar as well as a tipsy woman who sounded upset or stressed yelling at someone down her phone, a couple of door men stood right near the doorway outside, they smiled at her.

'Come on in Jess, good to see ya girl.' the one on the left named Connor O'Brien winked. She smiled at him and then he signaled her to enter with his hands, once inside she spotted her friends Ashley, Kate and Mary standing at the bar waiting to be served, while a young lad with a skin head (who looked to be in his late teens) stood shyly by, daring himself to talk to them. When Mary spotted Jessica, her eyes lit up and a huge smile spread across her face.

'Jessica! Oh my god, so good to see you!' Mary yelled as she gave Jess a big hug, Mary was the prettiest girl in their group, she was fairly short and had short blonde her that was cut just above her shoulders, she always had her make up done perfectly and always seemed to get the most attention off of the lads in town. Her other mates smiled too, they all gave Jess welcoming hugs as it had been a long time since they had all seen each other. Kate had ginger hair and Ashley looked almost identical to Jessica with them both having blue eyes and brown hair.

'It's a shame Lindsay Evan's isn't out with us tonight, I hope she's ok?' Ashley brought up the subject.

'Yeah I know it's a shame, but I'm sure she'll be alright, she's a tough girl our Linds.' Kate smiled.

'Anyway, we should get our drinks and go have a dance, maybe meet some lads, eh?' Mary giggled, the teenage lad standing behind her smirked. The girls waited at the bar for their drinks and while they waited the lad that Jessica spotted on the way in finally took up the courage to say something.

'So, do you come here often?' the lad asked nervously.

'Yeah, a bit...' Mary responded, not really interested.

'alright cool, cool. I haven't seen you around here before.' He yelled over the music, Mary gave him an uncomfortable smile and then looked straight ahead at the bar, the boy ground his teeth and stared at her menacingly, now Mary didn't notice this but Jessica did and a sense of unnerving crept over her, eventually the lad stepped away and blended in with the dancers on the dance floor like a ghost disappearing into the fog.

'Bit cold, Mary.' Kate joked.

'Eh, he's not my type like...' Mary admitted, the group chuckled. It took a while for them to get served as the pub was crowded that night, but eventually they got their WKs and a few Jager Bombs too. After downing their bombs, they were buzzing and all in the mood for dancing. On the dancefloor and a after a few sips of her WK, Jessica began to let her hair down and party. She noticed a few guys looking her way, but she didn't care, she kind of liked the attention anyway. But somebody unsettled her as she soon noticed one guy looking at her who wasn't smiling, a scruffy looking bearded man stood in the background, creepily behind a bunch of other young lads that were busy ogling her and her gorgeous friends. She looked back at the guy who appeared to be staring right at her without even blinking and he appeared to be mumbling to himself.

'Sorry!' a man bumped into her holding two pints of larger, one spilled on the floor a bit and he nodded in apology before heading to what must have been his girlfriend since he didn't bother chatting Jess up. When Jess looked back towards where the scruffy man was standing, he was gone, the whole situation reminded her of a slasher movie see seen years ago where a masked killer named Mike stalked a girl and her friends on a Halloween night. She found herself standing there awkwardly and fully aware of herself and she remembered what her dad had told her that night before she went out; *Don't go off with any strange lads or travel home alone.* The words rung in her head like an unanswered telephone call.

'Hey, Jess, what's the matter, babes?' Ashley asked, with concern in her voice.

'Oh nothing, I was just... let's just... dance.'

'Ok, no worries girl, it's been a bit… *difficult* hasn't it? You'll be in full swing in no time though, I tell ya!' Ashley laughed, Jess smiled and began to dance again. Ashley and Jess were close friends, they looked so alike that people often mistaken them for each other in college sometimes, they had been friends since secondary school, same year, same age and on top of that their birthdays were close by too; they were like sisters from other mothers. Later on; they sat down at a table, after a good session dancing, they were exhausted and needed a rest. Mary soon noticed a couple of the lads that Lindsay knew. Steve, Josh and Jordan were on a night out. She waved at them and they came over.

'Alright fellas, what are you lads doing here, I thought you wouldn't want to come out? What with Kyle and Lindsay going missing and all.' she chuckled, nervously.

'Could say the same about you lot too.' Steve smirked.

'Fair enough…' Mary winked, flirtatiously.

'I guess we just needed to get our mind off the whole thing really.' Jordan admitted.

'Doesn't really help that this is the town where he went missing though.' Josh sighed.

'I know what you mean lad.' Jess agreed with him, they both nodded their heads in agreement and they both cracked a smile each. Soon after the lads sat down with the girls and they all sat facing the dancefloor, the place was crowded and full of thirsty teens as well as total players, sexy ladies and overly drunk dancers. Later though Steve noticed a guy he remembered from when Lindsay Evans was

still around, he remembered her saying that this strange lad with a skin head was always staring and smiling at her and that was him right there in the middle of the dancefloor trying to get "lucky", but no girls liked him. Now with Steve having a lot of booze in his system and with The Disappearance of Lindsay Evans (a girl that he really liked) on his mind, he decided to take action. Steve stood up abruptly.
'Hey, where are you going?' Kate asked him quickly, Steve's expression was a snarl, but he quickly forced a smile before turning around to talk to Kate.
'I'm just going to have a little chat... with an old friend of mine...' He slurred his words a bit and sounded a little sarcastic, he then turned to face this mysterious stranger on the dancefloor and head over to him. From Jessica's point of view, she couldn't hear exactly what Steve was saying to the skin head, but soon enough she started to hear him shout.
'Where is she?! Where's Lindsay?!' Steven yelled, the skinhead looked frightened and Josh gasped.
'Hold on guys, he's had a bit much, I better go and stop him quick!' Josh jumped off from his seat and near enough ran over to Steve, Josh pulled him back and Steve just snarled and let Josh take him back to the girls. A couple of minutes later the doorman Jess knew came over to the gang of friends.
'Look guys, I like you all, but you can't just go up to lads in this place and start fights, ok? Now I'll let you off Ste, but if I see you do it again, you're out. You're lucky I'm already letting you off. Because if I didn't know you all, I'll probably would have kicked you out for that.' Connor warned the group.
'But that-that's the guy who took Lindsay, I know it!' Steve rose his voice, Connor chuckled slightly.
'I don't think so lad, he's only 19, just leave him alone, alright?' Connor asked before leaving the area and continuing his shift

elsewhere inside the club.

'Just let it go, Ste.' Jordan begged.

'Alright... alright.' Steve apologized. Jessica took her eyes away from all the commotion and noticed that same scruffy looking man with the beard staring right at her, mumbling a few words she couldn't comprehend from the back of the dancefloor. She squirmed in her seat and forced herself to look at her friends and away from where he was standing.

After The Kings Bar closed, Mary, Kate, Jordan, Connor and Josh left the Old Town, but Ashley, Jessica and Steven were still up for a good drink or two, so they stayed out. They skipped the 80s bar next door to The Kings Bar, not because they didn't like 80s music, but more because the place was small, and the alcohol was overpriced and nasty, (not to mention it was more for older folks rather than the young.) So, they headed straight towards the second biggest club in town, The Dungeons nightclub.

Once they reached the entrance, the three of them had to get patted down by the security guard on shift, pay the entry fee and get "THE DUNGEONS" stamped onto their fists so that they could come back and too from the club whenever they pleased. Once inside, they could see that the place was crowded and loud techno music played from the speakers that the DJ was busy mixing inside of a stall that stood high above the dancers on the dancefloor. Multi-coloured strobe lights lit the place up in blue, red, green and yellow flashes.

'I'm getting a drink, want any?' Steve offered to pay for the girls.

'No, it's alright lad, I'll get my own.' Jess told him, Ashley smirked.

'I'll have one, love.' Ashley winked at Steve, he nodded back with a cheeky smile.

'I'll get you a WK!' He said before heading off towards the bar.

Suddenly Jessica felt someone tap her on the shoulder and she remembered that creepy guy in The Kings Bar with the beard that kept staring at her and mumbling strange words, she held her breath, closed her eyes, turned around and opened them expecting to see that weirdo, but she was only pleasantly surprised to see that the man who stood in front of her was that handsome Doctor that she liked, Samuel Davidson.

'Oh my god! Hi!' Jessica screamed happily as she gave him a big hug, her reaction came to Samuel as a bit of a surprise, but she was pretty drunk by this point in time and she did fancy the dude a lot mind you.

'Hey... it's good to see you too.' He chuckled, Jessica leant back and let go of the Doc, she then looked up at him and smiled.

'Didn't fancy you the partying type, Doctor.' she drunkenly flirted.

Ashley stood in the background with a cheeky grin on her face, she thought Samuel was a real good looking chap.

'This is my friend, Ashley!' Jessica introduced Ashley to Samuel, he smiled, nodding his head.

'Hey there, nice to meet you.' he smiled.

'Nice to meet you too, hon.' Ashley winked.

'This guy saved my life!' Jess said to Ashley.

'Wow, really?' Ashley asked with astonishment.

'Well I wouldn't say that, it was more of a team effort but... yeah I guess you could say I saved you.' Samuel chuckled, Ashley looked confused and Jessica seen this.

'Oh right, forgot to mention, Samuel right here was my Doctor that saved me after my car accident.' Jessica explained.

'Oh right, now I see!' Ashley laughed.

'Well done saving her lad!' Ashley gave him a thumbs up, he gave her one back with a wide smile.

'Just doing my job.' he winked.

'Oh, so modest, isn't he?' Ashley smirked.

'He sure is...' Jess smiled as she began to rub her hand against his back. But as Jessica done this she felt that same weird cold chill that unsettled her back at the hospital and when she turned around, all she could see were a bunch of other people, mostly men dancing around, but then she seen him in the background, just standing there again with his jaw hanging loosely, the man with the scruffy beard stood staring at her behind them all, his head tilted forwards and his eyes looking up at her in an intimidating manner. Jessica had enough of this creep, so she decided to show him that she was taken. Jessica looked into Samuel's eyes with a look of absolute lust and he knew too what she wanted, soon enough the two of them were kissing and putting their hands all over each other and as Samuel held her closer. Jessica looked over his shoulder and the bearded man that was staring at her, now appeared to be in some kind of distress, he still stood there staring at her but now his eyes showed terror and he looked as though he was about to cry and he stood there squirming too like there was someone in front of him, screaming and yelling at him something fierce, but nobody was yelling at him, this man was clearly insane and Jess thought kissing Samuel would've made things better by telling this creep that she was taken, but now, she was all the more scared, but she knew if she stayed with Samuel, he would keep her safe.

'I'm just going to get a drink, I'll be right back.' Samuel smiled.

'Ok...' Jessica leaned into his ear.

'Don't be long...' She whispered, Samuel grinned, he thought Jess said that to be seductive but in reality, she said that because she needed him to protect her. Samuel walked passed Jessica on the way to the bar and when her vision was clear again, the scruffy man was nowhere to be seen.

'Jess...' Ashley said but she didn't sound so joyful as usual, Jessica looked at her friend.

'I know Samuel is a good looking lad and all, but don't you think this a little too soon... I mean it's barely been a week since Jacob died, maybe you should just wait a bit before getting off with him, yeah?' Ashley bit her bottom lip, she was glad that Jess was moving on, but she had to admit, this was a bit too soon.

'I know what you mean, Ash. But I've been seeing this strange man follow me everywhere, he has this crazy look to him and I don't know... but I feel like I might be in danger, I only really want to stay with Samuel tonight because I don't want that weirdo to come anywhere near me.' Jessica admitted.

'Ok Jess, I get you, just... I don't know, take things slow?' Ashley pleaded with her.

'I will, don't worry' Jessica winked. Steve came back shortly after with three drinks, two WKs and a Larger for himself.

'Hey, Jess, I know you didn't want one, but I got you one anyway. Don't worry, I got paid this Friday and I think we all need a good drink or two after what's been going on around town, you know?' Steve smiled as he handed a WK each to Jessica and Ashley.

'Alright lad, thanks. I'll get you one next time.' Jess smiled.

'It's no problem, Jess, really.' Steve held is hand up in protest.

'Alright... cool, cheers!' She chuckled. Shortly after, Samuel came back with several shots for himself, Ashley and Jess.

'Oh, hey there, this is Samuel, the Doctor who saved my life!' Jessica introduced Samuel to Steve, they shook hands.

'Alright mate, nice one for saving her.' Steve thanked him.

'No worries mate, what's your name by the way?' Samuel asked.

'Oh, my name is Steve, but most people just call me Ste.' he chuckled.

As the night went on, Jess got so drunk and caught up with all the fun of the night that she had completely forgot about her creepy stalker from The Kings Bar and come to think of it, she hadn't even realized that Steve and Samuel had parted ways hours ago and it was just Jessica and Ashley that were left in the soon to be closed nightclub. They were both dancing like crazy and didn't really care to notice if anybody was looking, they had denied several lads who had come up to them earlier on to try and get "lucky" so, everybody knew they weren't interested and the girls mostly went on with their night having fun with little interruption. Before Jessica and Ashley even realized it though, the nightclub's strobe lights cut off and the main lights on the ceiling turned on, lighting the club in a bright yellow so that all the cleaners could see what they were doing once everybody left the club.

'Come on, come on! Everybody out!' A Bouncer yelled at everyone on the dancefloor and there was a collective sigh as everyone picked up their belongings and exited the club.

Jessica and Ashley waited at the taxi rank nearby for a taxi each, but when Jessica reached for her purse, she found that she had blown all her money on booze and she didn't have any money at home and her bank card had gone missing after her car accident.

'Lis-Listen Ash... I... won't have enough money for a ta- taxi, so I'll just walk home.' Jessica drunkenly slurred her words to her friend Ashley, (who was also a little too drunk as well and none the wiser to realize that this may have been a bad idea to let her friend go.)

'Ok, Jess... see ya, next, next, next week... love.' Ashley laughed drunkenly.

'Alright, see ya later, babes!' Jessica burst out laughing before drunkenly stumbling over to where the canal was, the sky was just now beginning to brighten up and by the time she had walked home it would've been daylight, but only if she managed to get that far. Now you see this canal was hidden behind tall buildings and nobody else was walking along the canal and just as she left the Old Town area and under the bridge that led out of town, she heard some footsteps behind her. Jessica turned around, but she couldn't see anybody behind her, yet she had this strange feeling that somebody was standing there in the darkness of the bridge's shadow that shrouded the area in darkness. Jessica held her breath, feeling a little soberer now, but still drunk, she walked over towards where the sound came from underneath the darkness of the bridge's shadow. She stood just outside of the darkness and asked,

'Hello, is anybody there?' There was a short pause, but then she heard somebody say;

'Are you, Jessica McKenzie?' The voice asked, it was a man's voice and it sounded croaky like he had been smoking but there was also a hint of fear within that unsettled Jessica deeply and against her better judgement she said;

'Yes I am her.' Soon after this she seen something that she would soon regret as the man from earlier, (the one with the scruffy beard) crept out of the shadows revealing himself like a killer in a slasher.

'You... what do you...' Jessica stood there shyly, backing away slowly. 'Please... leave me alone...' She started to whimper.

'I am so, so sorry for this, but he won't leave me alone, I have to...' The bearded man rose his hands out in front of her and into a strangling pose, Jessica gasped, she spun around quickly and began to scream hysterically and as loud as possible as she ran down the canal, occasionally tripping over her high heels and falling into the muddy grass to the left of her. All the while the bearded man ran after her shouting, with a look on his face so fierce that even the way he growled would have sent a small child into tears. Eventually and unfortunately the man caught up with her, he hit her so hard she flew to the side wall and she let out a loud wallowing cry of pain that was quickly cut off as he forced his big, rough hands around her little neck and mouth, her eyes bulged open in absolute terror as the grip on her neck began to tighten and tighten. through all the pain and misery, she could see that the man who was strangling her, he did not have a look of satisfaction on his face but a look of sorrow and guilt that rose from his tear filled eyes.

'I am so sorry. But I had no choice, he wouldn't leave me alone!' The man cried and these were the last words the living soul of Jessica McKenzie ever heard.

Chapter 25:
Karma

22nd of August 2001,
5:12am, Sunday Morning.

'It is done... I did what you asked, now please, leave me...' Daniel Harriot asked the ghost of Jacob Kennedy who had been standing beside him the whole night, leading him towards his ex, Jessica McKenzie, a girl who now lay dead beneath Daniel on the Runcorn canal leading outside of the Old Town.
'Excel- el- lent.' The creature that was once Jacob Kennedy smiled, it's grotesque upper lips curved upwards as if to give a smile, but it's lower jaw hung in place with it's tongue curling up to the left side of it's face.
'Well... are YOU GOING TO LEAVE ME ALONE!' Daniel shouted, tears still falling from his eyes. The wicked creature just laughed.
'Oh, not yet... no. Just wait... one sec-second now.' Jacob pointed at an immerging apparition that lay beside the now dead body of Jessica McKenzie. The image was not clear at first but soon the shape began to take on the form of a transparent female body a similar size to that of the body that lay beside it. As the image came into existence, it's features became more apparent and the clothes the body wore were those of Jessica McKenzie's with the same muddy brown leather jacket, silk red skirt and red high heels and the facial features the body had were un-mistakenly those of the girl that lay beside it.

Jessica McKenzie awoke to see that same horrible man stand above her, his face was red with terror and some kind of disfigured monster of a man stood beside him staring down at her with a look of satisfaction that she could still recognize even with the blackened eyes and destroyed face. Jessica attempted to scream but only an echoed whisper escaped, she would have cried but no tears came, yet her vision was blurred and she felt her cheeks tighten with the same heat that you feel in immense sadness. Yet the tears refused to flow as if her body was now an empty shell and not that of the living. She sat there confused and looked up to the two men that stood above her, she sat there looking up at them like a confused toddler who had gotten lost and had no understanding of what the world was and what horrors it had in stock. But of course, this was exactly what Jacob wanted to see, as he knew it was the fear of the unknown that terrified her the most. The monster that stood beside the man looked down at Jessica and it nodded at something to her left with a sinister smile, Jessica looked to her left and immediately squirmed to her right and covered her face and eyes. She seen her own dead body lay beside her, the eyes of her body were bulged with a look of terror on her now dead face, the jaw hung wide open as if attempting to scream, her body's hair was wet with sweat and the makeup she applied had been smudged by her killer's hands. She looked up at the two men that stood above her.

'Why... oh god, why!?' she attempted to cry again, but with no tears to shed.

'You kn-know why...' The monster spoke to her, she had no response, but she looked at the disfigured man again, she didn't understand why, but she felt a familiar presence when with this man that she just couldn't figure out, but then she studied the monster's clothing and soon enough she began to realize who it was.

'Jacob...' She gasped, the creature's smile diminished, the upper lips sloping down and jaw hanging even lower with his eyelids closing slightly.

'I told you... that I would ma- ma- ma- MAKE YOU PA- pa- pa- pay for this...' it's growling voice lowered and for the first time in a long time, Jacob finally let his guard down, his eyes, although empty and full of darkness somehow managed to show her a look of deep sadness and shame. Jacob looked down at the dead girl he used to love, now a dead soul with her eyes as dark as his, an empty shell walking around with no goal and no purpose, just like himself. He had let the hatred for what she had done to him take over and he had bullied Daniel Harriot into killing her for his stupid revenge, but now that she was dead, he realized that what he had done only brought more pain into this world. Although her actions were rash and led to his own death, he thought ending her would bring some kind of justice or satisfy his lust for life, but no, it only brought more sorrow. *Hadn't I done enough in the world of the living? Now, even in death, I am still no saint.* Jacob thought and a tear would've fallen if he wasn't dead. Jessica's ghost stood up from the ground and looked at him with a mixed look of regret, sorrow and guilt. She had no idea that this whole time, even in death, Jacob had to live with the mistakes she had made that unfortunate morning. She was mad, she was distressed, but at the same time a part of her knew that something was coming, from the creepy messages on the hospital window, the chills that crept up on her and the creepy things she had been hearing about people going missing all the time, it just seemed unescapable no matter how hard she tried to avoid it that something, or someone, would eventually get to her in the end. *plop!* A quiet sound came from the water in the canal, the two men looked behind Jessica's ghost and inside of the water, it appeared as though some dark red hands covered in blood were rising to the surface. Jessica's ghost turned her head around to see what was inside, she gasped as the hands rose out of the water slowly towards where she was standing. The hands' arms appeared to extraordinarily long in size as they stretched out from the water like spider legs, Jessica turned her head back towards Jacob and Daniel, when she began to run the hands leaped out at her and the right hand's fingers dug into her mouth while the left hand's fingers had their sharp nails dug inside of her upper eye lids, an echoed scream erupted from Jessica's ghost the moment the spider length hands ripped her face apart, souring her beautiful subtle face into an ugly, bloody mess before pulling her into the waters below. A loud and huge splash could be heard as she fell into the water, then those horrible, devilish hands grabbed her again and pulled her down into the abyss. Daniel stood there in silence, he couldn't believe his eyes, the ghost of Jacob Kennedy however seemed more saddened by the whole ordeal rather than shocked, almost like he was expecting this to happen.

Somebody yelled "Hey!" in the distance. Daniel awoke from his trance and looked up, high above him stood a middle aged obese looking man with greying blonde hair. Daniel looked around quickly and realized that this man had seen Jessica's dead body in front of him, Daniel took a deep breath and quickly legged it down the canal, away from the Old Town and out of sight before the older man could make his way downstairs. The man from above the bridge investigated the girl's body. At first, he thought she was unconscious, but the more he looked, the more apparent things became. He eventually came to the shocking conclusion that the girl was indeed dead.

Chapter 26:
The Results

```
22nd of August 2001,
8:45 am, Monday.
```

Stacy Evans arrived at the Runcorn Police Station early for her shift at 9:00am in order to get changed into her surgical outfit, so that she could begin her studies on the body that was found near Hallwood Park yesterday afternoon by Donald Parker. She walked into the station and was greeted by other staff as they looked up at her while sitting behind their office desks, she nodded back at them and entered the women's changing room. Once she was ready, she walked towards the Coroner Office, she unlocked the white door that led inside and then she put on a surgical mask from out of one of the drawers inside of her desk, she then walked over towards the door that led into the Morgue Room inside of her office. Once inside, she began to open the vault that had the words;

`"Male body, 16-20 years of age"` labeled onto the bottom right hand corner of the vault, she carefully opened the vault and inside lay the body of the teenage male wrapped up inside of a body bag, she gently slid the body onto a assistance trolley and pushed it to towards a more spacious area inside the room. She grabbed a pair of white gloves and scalpel in order to perform the surgery on the body, the first thing she needed to do was take a blood sample in order to test the blood to see if it had any relation to Erin's. So, she turned around and grabbed a syringe out of the tray she kept all of the clean surgical equipment inside of, she walked back to the trolley she kept the teenage body on top of and placed the syringe and scalpel on top of an empty area on the trolley. She then began to remove the body bag that was covering the skinned body of the teenager found near

Hallwood Park, she had to admit, even for her, this sight was truly horrific as she had never imagined that something like this could ever happen in a town like Runcorn. But with all of her surgical background and history she managed to take it all in without feeling squeamish. The horrendous smell, however, was something that she had yet to get to use to. She thought regular corpses smelt bad enough, but this amount of decaying flesh was something else entirely, however she had no choice but to continue her operation regardless. The first thing she needed to do was take a blood sample in order to compare the blood type with Erin's (they had already taken a sample of Erin's blood when they brought her in for questioning a few days ago.) So, Stacy picked up the scalpel with her right hand and she then began to make a small incision into the specimen's right wrist, after this a small amount of blood poured from the wound, she quickly dapped the wound with her fingers before entering the syringe into the cut. She then began to pull up the pump that extracted the blood from the body and into the syringe's tubing. After this, Stacy walked over to where the test tubes were held with the blood filled syringe held gently in her left hand, once over there she slowly and carefully poured the blood into a test tube. After this, she screwed on a lid so that the blood would not spill or cross contaminate into any of the other tubes and after that she plastered a note onto the test tube saying;

"*Skinned Male Body age: 16 – 20*", once this was done, she then proceeded to put the tube onto an empty test tube rack as it was important to keep things separate. Once this was done, she walked back to the specimen that lay on the trolley behind her, she decided it would be best to examine the body for any cuts or wounds that would indicate how this body came to be skinned. The first thing she noticed (as did the Police Officers and civilians at the scene) that there had been large chunks of muscle and fat missing from the body like as if it had not been skinned gently but ripped apart by some carnivorous beast. On closer inspection she noticed small cuts around the specimen's lips, eyes and facial area that reminded her of the scars found on the body of Tiffany Wright, she wasn't completely sold on the idea however and she had to be sure they were the same. Unfortunately for Stacy, Tiffany's body had already been sent to Funeral Care. However, it was mandatory that the Coroner must take photographs of any suspicious wounds on the bodies examined, so there were some photos of Tiffany's wounds inside of the drawers at Stacy's office desk. Stacy then proceeded to cover the body of the teenage male, remove her surgical gloves and throw them into the waste bin, before pulling down her surgical mask and exiting the Morgue Room. Once inside of her office, Stacy opened the drawers containing the photographs of Tiffany Wright's wounds, she held them in her hands carefully and once back inside of the Morgue Room, she lay the photos on top of a clean surface. After that she removed the body bag that she used to cover the body and then she walked back to the photographs, picked them up and walked over to the body again to compare the cuts and wounds on the photographs to those that were on this skinned body. The cuts were similar in shape, however they appeared to be larger as well as deeper into the body of this specimen, also by the roughness of the cuts, Stacy concluded that the murderer or possible animal that killed this young boy must have been in a rush. She guessed that it must have been an animal of some kind due to the curved and ragged cuts on both of the bodies that were examined. Either this was some crazed animal let loose on the streets of Runcorn or some sicko using some kind of tusk as a weapon instead of a knife of some kind, *quite clever...* Stacy thought, *by using some kind of tusk, there is no way that I could ever get an imprint of the weapon used on the body.* The thought angered Stacy as this was only going to make the entire Investigation all the more impossible and with her little sister, Lindsay Evans going missing as well? Well let's just say, Stacy Evans was beyond stressed, but she took a deep breath, remained calm and continued with her investigation. Her final observation was to investigate the insides of the specimen, she needed to see if the body had the same cuts inside. So, Stacy Evans put the photographs back down onto a clear surface, she then put on another pair of surgical gloves and equipped her scalpel, she then began to examine the inside of the specimen's throat, and what would you know? Similar looking cuts were leading all the way down the specimen's throat, just like the wounds inside of Tiffany's body, only bigger, deeper and rougher. After this, Stacy then proceeded to gather some surgical suture to stitch up the body's recently cut wounds, once the stitching was complete, Stacy pulled the body back into the body bag carefully, before sliding it off of the trolley and into the vault it came from. Once this was done, she locked the vault's door. Now after all this, Stacy Evans only had one more objective to complete before writing her report and that was to check the blood extracted from the specimen and to compare it with the blood of Erin Cross. So, Stacy walked over to where the test tubes were held, she picked up both tubes containing the bloods of the teenage male and Erin. She took them under a microscope each, the results were upsetting as the blood taken from both bodies appeared to be an almost identical match, being the same blood type: B. With all of this evidence backed up it appeared to Stacy Evans that this body was indeed that of Kyle Cross himself, from his cellphone being found nearby, and the fact that the specimen died in a similar fashion to Tiffany Wright, the fact he went missing the same night Tiffany died and with the blood type being the same as Erin's, it became obvious to her that this was indeed the unfortunate truth.

Chapter 27:
The Unfortunate Truth

```
22nd of August 2001,
3:40 pm, Monday.
```

Erin Cross awoke from her slumber by a loud knock on her door, she had been sleeping more often since Kyle disappeared and the swines over at Runcorn Police Station had put her on house arrest. She slowly rose out of bed and to her feet, she then put on the same old clothes she had been wearing for the last 4 days and looked out of her bedroom window, there were two Police Officers that she recognized, Officers Carr and White, who were standing at her door with concerned expressions upon their faces. Now this worried Erin, so she quickly ran down the stairs without washing her hair or brushing her teeth, not caring about her appearance, but at the same time she didn't mind these two officers as they had been nice to her before, *unlike that Detective, John Prescott from Liverpool.* Erin snarled at the thought. She opened her front door and was greeted by the two officers who looked even more anxious and worrisome than before.
'Miss Cross, we have some unfortunate news...' Officer Carr announced. Now, Erin had a feeling that what they were saying was about her son, but after the incident she had with John Prescott she allowed them to continue.
'What's the matter?' Erin asked with her arms folded, trying to hide her vulnerability.
'I am sorry to deliver this news to you, Miss Cross, but we... found your son and, well-' Before Officer Carr could finish his sentence, tear drops began to fall from Erin's eyes and the Officer leant his left hand

onto her shoulder to give Erin some comfort, she leaned into him in response and Officer Carr wrapped his arms around her, holding her in his arms as she quietly wept. He looked at Officer White and she gave him a sad, yet approving nod, letting him know that what he was doing was right, Officer Carr nodded back with a sad smile and stroked Erin's upper back and whispered,

'It's going to be alright, it's going to be alright...' several times. After a while, Erin Cross stood back and away from Officer Carr. She stood there staring at the two Police Officers as her tears began to dry, still shocked by the news.

Eventually she asked the two Officers to come inside and she led them into her living room where they sat on the same sofa, while Erin sat on an arm chair opposite, Erin had her face buried into her hands, breathing heavily, almost sobbing again.
'So...' Erin sniffed.
'Where did you find him.' she asked. Officers Carr and White looked at each other briefly, Carr nodded at White then she looked back at Erin.
'Two civilians found him. His body lay hidden at Hallwood Park, we weren't sure of the identification, so we had the body analyzed at the station by our Coroner-'
'What do you mean you weren't sure of the identification! You had photos of Kyle Cross didn't you?' Erin Snapped, interrupting Officer White, Officer White paused for a moment, then continued.
'...Miss Cross... the body we found was...' Officer White took a deep breath and then looked at Erin in the eyes, the look gave her chills.
'...Disfigured.' Officer White finished her sentence, Erin Cross nodded her head with her eyes looking down, red and watered up, she looked back up at Officer White and a look of absolute sorrow rose from her stained red face and emotional eyes, shaking slightly

she struggled to speak.

'My... beautiful baby boy, oh god...' Erin tilted her head down and began to weep quietly for a short period, the Officers let her cry without interruption.

'Then how...?' Erin asked through her unsettling sobs.

'How...?' Officer White asked carefully, trying not to upset or anger Miss Cross any further. Erin wiped her eyes and painfully, heavily lifted her head up to face them, her eyes now even redder than before.

'How do you know that the body is my son?' She asked.

'We had the blood tested at the station, it came up matching with yours and we also found his mobile flip phone with photos and videos of him inside, we found it at the scene of the crime. The Coroner also came up with the conclusion that the body found was around the same age as your son. We will have to keep his mobile phone at the station for now as we will need it for evidence that could further help us solve this case, I hope you can understand.' Officer White said to Erin, Erin nodded her head, her tears fading now.

'I understand Officer... thank you.' Erin spoke through her tears.

'It's alright Ma'am, when you are ready to host Kyle's Funeral call this number.' Officer White took out her notepad and wrote down a number onto it, she ripped off the page she had written on and then placed the note on top of Erin's coffee table that stood between them.

'...and if you'd like to ask us any further questions, we are happy to oblige.' Officer White said, professionally.

'Yes, one more thing before you go...' Erin spoke.

'Of course, Ma'am.' Officer White replied.

'Promise me, you will find the man responsible for this!' Erin Cross asked the Officers, they both just sat there in silence for a few moments, eventually Officer White spoke.

'Miss Cross, you know we can't promise that... but believe me when I say it, I will make it our sole purpose. As long as I'm around, I will NEVER give up on this investigation, I and Officer Carr here will try our damned best to find him, won't we, Mike?' Officer White asked Carr.

'We will.' he nodded with a firm and reassuring look that somehow brought a glimpse of light and hope into Erin's eyes that shortly faded as she remembered that her son was gone, and nothing was ever going to bring him back.

'Thank you.' Erin said, her voice more clear now but still far and distant, quiet but firm.

'You're welcome.' Officer White nodded as she and Officer Carr rose from the sofa and approached the hallway leading to the front door.

'Here…' Erin quickly rose to her feet and beat them to the front door and opened it for the Officers.

'Thank you, Ma'am.' Officer Carr tilted his hat to her as they both exited the front door, once the Officers were outside, Erin slowly closed the door behind them. Afterwards she turned around, kneeled down onto the floor and she couldn't stop herself from crying as images of Kyle Cross scattered across her mind like film against a projector screen. She remembered all the good times she had with him, his birthdays, the first time he went to school, the last day he finished school, how excited he was to go to college and she remembered how proud she was of him, the art he created and the awards he won and the friends he had. He was so popular and smart too, Erin had her hard times with him, like any mother would with any child, but he had so much potential and he was the greatest thing that had ever happened to her, he was her only child, but still she loved him like no other. Not even the man that she had married compared to the love she had for Kyle and now that he was gone, she just simply saw no point in living, with her husband divorced and her son gone with little to no friends left. With all this sorrow that she had gone through, there was still one thing that haunted her the most and that was being alone. With no one to love or talk to she wondered;

How did my life get here? I used to be so happy, I had everything, a family, a son, a husband, friends. I used to be somebody, people cared, but now... I'm all alone and I don't know what to do.

Chapter 28:
The News Broadcast

```
23rd of August 2001,
11:45 am, Tuesday.
```

Lucas Miller sat on the living room sofa inside of his parents' house, he finally got a day off from that shitty job he hated at McRoonies and he was bored watching television, flicking through the channels looking for something interesting to watch, he could've just turned on his video game console upstairs and play some shooters but work left him so exhausted that he honestly couldn't even be bothered playing it. It was a relatively sunny day and the heat was immense, however he was glad that he wasn't in work today, Graham McDonald seemed so stressed, aggressive and impatient since Lindsay Evans went missing. He had been acting strange in other ways as well come to think of it. Graham was always second guessing everyone and that suspicious look in his eyes always rubbed Lucas the wrong way, he hated his boss more than ever in all honesty. Anyway, so here Lucas was flicking through the channels, his parents out of the house and the volume on high, the fact he couldn't find anything good to watch was annoying, but what really ticked him off was the fact that his boss didn't give him a Saturday or Sunday off this week, but regardless, he was still glad to have the day off and forget about work for a bit. He could've gone outside in this weather but with all the missing person posters and Police everywhere after the recent disappearances in town, Lucas decided he'd feel a lot better staying in watching TV instead, he wanted to relax and escape reality for a bit. Eventually the teenager came across BBN News, usually Lucas never really liked the News, but it beat the usual morning shows that were playing on every other station, so he gave it a watch. *It would be interesting to see what else is going on in the world* Lucas thought with a shrug as he put the TV remote on top of the coffee table in front of him and allowed the News to run.

'Today on BBN, recent terrorist attacks have led to multiple deaths in the streets of Berlin. Government Officials are working on cracking down the whereabouts of the terrorist group.'

'In other news today, British celebrity Daniel King has been found dead in his luxury apartment in Los Angeles this morning, after celebrating with friends and fans last night after the success of his third book, Ritual. Police are currently investigating the Author's death; however guests believe that he may have overdosed on some form of drug.'

'Also in LA; six churches have been burned down in a suspicious arson attack last night, several bodies have been found as the arsonist committed the crimes during several church services, Police are currently investigating the crime scenes.'

'Several teenagers have also gone missing in the north west of Britain. Three teenagers by the names of Kyle Cross, Jessica McKenzie and Tiffany Wright have been found dead in the town of Runcorn and Police are currently on the lookout for any suspicious characters in the local area.' A young female News Anchor announced this news as images and videos matching the subjects mentioned flashed on the screen to dramatic music. Lucas gasped when he heard that the local news had made it to television, even though he wanted to get away from it all, he was still curious to see what the News had to say about it and the deaths came to him as a huge shock, he watched patiently as the News Anchors went through the two previous stories in full detail. When it came to the story about Runcorn he turned up the volume and listened in carefully. A News Reporter stood outside Runcorn Old Town, Lucas could tell where the clean cut, middle aged man was standing because of the Silver Jubilee Bridge that stood in the far distance behind him, Lucas could also hear the distant sounds of traffic and street life in the background.

'I am here today, in Runcorn where, unfortunately, two teenagers have been found dead in this part of town. Another was found in an area named Hallwood Park a couple of days before the most recent discovery of a Miss Jessica McKenzie, who was on a night out with friends the night of her death. I stand in Runcorn's Old Town Centre right now with the town's Chief of Police, Mark Spencer... now Mister Spencer...' The News Anchor turned to his left and approached a bold headed Police Officer who appeared to be in his mid-fifties, the camera followed the News Anchor so that both men were in shot.

'...According to our reports, you suspect that the Victims may have been killed by the same culprit, is that statement correct?' The News Anchor asked the Chief, he nodded his head.

'Yes, we believe that all of the Victims in town have been murdered by the same culprit. The bodies all have several things in common, this evidence has led us to believe that whoever it is, may be targeting certain individuals. So far, they have all been in their late teens or early twenties, all of which were also last seen leaving the town after drinking in the local nightclub, The Dungeons. Another thing we have noticed is that a couple of the victims also knew each other and hanged out in similar circles, so we also have the suspicion that the Killer may be after a particular group of people. We suspect that these killings are not random, but rather planned and well executed as we have found it difficult determining the causes of death, there have been no traces of DNA or evidence found on the bodies either, so we believe that this person is extremely dangerous and highly intelligent.' Chief Spencer explained.

'We are sorry to hear about the unfortunate news in your town, Officer Spencer. Do you have any idea who this killer may be? Is there anything our viewers should keep on the lookout for if they were to visit Runcorn? How can people avoid an unfortunate end in your town?' The News Reporter asked, the Chief paused.

'The Killer seems to be targeting young men and women who go on nights out in town, the killings seem to only happen at night. We suggest to young persons between the ages of 16 to 25 that you spend your weekends indoors and keep a look out for any strange out of place characters. I will be closing down the local pubs, clubs and bars in town during the weekends until we have a confirmed ID of the target.' Chief Spencer spoke and nodded his head at the camera, the Reporter then thanked the Chief for his time, then he walked out of sight while the Reporter turned around to face the camera directly.

'If anyone has any information regarding the identity of this *mysterious* killer, please do not hesitate to call into our News Station or if you live in the local area, please visit the Runcorn Police Station. If you have any suspicion that you may know or have an idea who the Killer may be, we seriously advise that you give in any and all information you may have, even the smallest detail can lead to successful results. I am Peter Sanders with BBN News, Runcorn.' The News Report then cut to the studio where the female Anchor from before continued to talk about the events in Runcorn.

Lucas Miller shut off the TV, he sat on the couch thinking. He thought about the people he had met in Runcorn, several characters came to mind, but one name in particular seemed to stand out from the rest; Graham McDonald, the Manager at Runcorn's McRoonies. He seemed off since Lindsay's disappearance and refused to speak of her, she vanished sometime after getting the job at McRoonies and she seemed distracted the day she left work too. Lucas remembered her rushing passed everyone, nearly bumping into a customer on the way out. *Something Graham said may have spooked her?* Lucas thought to himself, he paused for a few moments before standing up and walking over towards the house telephone. He picked it up and dialed the number for the Runcorn Police Department. He brought the phone up to his ear and he could hear the phone ringing, soon enough an operator answered the call.

'Hello, Runcorn Police Department, what is your emergency?' A young sounding female answered.

'No emergency, I am calling because... I heard that you are looking for any... erm... what is it? Suspects who may be responsible for the disappearances around Runcorn. I have a feeling I might know the guy.'

'Right...' The female operator replied and there was a short pause with a few typing sounds in the background.

'Ok, Mister...?'

'Lucas Miller.' Lucas replied,

'Right, ok...' (more typing sounds.)

'I have sent a message to the Chief of Police, Mark Spencer. He will be calling you up shortly for a meeting at the station as we'll need you to give us a full detailed description of the possible suspect. Now before you go, can you tell us the identity of this individual?' The woman asked.

'Yes, I know this person's name and profession.'

'Excellent!' The woman replied in a cheery tone.

'His name is Graham McDonald and he is the Manager at the McRoonies fast food restaurant in Runcorn.' Lucas replied, there was a pause and more typing sounds on the other end.

'...That's great... how do you know, this Graham McDonald? What is his relation to you?' The woman asked.

'I work at McRoonies, I am not related to him in anyway.' Lucas answered.

'Hmm... ok, what makes you believe that Graham may be the Suspect?'

'Before Lindsay Evans went missing, she worked at McRoonies with me. She was new there before she went missing, she only worked there for a few days. I noticed that the Manager was extremely nice to her, nicer to her than he was to the other girls too. The last time I seen her, Graham MacDonald asked her into his office for a "meeting". Shortly after, Lindsay came jogging out of the office and out of the restaurant, she seemed distracted. I watched as she ran out of sight, and that was the last time I saw her.' Lucas explained to the Operator. The woman on the other end paused, he then heard typing again on her side, then she answered.

'So... do you believe that what Graham McDonald said to her in his office, it has something to do with her disappearance?' The woman asked.

'Yes, I believe so...' Lucas replied, there was another pause on her end with more typing.

'Ok then, I will be forwarding this information to our Chief, he will be calling you shortly to schedule a meeting at the station. There you will be giving us a full description of the Suspect. One of our illustrators will be there to draw up an image of the Suspect that you'll be describing. Chief Spencer will be calling you in the next couple of hours, do you think you may be able to come to the Station today if possible?' The woman asked.

'Sure, that's fine.' Lucas replied.

'Excellent!' she said again before hanging up. Lucas put the phone down and walked into the living room, he then sat on the couch facing the TV, waiting patiently for the Chief to ring.

Not even an hour later, the telephone rang. Lucas stood up abruptly and jogged over to the telephone, he picked it up quickly and answered.

'Hello...'

'Hello, is this a Mister Lucas Miller?' A familiar voice from TV spoke through the phone.

'Yes, it is, is this the Chief of Police?' Lucas asked.

'Yes, Mister Miller, I have been informed that you may have some information regarding the possible identity of the Culprit that may be behind the Murders that have been going on in Runcorn. Is that correct?'

'Well not exactly... I don't believe I know the Killer, but I do believe that the Manager at McRoonies may be involved somehow.' Lucas Miller replied and then there was an un-nerving pause that came from the Chief on the other end, Lucas felt a little guilty ratting out his boss like this. *He could get in a lot of trouble for this, he might not have anything to do with it and I just know this won't go down well if he's not guilty. I better ask if the Chief will keep my identity a secret, I'm not sure if I want this responsibility* Lucas thought.

'Hey!' Lucas broke the silence.

'Yes...?' The Chief asked, sounding a little annoyed.

'I'm sorry, I just... you won't tell him I told you this info, right?' Lucas asked as politely as possible. Lucas could hear a light chuckle on the Chief's end.

'No, of course not. Don't worry, nobody will know that you were the one who gave us the tip. you will be sat in an Interrogation Room where we will be asking you a series of questions about that manager of yours, the only people who will know that you have given us this tip will be the Officers who will be with you during the questioning.' The Chief explained, Lucas sighed with relief.

'Ok, I understand. When should I arrive at the Station?' Lucas asked, in a polite yet shy and respectful manner. The Chief paused yet again.

'...Well, as you may imagine, we have been extremely busy following any possible leads this passing week, so we will need you to come in tomorrow. Before I can book you in for questioning, I must ask you, do you have any plans scheduled for tomorrow?'

'I have work tomorrow in the afternoon, at around... 3pm.' Lucas replied.

'Hmm... alright then, we can schedule a meeting at the station tomorrow at...' (again, typing could be heard in the background on the Chief's side of the line) '...11:30am, I understand that you are a young man, so please explain to your parents that you are not in any trouble tomorrow, just that we believe you may have some information that may be vital to the Investigation. Do you know where the Station is and how to get here?' The Chief asked.

'Yeah alright, I'll explain the situation to my parents. I also know where the station is, it's near the Courts around the Runcorn Shopping City, isn't it?'

'Yes, that's correct, Mister Miller. We will be expecting you at the station tomorrow, thank you for your time...' Chief Spencer then hung up, Lucas slowly lay the phone down into its place and returned to the living room, he then sat down on the sofa and proceeded to turn on the television.

Chapter: 29
The Witness

Chief Spencer could not spare the time to schedule a meeting with that Lucas Miller today because he had another matter to attend to, he was to question an eye witness that had seen the latest murder in town. The Chief asked the Witness to meet today at 1:30pm after Police came to the crime scene yesterday, where the latest body had been found, that of a Jessica McKenzie, a young woman with dark hair who had been found dead by Runcorn's canal that morning. The similarities to Tiffany Wright's murder were all too apparent; they were both young women on a night out, dressed up, walking home from The Dungeons nightclub along the canal. *They were both brutally murdered and dumped there by the same killer!* Spencer thought, clenching his right fist. It seemed all too obvious to Chief Spencer that whoever killed Jessica, also murdered Tiffany, now all they needed was a description of the Culprit and then they could really start to solve this case once and for all. *Then again...* The Chief thought, *what about that Graham McDonald, the Manager at McRoonies? Perhaps he had something to do with it?* He second guessed himself. He had been sitting behind his desk for hours, playing with pens, thinking, trying to understand what was going on and what his next step should be, time was of the essence and if he didn't act quick, the Killer would strike again, he had no doubt about that. But for now, all he could do was wait and come up with some questions that needed answering, he had his Illustrator ready to draw up an image of the Witness's description of the Suspect and he also had the Interrogation Room ready for use.

Eventually 1:30pm came and the Chief was informed that a Mister Richard Page had arrived at the station, he then told the Receptionist at his door to send Richard to Interrogation Room Number 3 with the Illustrator.

'Understood, sir.' The woman said as she held the door open for the Chief to exit, he exited his office and walked towards the Interrogation Room, he entered the room and sat behind the table waiting for the Illustrator and the Witness to arrive. Shortly after the Illustrator entered the room with a middle aged obese man dressed in black track suit bottoms and a white t-shirt, the Illustrator led him to a chair facing the Chief and once Richard sat down, Chief Spencer recognized him almost instantly.

'I remember who you are, you were at the scene of that accident a while ago at Heath Road, right? that car that crashed into your truck, did you know that the driver was the same girl you found at Runcorn Canal?' The Chief asked. Richard was awestruck,

'I had no idea... I thought I recognized the girl, but... Christ, Runcorn's a small town isn't it?' Richard asked, rhetorically. Chief Spencer sat in silence allowing the Witness to comprehend what was happening, after a while he then continued.

'Yes... this is a strange coincidence, I must admit. However, that is irrelevant, and I know this may be hard for you, but I need you to describe to us the identity of this man you found at the canal.' The Chief asked Richard, delicately.

'Ok, I don't know where to begin... he-'

'Let's just start with the Culprit's face, can you describe to us what he looked like?' The Illustrator asked, holding a sketchbook and pencil in his hands.

'Ok, I did get a good look at the man's face. He was scruffy looking... he had a short beard around this height...' Richard touched the bottom of his second chin to symbolize how long the beard was.

'He had a... I guess you could say, small face? His eyes, mouth and nose were pretty close together, he had a tall forehead, I suppose, brown eyes too.' Richard told the Illustrator, the Illustrator nodded his head and drew something on the sketchbook that Richard could not see from his side as the man was standing in front of him, next to Chief Spencer.

'That's very good, Mister Page, is there anything else you could tell us about him, the shape of his nose, hair style, what was his ethnicity?' The Chief asked.

'Oh yes, well, he was white, but I never heard him speak so I can't say where he was from. He had a stubby nose, flat and round, short too, his hair was just as scruffy as his beard, medium length and unkempt.' Richard told him, the Chief and Illustrator both smiled slightly.

'That's great, Mister Page, can you tell us what kind of clothes he was wearing?' The Chief asked.

'Yeah... he was wearing a pair of jeans that looked new, but his jacket and shoes looked old, I wouldn't say he looked homeless, but the man was clearly... dirty? I suppose you could say, that you could tell he hadn't had a shower in a while, do you know what I mean? The jacket was green, and he wore a red hoodie underneath it, his jeans were light blue and his shoes were brown, he was about my height, but... a lot skinnier than I am...' Richard chuckled slightly.

'That's excellent, Mister Page. So, I say, you're about 5 foot 2? something like that, right?' The Chief asked.

'No... I'm 5 foot 4.' Richard told him, the Chief nodded and then he gestured towards the Illustrator, the Illustrator then showed the Chief his sketch, Chief Spencer nodded again and then the Illustrator showed Richard the sketch.

'So, does this look anything like the man you seen yesterday morning?' The Illustrator asked him.

'Almost... he was wearing a leather jacket, not a puffy one. Other than that though, that's pretty spot on, to be honest.' Richard smiled slightly.

'Ok great... I'll just adjust that little detail now...' The Illustrator said as he began to rub out the jacket and change it into a straighter looking leather one with his pencil.

'Yeah... that's the one, now that's what he looked like, dead on, pretty much.' Richard smiled a little again as he crossed his arms.

'Excellent, Mister Page, thank you for coming in, this information will come in handy I can tell you that now. So, we'll be looking for a man around 5 foot 4 matching this description and we'll also be plastering copies of this sketch around Runcorn on streetlights and in shop windows, etcetera.' The Chief said, then he looked at the mirror in the Interrogation Room and clicked his fingers, then the Receptionist from before came into the room and led Richard out of the room and out of the Police Station.

The time was now 3:44pm and Chief Spencer began photocopying the Illustrator's sketch onto wanted posters that would later be posted around town. Tomorrow he'll meet Lucas Miller, and the Illustrator will be there too, so that they can get a good idea of what Graham McDonald looks like in case he disappears for some reason. Chief Spencer leaned back in his chair, *it looks like we might be able to solve this case after all.* he grinned.

Chapter 30:
Graham McDonald

```
24th of August 2001,
11:45 am, Wednesday.
```

Lucas Miller sat in an interrogation room with Chief Spencer and his Illustrator, he sat facing the two from behind the table in the middle of the small room. The Chief and the Illustrator both had comforting/reassuring smiles on their faces as not to make Lucas Miller feel like he was under pressure as they wanted him to feel comfortable handing over essential information to them. Lucas Miller sat visibly stressed in his chair, he kept asking them if they would keep his identity a secret and he often hesitated before telling them things about his manager, Graham McDonald.
'Do not worry, Lucas Miller. We will be handing this information over to a Detective of ours, we just need a description of Graham and a proof of address, if possible.' The Chief smiled, sincerely.
'Well... ok, my manager is balding, he's quite big, wouldn't say he was obese, but you know... pretty large. He has a stubby nose. Big, wide eyes. He always wears a shirt and tie, he looks professional enough, at least for a McRoonies Manager. As for a proof of address? I don't know, but he has a car, a red convertible, you should be able to get his address from his registration plate, right?' Lucas Miller told them. Chief Spencer nodded then looked at his Illustrator who was still busy drawing up an Illustration of the Suspect. Once the Illustrator was done, he showed it to the Chief, Chief Spencer turned the page over to Lucas Miller and asked,
'So... does this look anything like your Manager?' He asked Lucas Miller, Lucas nodded. The picture showed a fairly decent drawing of a large man in a smart shirt and tie, the face looked similar to that of

his Manager and the balding hair looked spot on too.

'Yeah... that's him alright.' Lucas scratched his cheek a little nervously, the Chief could tell Lucas was stressed about ratting his boss out.

'...Thank you for your time, Mister Miller. The information you have given us will be most helpful, will your Manager be in work today?' The Chief asked, Lucas nodded back in response.

'Yeah he'll be in now, he'll be out up front helping the new employees he just hired last week.' Lucas told them. There was a short pause as Chief Spencer sat back in his chair, thinking about the situation.

'Ok then.' Chief Spencer spoke loudly as he leant forward quickly, gently slamming his hands against the table, unintentionally scaring Lucas Miller.

'...Again, thank you for your time, the information you have given us has been great, I'll be sending an officer down there to look up the registration plate and then we'll call you again if we have any more questions that need answering. Now if there's anything else that you believe may be helpful to us, let us know now, otherwise... you're free to go.' Chief Spencer spoke, with a slight smile.

'No Officer, thanks... but I can't think of anything else that may be helpful. I'm sorry.' Lucas apologized.

'No, no, it's alright mate. Again, thanks...' The Chief then looked over to the mirror behind Lucas, he nodded at the mirror and the door exiting the Interrogation Room opened as an Officer stood in the doorway.

'...Officer Phillips here will lead you out, and don't worry Lucas Miller, nobody will know you gave us this information, only us officers will know and we won't tell anyone outside of work. The information you have given us will be strictly confidential and nobody will suspect that you gave us this.' Chief Spencer waved his hands over to the officer in a friendly fashion and then the officer came over to Lucas Miller and led him outside of the room.

```
11:55am, later that day.
```
Officers Carr and White were on patrol through Murdishaw in Runcorn, looking around for any suspicious characters in town. Suddenly a call came through on the Police Cruiser's Radio, Officer Carr answered while Officer White continued to drive.
'Hello, Officer Carr. It's me, Inspector Miranda Carlton. We've just received some valuable information regarding the disappearance of a Miss Lindsay Evans. An employee at the McRoonies fast food restaurant in Runcorn suspects that the Manager there, may be behind the disappearances in town. She said that Lindsay Evans went missing sometime after a "meeting" in his office. So, we'll need you two to go to the restaurant and write down the Manager's registration plate number that can be found on his car, *obviously*. It's a red convertible that should be parked in the restaurant's parking area, just... try not to get the Manager's attention, we can't afford him knowing that we find him suspicious, if he is the Killer, he may try to skip town, you understand?' Inspector Carlton ordered them through the Police Radio.
Officer Carr held the radio's call button down and a static sound escaped from the speakers, allowing Officer Carr to reply,
'Understood Inspector, we will be heading over to the McRoonies restaurant right now.'
'That's great Officer Carr, let us know what his registration number is ASAP.' Inspector Carlton said before the radio cut off. Officer Carr then put the radio transceiver away and nodded at Officer White. She nodded her head but kept her eyes on the road, Officer Carr sat back in his seat and watched the road in front of them as she drove the Police Cruiser towards the McRoonies. On the way, Officer White came up with a plan.

'Michael...' She said to Officer Carr, he looked at her with genuine interest.

'...I've got an idea. Once we are near the McRoonies, I will be pulling up at the car park just outside of the restaurant. From there I want to scan the parking area from our view and see if we can find the red convertible that Carlton was on about...' Officer White paused for a while as she focused on the road (there were a lot of children playing outside and a lorry was coming along on her right) once the road was clear, she continued.

'... I want you to write down the registration number if you see it, or I'll say it out loud in our car if I spot it before you, it'll be like a little game I suppose. Who can spot the car first?' Officer White chuckled, Carr smirked (they often liked to play little games like that, it made the job more entertaining.)

'I don't want the Manager knowing that we are watching, if he really is behind the disappearance of Lindsay Evans.... there's a good chance he'll skip town if he knows we're suspicious.' Officer White continued.

'I understand, Sarah. That's good thinking. You really think outside the box!' Officer Carr smiled, White blushed slightly with a faint smile.

'Thanks.' she said quickly before driving in silence towards the restaurant, they were nearly there now, just taking the road through Halton Village, round the roundabout and passed the hospital, not even five minutes away from their destination. Once they arrived, they parked up outside the restaurant, just out of sight from the employees inside, both Officers Carr and White were almost certain that none of the members of staff could see their car, there were so far away that they both had to squint their eyes from where they were parked to clearly see the registration plates of the cars parked directly outside the tiny restaurant.

'Found it!' Officer Carr snapped with delight. Officer White sighed, jokingly.

'I guess you win...' she chuckled.

'...So, what's number then?'

'...it's D78 45N, I'll make a note of it.' Officer Carr replied as he drawn out a pen and proceeded to write down the registration plate number on a piece of white paper that was attached to the notebook he always carried around. Once he was done, he nodded at Officer White and showed her the numbers he had written down, she nodded back and then he turned to face the Police Radio. Officer Carr dialed the number for the Inspector and Inspector Carlton picked up almost immediately.

'You have reached Inspector Carlton, what is the situation?' she answered.

'It's me, Officer Carr here with Officer White, we have the registration plate number for the red convertible outside of the McRoonies.'

'Excellent, Officer Carr. What is the number?'

'The registration plate number is... D78 45N, Ma'am.' There was a pause on the Inspector's line and Officer Carr could hear Carlton say the numbers to herself and the faint sounds of a pen writing against paper could be heard through the radio.

'Ok then, that's great... I will be putting Detective John Prescott on this case. Just proceed with your regular patrol and get out of that area quick, before that Manager suspects anything.' Inspector Carlton ordered the two of them.

'Understood, Ma'am. We are on our way out, over.' Officer White said as she turned off the Police Radio, she then rebooted the car into ignition and proceeded to exit the area.

However, as they were about to exit, a bolding obese man in a smart shirt and tie exited the McRoonies building with a cigarette in hand, he stopped in his tracks and stood still with his jaw dropped as he spotted the Police car exit the area. The officers didn't notice him as he quickly ran back inside the building, dropping his cigarette on the way back inside.

Chapter 31:
The Chase

```
25th of August 2001,
7:45 am, Thursday.

I have been sent to an address today at 4 Pitchford
Road, Beechwood. The Inspector, Miranda Carlton has
asked me to investigate the house belonging to a
Mister Graham MacDonald, the Manager at a McRoonies
fast food restaurant stationed in Runcorn. I write
this out before heading towards the address, I
believe that this lead may be the straw that
finally breaks the camel's back. I have been told
that this man has been acting rather strange since
the disappearance of Lindsay Evans, he tends to
strike out and avoid talking about the subject
every time her name is brought up by staff at the
restaurant.
I am just having a coffee, black, at a local café
in town. It's not the best I must admit, everything
here has been most un-satisfactory indeed, I cannot
wait to leave this town and continue my work back
in Liverpool. Anyway, enough with the pleasantries,
I will be making a new report once I have
investigated this new lead, I have a feeling that
this case is almost at a close.
```

John Prescott finished his coffee, shut down his laptop and closed it shut, he stood up from the table he was sat behind and tucked the laptop under his right arm like a newspaper. He left the empty cup of coffee on the table and thanked the waitress on the way out, she smiled slightly, it was forced but John smiled back and left the café with his laptop in hand. He opened the passenger side door of his car and gently lay the laptop down on the passenger seat, he then closed the door and looked up at the sky, it was cloudier than usual, but still rather sunny for a day in England, however it was obvious that this sunshine would not last forever. He then walked around to the driver's side of his car, opened the door, entered the car, sat in the driver's seat, turned on the ignition, put on his seatbelt and began to drive his car towards the address Inspector Carlton had given him earlier that morning.

As Detective John Prescott drove towards the address, he noticed a red coloured convertible (with the roof closed) heading his way on the opposite side of the road, the car seemed to speed up a little when approaching John's car, it wasn't speeding, but John found this behavior suspicious, so as the car passed him, John turned around and looked inside the car. There was a blonde teenager, a girl, who matched the description of that of a Lindsay Evans, she looked terrified and it looked like she was pleading for help behind the car's windows. John Prescott immediately spun his car around and turned on the hidden siren to chase down this car, but just as John did this the convertible began to speed up and drive out of sight, John quickly revved the engine and chased down the red car.

They were speeding through Beechwood now and the red car seemed to be driving towards the next town over, which was Frodsham. John could see the car in his sights now, he had just turned a corner and the red car was about to skip a red traffic light with a Lollipop Lady and school children crossing the road, if John didn't catch up soon, there would be more blood to pay. The red car beeped loudly before crossing the red light, the children and Lollipop Lady ran to the left side of the road quickly as the red car rushed passed, barely missing the children on the way, the pedestrians then heard John's siren and remained on the side walk watching on in absolute terror, some of the younger children were in tears, but John didn't have time to look. John was close enough to see the girl screaming and the frustrated face on the driver, who was a large balding bloke that matched the description that the Chief had given him earlier, the driver was Graham McDonald alright, and Lindsay Evans sat in the back seat. The red convertible suddenly turned right after skipping the traffic lights, and other cars on the road beeped in a panic and swerved out of the way of Graham's red car, they stayed still when they saw John's car flashing red lights with the siren blazing, chasing after the crazed driver. The red car drove up towards a motor way on the right and John Prescott followed closely behind at full speed, (It seemed the red convertible far outmatched John's car when it came to speed.) John quickly turned on the Police Radio in his car while keeping one hand on the steering wheel as not to steer off the road. Once the radio turned on, he yelled down the speaker saying,

'There is a red convertible on the M4 coming out of Runcorn, I am an Officer chasing the culprit, but I can't seem to catch up, I need back up ASAP!'

'Understood, we're sending out a dispatch right now!' The Police Operator replied before the radio cut out to static.

'Great...' John said to himself as he continued to pursue the red car in front of him. John noticed the car seemed to swerve from the left and right side of the motorway, he looked deeper into Grahams' car and he could see that Lindsay was trying to fight with her kidnapper, which resulted in the car losing control, making it swerve from left to right. There weren't many cars on the motorway at this time, (thank god) but if there were, there would surely be an accident. Graham hit Lindsay real hard, and she fell back in her seat, John could see that she was crying and holding her nose with both hands as blood poured out slowly between the gaps of her fingers. John was close but not close enough to stop him. John decided to use the speaker attached to his car in order to tell Graham there was no point in running. He turned the speaker on and a loud static sound escaped the car from the microphone.

'Graham McDonald. We know who you are, what you've done. There is no point in running, you will only get yourself and Lindsay killed, including others. Nobody needs to die today, there has been enough blood in this town!' John yelled through the microphone, he could see Graham getting emotional as he said this. In the far distance John could see a Police Road Block far ahead, but it seemed like Graham McDonald was far too distracted and distressed to notice, John could see that he was getting through to him.

'More Police cars will be coming, Graham, you can't out run us all. Let the girl go, pull over and we'll talk. There is no need for violence, we can get you help!' John yelled through the microphone again, but Graham ignored it and continued to drive down the motorway, at full speed. Two Police cars drove up on the left-hand side where John was chasing Graham. Graham swerved passed the two Police cars as they tried to block his path, he nearly crashed into the side banisters on the road and John could hear Lindsay scream as they nearly crashed, but Graham quickly gained control of the car again and the chase continued. The Police cars turned around quickly and joined the chase with John Prescott. The chase continued for what must have been another 5 or so minutes, Police were on the motorway ahead, they had Police Spikes laid out across the road, Graham turned around and looked at John Prescott and the other Police cars, he then looked forward and slowed down slightly near the Spike Strip. Graham's car lost control almost instantly, Graham tried to gain control of the car again, but a Police Cruiser cut in front of him, while two more blocked his right and left side, John took the opportunity to block Graham's exit from behind. The red car was trapped and now all the Police had to do was exit their vehicles, arrest Graham McDonald and escort Lindsay Evans to safety. Two Police officers quickly ran out their Police car in front of Graham with Tasers in hand, aiming at the passenger, he held his hands up while still sitting in the driver's seat, his face and hands covered in blood. The first officer pulled him out of the car aggressively while the other stood back, aiming his Taser at Graham, they cuffed him and put him in their Police Cruiser. The car blocking Graham's right opened and two officers that John Prescott recognized exited the car, they were none other than Officer White and Carr. They both opened the passenger seat that Lindsay Evans was sitting in and at this point John Prescott had exited his car and walked over towards the passenger side to help out the two officers. Lindsay Evans sat in the back seat shaking slightly due to shock, she sat there in nothing but her underwear, she looked starved, pale and weak. Severe rope burns were clearly visible on her ankles and wrists and she also had cuts on her right and left forearms that sadly, appeared to be self-inflicted. There were also small rashes on her neck and the seat she was sitting in appeared to be wet with sweat. Officer White took her Hi-Vis Police Jacket off and wrapped it around Lindsay Evans. John Prescott, Michael Carr and Sarah White all helped Lindsay out of the car.

'We'll take it from here...' Officer Carr told John, he nodded in agreement and got back into his car. The Police car in front of the red convertible took Graham away and Officers Carr and White helped Lindsay into their Police Cruiser while the car on the left stayed behind to secure the crime scene. John Prescott drove off shortly after, he still had to investigate Graham McDonald's house.

Chapter 32:
The Old House

25th of August 2001,
9:52 am, Thursday.

John Prescott drove towards the McDonald Residence after the chase that had followed earlier that morning, it began to rain slightly, but the sun was still high in the sky, making the wet tarmac below shine like glitter. Despite the horror that he had just witnessed, John Prescott always found this type of weather rather spectacular. Summer was almost at a close, but the rain had come in early before Autumn. Passing cars seemed to shine as light sprinkles of rain glittered their windows and chrome for a moment. It took his mind of off the unfortunate events that had just happened earlier. John sighed to himself as he approached the McDonald Residence, fully aware that he was about discover something truly disturbing and barbaric inside of that tall, threatening and creepy house of Graham McDonald's. The house was rather Victorian looking and large, it became apparent to Mister Prescott that Graham must have been a rather successful man to own such a grand house like this one, the house must have been about a hundred years old. John guessed that Graham must have inherited this house from his parents or something like that. Now this wasn't a mansion per se, it was a standard two story house from the Victorian era, built mostly out of white painted cobble bricks with oak wooden windows, doors and roofing. There were other houses just like this one around Beechwood, but there was something particularly un-nerving about this house, almost like John could sense that something wasn't right, like there was something abnormal waiting inside. John drove onto

Graham MacDonald's driveway and parked his car, he switched off the engine and exited the vehicle, gently shutting the car door behind him as he approached the house and attempted to open the tall olive green door made of oak wood. It opened without much force, like Graham was in such a hurry that he had forgotten to lock the door on the way out, *those stupid Coppers, White and Carr. Graham spotted them yesterday and he made a run for it.* John snarled to himself before entering the now derelict building.

An immediate stench of rotting meat came from the back of the house as he entered, at least, that's what he thought it smelt like. *Anything foul enough smelt like that anyway* he thought as he covered his nose, it was a smell that after all this time, he still couldn't get used to. A tear rolled down his cheek, not just from the stench but from the fear that would follow as he knew that there was a good chance that he may come across a dead body or something equally disturbing. He had seen it, smelt it and dealt with it all the same before and it never got any easier. He stood inside the hall of the house and he had two options, go inside the living room or go upstairs, John decided it would be best to check the upstairs first before looking around downstairs, the stench seemed to come from the upstairs as well as the downstairs area, but John had no choice but to proceed further. He walked up the long dark stairway inside of this old Victorian house, the outside may have seemed fancy, but inside; it was quite the opposite. The white wallpaper leading upstairs was peeling and moldy in parts with bloody scratches in the paper, John came up with the conclusion that the scratches must have come from a victim trying to escape, one that Graham must have dragged upstairs forcefully. Lindsay Evans was a possible suspect, but John would have to look for finger nail parts inside of the wallpaper for proof, he could also extract the blood and get that tested. He continued up the stairs and entered the main bedroom. This is where the most horrific piece of evidence was found; the bedsheets appeared to be covered in a dark red and brown substance, possibly blood that had dried up on the sheets over a period of weeks, or possibly months. On the bed post there were blood stained ropes that must have been used to keep Lindsay's hands bounded on the left and right side of the bed, but there was also another on the center of the bedpost that would explain the rashes on her neck, they were also rope burns, the blood must have come from the cuts on her arms that she either self-inflicted, or maybe they were from Graham who inflicted them upon her. John imagined her screaming, *her hair wet with sweat, blood and tears as Graham cut her arms out of some sick and twisted perversion, Lindsay burying her face into the pillows with shame and guilt while Graham got on top...* tears fell from John's eyes as the thought crossed his mind, but this time it wasn't because of fear, it was sorrow. He wiped his eyes clean and continued to investigate. John followed the stench into the bathroom nearby, this is where he found pieces of sharp knives and glass that had been soaked with blood inside the sink, a sickly smell of bleach also filled the air, it became obvious to John that Graham tried to clean the evidence. The bath was also filled with bloody water and a messy red handprint could be seen on the side wall of the bathtub. John was careful not to touch the crime scene with his bare hands as he did not want to misplace Graham's handprints with his own. So, he put on a pair of white plastic gloves from inside his blazer and reached inside the bathtub to unplug it. When the water was drained, he could see clear leg imprints, those of a female, possibly Lindsay Evans, laid out upon the bottom of the bathtub (they were outlined within the thickness of the blood that lay at the bottom). John exited the room shortly after and headed downstairs, the living room seemed barren (apart from an empty couch and dusty TV that stood facing it) the room lay in darkness, in fact, all the rooms were like this, cold, dark and stuffy. The windows looked old and decrepit like they had not been opened in some time and the dust that lay upon them, darkened the rooms in a dark orange glow that was deeply unsettling, yet somehow comforting at the same time. This place was safe, away from prying eyes, where you had the freedom to do whatever you desired, that aspect seemed nice. But unfortunately, it was used for sick perversions and Taboo desires, by a man with no shame. A man named Graham who felt no mercy or remorse for any other human, he was a complete and utter Psychopath. John Prescott continued. He walked passed the living room and into the kitchen area, this part of the house seemed the most normal, but even that was a far cry from the standard kitchen you'd see in a regular old house. There were cobwebs around the window sills and the taps looked a little rusty, moldy food also lay out upon the surfaces with maggots and flies buzzing around them, strange black and slimly substances also covered the walls, the smells and ugly sights made John feel sick. He tried to turn on the kitchen light to brighten the room up a bit, but the light bulb flickered briefly before smashing to pieces, the glass fell on the floor with a loud shatter in the center of the room. John jumped back in shock, it was like a jump scare in a mediocre "Horror Flick". John chuckled at the thought but cut himself off soon after, *this is no time for jokes, Detective.* He told himself, before carefully treading passed the broken glass and entering the utility room in front of him. Inside this room there appeared to be more evidence; that old smell of rotten blood came back to him as disgusting laundry lay out everywhere, covered in fresher blood and other substances, some clothing and bed sheets were shoved into the washing machine, they looked clean and out of place next to the dirty walls and bloody laundry everywhere, *another attempt at hiding more evidence again, I see.* John made a mental note.

He left the house shortly after and called Inspector Carlton in order to give her a full detailed description of the house that belonged to Graham McDonald.

'I understand, Detective. It seems like Graham was trying to hide something in that house of his, all the cleaning suggests that he was in the middle of hiding the evidence, but he must have realized it was no use and tried to skip town in the end with Lindsay Evans... it is a good thing you found him when you did, who knows what he would have done to Lindsay if we didn't catch him.' The Inspector thanked John Prescott over the phone.

'It's quite alright, Miranda. I told you I would handle this. I know my methods have been a bit rough in the past, but they get results. I think Officers Sarah White and Michael Carr were spotted by Graham and he tried to make a run for it. Anyway, it doesn't matter now, I suppose. We've got the target and we caught him red handed with Lindsay Evans in the back of his car. Once the Forensics Team gets to this place, we'll have enough evidence to put him behind bars and this case should be closed.' John Prescott explained, there was a short pause on the other side from Inspector Carlton.

'Well... not quite, Detective. You see we have witness reports of another Killer in town, a man with a scruffy beard dressed in trashy clothes. He was found a couple days ago strangling another girl by the name of Jessica McKenzie. We suspect that Graham is a killer too but another one is on the loose. Perhaps Graham knows the other killer, it seems like a stretch, but I'm afraid this case is far from over, John.' The Inspector explained.

'I understand...' The Detective sighed.

'Don't worry about it, you've done us proud today catching that bastard and saving that girl... I'm sure Graham will spit it out if he knows the other guy, if not we keep looking, but we've got a detailed description of that target, so he should be easy to find. Secure the area until the Forensics Team comes by, you'll be discussing your finding in more detail at Mark's Office once they're there and you're ready to leave.'

'Understood, Inspector.' John Prescott hung up after saying that and waited for the Forensics to arrive. Once they arrived, he helped them gather evidence and then he left the premises shortly after.

Chapter 33:
A Wanted Man

```
25th of August 2001,
8:52pm, Thursday.
```

Donald Parker had a terrible week, not only had he found working at the local convenience store in Halton Lodge difficult, he also seen the dead body of that teenage boy who had been skinned near Hallwood Park. Even his dog, Georgia, seemed a little distant since the incident. Working here didn't help much either, it was minimum wage and he always got some snotty teens come in robbing stuff, like a bar of Kickers or a can of Cola. Some of them would try and buy Cigarettes or Alcohol without ID and he would have to explain to them over and over again; "I can't sell you them without a proper ID." and they would often say, "I haven't got one yet" or the classic "Ah man... I left it at home, I am 18, honest..." and then Donald would resist, and they'll freak out and start arguing with him, it was an absolute chore, but he knew there were worse jobs out there, so he put up with it. There were other things that Donald hated about the job but dealing with those teens was a big one. The job wasn't so bad though, the adults that would come in were fine and always had an interesting tale to tell, like how their day in work sucked, or how their kids were a nightmare and Donald having a daughter himself, could often relate. His daughter had just turned 8 recently and with Donald being in his late thirties he had a hard time keeping up with her shenanigans and Pop Culture references. He liked Vintage Scooters and Motown music, while she liked pretty boy pop bands and all those music based TV channels. Donald often thought about his daughter, the kind of shows she watched were trashy, women dressing up like sluts, acting like them too while all the boys she liked were all "Gangster" rappers with backwards caps and baggy trousers, objectifying women with words like "Sweet ass" or "Damn girl..." while they whistled. He found it discomforting seeing his daughter watch such teen shows, she may have only been 8 but she was growing out of all that kiddy stuff and found the late teen entertainment more up her alley, which was a worry but, *what makes her happy, makes her happy...* he often thought. If he didn't let her watch what she wanted, she'll have a temper tantrum. Still, seeing all these teens, hanging around this shop, the boys acting like thugs and the young girls and acting "mature", it worried him greatly. It wasn't just his daughter that he worried about, his wife seemed distant too, come to think of it she had been for a while, but at least before, she seemed happy. Being a mother always put a smile on her face, but now, after 8 years of it, she seemed kind of drained. Donald thought about his family while he was busy cleaning the shelves around the store, he had worked there about 4 years now and was close friends with the Boss, Charlotte, who was a slim, blonde woman in her early forties who came to Runcorn from Liverpool back in the 1987. She stood behind the till waiting for other customers to come in through the door before they closed at 10:00pm. It had been a quiet day and a quiet night too, and with it being a Wednesday, they didn't get a lot of school kids coming in either, the kids just wanted to go home and get some rest after school and it was the same for Charlotte and Donald too. Donald noticed Charlotte looking at the Wanted Poster that the Police had put up of a Suspect Illustration, he stopped what he was doing and looked at her from where he was standing, Charlotte began to speak while she kept her eyes on the poster. 'Funny looking fella, isn't he?' she said, Donald looked at the poster, the man in the picture had a small nose, buggy eyes, a scruffy looking beard and unkempt hair.

'Looks like a homeless.' Donald chuckled. Charlotte laughed,

'Yeah...' she sighed.

Some time passed and Donald went back to cleaning and Charlotte opened the tills so that she could begin the count, it was now 9:48pm and they were about to close the store early when the door rang open and a customer came through the door, the two of them put on forced smiles and stiffened their backs to greet him. The man who came through the door was wet from the rain, wearing a brown leather jacket, a red hoodie underneath, his sweat pants looked dirty and worn out, matching his tatty looking trainers. He also had a scruffy beard and unkempt hair. The two of them didn't make the connection straightaway, but they felt a little strange around this fellow. This guy kept on flinching and looking around his back with anxiety, Donald thought this guy was probably on drugs or something like that, while Charlotte thought he was a loony from the YMCA. The man mumbled to himself as well, Donald thought he heard the words "She didn't need to..." or something like that. Eventually the man picked up a large bottle of Whiskey from the back of the store and headed towards the counter, Charlotte stood behind the till with a smile, awaiting him. The man smiled forcefully and handed her the bottle, as she moved her head to open the till the man noticed the Wanted Poster and his eyes seemed to bulge with genuine fear, Donald caught this and looked at the poster again, it was a match. He was the Wanted Man.

'Hey!' Donald shouted at the man, he looked at him, his face a look of terror, the scruffy man snatched the bottle out of Charlotte's hands.

'What are you doing!?' she screamed as the man barged through the door.

'He's the Killer, call the Police!' Donald told her as he ran out after him. It was pitch black out doors and raining heavily, but Donald could see the man's silhouette disappear into the darkness that wasn't covered by street lights. Donald ran into the darkness after the man, he heard Police sirens through the sounds of rain and then blue and green flashing lights cut around the street corner, lightening the wet surfaces around them as he chased after the man who was heading towards the nearby school. The scruffy man ran into the road and a loud beep could be heard as a Police car approached at high speeds. The man put his hands up in the air to cover his face, but it was no use, before he could properly react, the car rammed straight into him. The man skid along the floor like a ragdoll, his arms thudding against the wet tarmac every time he flipped over. The Police car came to a thrashing halt and an officer exited the vehicle, Donald stood nearby on the sidewalk and watched on in horror. The scruffy man began to stand up from his accident and attempt to limp away from the officer, but he caught up and aimed his Taser at him. The man slowly lifted his arms in the air and the officer spun him around slowly and began to cuff him, the officer noticed Donald Parker watching in the rain, as he led the scruffy man towards the Police car.

'Thanks for calling us, don't worry, we'll take it from here. Stay put though, we'll need to ask you a few questions.' The officer told Donald, Donald nodded in response, so did the officer. The scruffy man limped in front of the officer towards the Police car, groaning with every step, once he was inside the car, the officer closed the door on him and walked over towards Donald Parker. Donald noticed that the officer's badge read "Constable Phillips" on his Hi-Vis Police Jacket.

'We got a call in the local area from that shop nearby, I assume you work there?' The officer asked with a stern look.

'Yes... I was in the store and I noticed that man come in, he seemed strange, off putting even. I noticed the Wanted Poster behind our counter and realized it was him. I told my boss to call the Police and I guess that's where you came in...' Donald told the officer. The young Police man smiled slightly and wrote something down on a note pad he had on him.

'That's great, thanks... so, who called us?' The officer asked.

'That was Charlotte, she owns the store.' Donald responded, the officer nodded his head again and proceeded to write that down.

'Ok... I'll send another officer down shortly to ask you and her a few questions. Before I go though, I'll need to write down your address and phone number in case we need to get in contact with you again.'

'Ok sure thing...' Donald told the officer his details, the officer thanked Donald and got back in his car, the scruffy man looked distressed in the back seat almost crying, Donald could see the officer yell at him behind the car's windows, he couldn't tell exactly what the officer said, but his best guess was that he told the scruffy man to "Shut up!" Donald couldn't blame him. Donald watched as the car drove off, the flashing lights driving further away leaving the area in darkness yet again.

Chapter 34:
Two Suspects, One Killer

26th of August 2001,
10:14am, Friday.

Officer White was called into the Runcorn Police Station by the Chief of Police, Mark Spencer. She arrived outside the station in her car and the Chief was waiting for her outside, smoking a cigarette. He nodded at her once she parked up and exited her car, she smiled slightly at the Chief, once she walked near him, he asked,
'You can stay out here while I smoke or wait inside my office if you like?'
Sarah White shrugged and took out a cigarette from her pocket, she was about to bring out a lighter but the Chief had his out already and held it out for her with the flame flickering on.
'Here, light it up.' he nodded.
'Thanks...' she said before putting the cigarette in her mouth, covering her hand over the flame and reaching into the flame with it held in her mouth. Once the cigarette was lit, Chief Spencer put his lighter away, switched off the flame and put it back in his pocket. Sarah took her first whiff of the cigarette then she pulled it away and let the smoke escape her mouth with a satisfied sigh, the smoke blew up in the air and evaporated into the sky.
'We're close you know...' Chief Spencer said to her, she looked at him and he continued.
'...We have two suspects today, Graham McDonald which you know and a Daniel Harriot. Daniel is the one Richard Page seen last Saturday, standing over Jessica McKenzie's body. Daniel's been acting strange, always looking over his shoulder, talking to himself...' The

Chief took another smoke before continuing,

'I think he's got something wrong with him, a mental condition, Schizophrenia or PTSD, something like that... I reckon he's our killer, but that Graham though... I don't know what his story is.' He paused and watched as Sarah smoked her cigarette, he looked around a bit, the sky was grey, it had been sunny all August but lately it had been raining and the temperature had dropped. The two of them smoked in silence for a while, soon enough though, it started raining again and the Chief sighed.

'...We better turn in, we haven't got all day, I'll see you inside my office, don't be long...' He said after finishing his cigarette, digging it into the station's walls and throwing the remains onto the rain drenched ground below, he turned around and entered the building. Sarah finished smoking shortly after and entered the building to meet the Chief in his office, reporting for duty.

Sarah walked into the Chief's Office. Mark Spencer was already sat behind his desk, he had a lot of paper work on the top of it. Sarah sat behind the small guest chair in front of his desk, he leant over the desk towards her once she sat down.

'So, Sarah... I've called you in today because I want you to interrogate the Suspects. I've noticed your Police work... you're a good cop, but you screwed up recently after getting Graham's license plate number. John suggests that he seen you on Tuesday and so he tried to run town with Lindsay Evans, we could have avoided that little incident yesterday on the M4 if you just got his number without him noticing... we can't have this happen again, you understand?' The Chief told her with a stern expression.

'Yes sir, I understand, it won't happen again...' she apologized anxiously. The Chief tightened his lips.

'Good... apart from that though, you've been doing well. You found the body of Tiffany Wright and you've been doing a good job questioning people, getting information out of them. So, I'm going to give you another chance today with the interrogations. Graham McDonald is in Interrogation Room 3 and Daniel in number 2, visit David Cartmen in the Coroner Office... he's a Coroner from Warrington, Stacy Evans is on a temporary absence, I'm letting her spend some time with her little sister, Lindsay, after the car accident yesterday. At least until she's ready for work again. David has some information on the evidence found in Graham's car and household, you already know the information on the bodies found, but if there's anything else you need knowing, he'll provide.' The Chief ordered her, she nodded and left the office. The station was busy that day, lots of officers behind desks doing paper work, phones going off every now and again, staff members rushing around. Once Sarah entered The Coroner Office, the loud noises behind her settled as the door closed. A rather large, elderly man dressed in white overalls with short brown greying hair stood in the room facing her.

'Hello you must be Officer White, I'm the Substitute Coroner, David Cartmen.' He introduced himself.

'Hi there, nice to meet you, so what can you tell me about Graham McDonald?' She asked.

'Well... we have a lot of information on him...' David Cartmen said as he walked towards Stacy's desk and picked up some photos from the crime scenes, he handed them over to Sarah. The first set of photos showed the ropes on Graham's bed.

'We found these ropes on Graham's bed and if you look at the rope burns on Lindsay's neck and arms, they're a match...' David explained as Sarah looked through the photos.

'So, Graham tied her up and kept her prisoner... for what reason? What does the Evidence suggest?' She asked, the Coroner gave her another set of photographs and took the ones in her hand off her and

back onto the desk, the new set of photos showed the inside of
Graham McDonald's car. The first photo showed the back seat, ropes
were also fastened into the right and left sides of the car, but her
hands were never tied to them as he must have been in such a rush he
forgot. In the center seat where she sat, the seat looked a little damp
and some blood stains could be found along the seats, not much to go
on, it appeared as though those bloodstains came from the crash.
'What about the ropes in the car, do they look old? Maybe he has
taken her around Runcorn a couple of times for some reason?' Sarah
asked, and the Coroner inspected the photos closer.
'The ropes look fairly new and un-used, I think he just fitted them in
quickly to keep her hands down on the ride to wherever he wanted to
take her.' The Coroner explained, Sarah sighed.
'Are there anymore photos?' she asked.
'Yes, there are two more sets...' He told her as he took those photos off
her and gave her a new set. These photos showed sharp pieces of
glass and knives with photographs of Lindsay's wounds on her
forearms that matched the objects' imprints.
'We found these in his house, they match the wounds on her arms
and the finger prints found on them belong to Graham, perhaps these
are the Murder Weapons?' The Coroner suggested, Sarah nodded in
agreement, it seemed plausible.
'What's the next set of photos?' she asked David, he handed her the
last set, she looked through them thoroughly. This set showed
photographs of the dirty laundry and blood stains on the walls
leading upstairs towards Graham's bedroom.
'The photos suggest, at least to me, that Lindsay lost a lot of blood
while imprisoned inside his house. I met the Detective from
Liverpool, John Prescott, yesterday. John thinks the scratches on the
wall means that she tried to escape multiple times, but Graham tied
her to the bed to keep her put. For what reason? I'm not sure, he

could just be some kidnapper but with the killings going on, there is a good chance he's done this before. This may be the place where Kyle was skinned, however, we have no DNA evidence supporting that claim.' David explained to her.
Officer White thanked the Coroner and asked him what his take on the situation was, David paused.
'...In my opinion... I think Daniel isn't the Infamous Killer around town, I know he killed that girl Jessica, but her death seemed sloppy and un-planned, his DNA all over her. No, the other killings have been well executed, or so I've been told... the murder Daniel committed seems too rushed and out of anger, while the first two killings appeared to be planned, the house was a wreck when John arrived, but I think, given enough time, Graham would have cleaned that place out and somehow wash his DNA off of Lindsay's body.' David explained to her, she sighed, thinking about his explanation, *it certainly has merit* she thought. She shook his hand and exited the office.

Sarah White entered Interrogation Room 3 to interrogate Graham McDonald. The McRoonies Manager seemed bitter, he sat there frowning behind the table at Sarah, a small stitched up scar lay upon his forehead from the car accident yesterday. Sarah White sat down on the table facing him and began to ask him a few questions.
'Mister McDonald, I am Officer White, we have a lot of questions... firstly we would like to know why Lindsay Evans was found inside your car yesterday morning, for what reason did you keep her hostage?' Sarah asked with stern confidence, Graham sighed.
'I have nothing to say...' he replied.
Sarah sat in silence facing him with a menacing expression, the McRoonies Manager chuckled at the attempt of her threat, she snarled.

'You know what I think, Mister McDonald... you're behind the killings in town and Lindsay Evans was your next victim.' She told him, the man growled slightly then let out a small amused cough.
'...and what proof have you got of that?' he grinned, full of himself that they had no proof tying him to the murders. Sarah crunched her knuckles.

'We found murder weapons in your household Mister McDonald, we have Photographic Evidence of the knives and pieces of glass used to cut Lindsay's arms... I think you were in the process of killing her but our Detective came just in time to stop you, then you were going to drive Lindsay Evans out somewhere, murder her like you did the rest and ditch her body off somewhere in Runcorn, we've got you now Graham and there's no escaping it, you killed Kyle Cross and Tiffany Wright, admit it! You killed them didn't you?!' Sarah slammed her fist against the table, Graham rose his finger and pointed it at her and screamed.

'No god damn it! I'm not the Killer, alright... Lindsay she was...' Graham paused trying to come out with the words, he took a deep breath, leaned back and looked at Sarah before continuing.

'Lindsay tried to escape, so... I punished her, told her if she kept trying to escape, I'd keep on cutting her, I didn't want her to go...' He choked on his words as if upset, Sarah continued with her enquiries.

'...and that's where the ropes come in, you kept her tied up, so she wouldn't escape while you were out?' she asked, he nodded in response, hiding his eyes as if ashamed.

'I see...' Sarah scratched the back of her head, thinking about what she should say next, then it came to her.

'Have you kidnapped before?' Sarah asked,

'no...' he mumbled.

'...You see... I'm rather lonely, I'm in my late thirties and I've never had... anyone in my life, I wasn't popular in school or college and my looks never helped. I saw Lindsay and well... I guess I just...' He squirmed uncomfortably in his seat, sweating slightly.

'Just what?!' Sarah snapped, Graham shook slightly and looked at her with expressed guilt.

'I wanted to know what it felt like to... be with a girl...' he admitted. Sarah drew a deep breath.

'You're not our *Killer* after all... just some desperate loser, who thought he could force a girl to love him, is that right?' Sarah spoke harshly, he looked away in shame.

'That's it isn't it... I've dealt with people like you, you think the world owes you, so you wallow in self-pity and blame everyone else instead of working on yourself.' Sarah said to him and he turned red and seemed to sweat more, Graham growled then screamed.

'You don't know what it's like! My parents were never there for me when I needed them, friends betrayed me, I was a laughing stock, even my employees hated me. I have a body issue where I can't lose weight and I just had to sit by and watch as everyone got married, had children and lived happy carefree lives while I was left behind, on my own, alone and unwanted... so I took Lindsay Evans and I kept her in my house, she hated me for it but I didn't care, at least I wasn't alone anymore. I thought in time she would grow to appreciate me, to love me even...' He choked, Sarah sat there frowning at him unmercifully while he spilled his confession.

'Then what were you going to do? Once you found out we were onto you? You were going to tie her up in your car and ditch it somewhere, burn it up or drive into a lake, killing the poor girl, you never cared about her, you were about to murder her and we stopped you just in time!' Sarah yelled again, Graham cried and shook his head.

'No... no I wasn't going to kill her! I was going to drive out of town and find a place for me and her to stay, I have a lot of money saved up and was going to buy a small flat somewhere to keep her in. I would never kill Lindsay...' he cried further.

'I don't believe that for one second Graham and you can cut the act, I know your type... you really think I'm going to be merciful after what I've just heard. No way, you're a *Monster* and if it was up to me, I would charge you for Abduction and Attempted Murder... but I guess that's for the Courts to decide.' Sarah spoke cruelly then stood up, high above Graham, looking down on him as he cried like a child. 'You're a sad and pathetic man, Graham McDonald. You'll have a long hard time to think about what you've done behind cold bars. You think it's lonely now? Wait until the Inmates here about your story.' Sarah White left the Interrogation Room shortly after, slamming the door shut on the way out.

Sarah walked towards Interrogation Room 2, she entered to the sight of Daniel Harriot, sitting behind his table with a deeply distressed expression upon his face, he was biting his finger nails on his right hand while his left was handcuffed to the table just like with Graham. (Both Suspects had been cuffed to stop them from attacking officers or from escaping the station.) Daniel looked at Officer White with a panicked expression as she walked over towards the table and sat down to interrogate him. Sarah felt confident with her approach, but that was until she sat down and seen the apparition of a form that looked all too familiar, standing behind the Suspect.

'You see him too, don't you?' Daniel cried a little. Sarah nodded in silence, a look of shock on her face, the monster turned around to face her and that dream she had with that crying man came back to her as she recognized the Demon from her dream, it was the disfigured man in the tracksuit with his face all ripped apart and lips dangling off like melted plastic.

'I remember you...' Daniel spoke, Sarah looked at him, the Suspect nodded his head in a fearful fashion.

'You're that little girl I seen in my dream, I know it...' he smiled slightly in the hopes that he was right and wasn't going insane after all, but Sarah White had a job to do and couldn't look like a Lunatic in front of the Chief, (who was most likely monitoring the conversation behind the one way mirror that stood inside the Interrogation Room.) Sarah had to pretend she couldn't see the disfigured ghost and act like Daniel was insane and hallucinating.

'I don't know what you are talking about, Daniel Harriot.' Sarah said, Daniel shook his head.

'No... no don't say that!' he pleaded.

'Daniel you're sick, you need help, we can put you in an Asylum for the Mentally Ill, this isn't your fault, but you need to let us help you...' She lied to the Suspect and he started panting, heavily.

'But you can see him, I saw your reaction when you came in, I recognize you from the dream!' he insisted,

'There is no man behind you, Daniel... your hallucinating, having disturbing visions. The voices in your head have been telling you to do things, to go around killing in town.' Sarah locked her eyes with his, he shook his head violently.

'No, no! *He* told me, the man made me kill her, I didn't want to, I had no choice!' Daniel screamed loudly and so did the ghost, the table even vibrated slightly. Sarah got up from her chair and grabbed Daniel by the shoulders and looked into his eyes.

'Daniel! Listen to me... there is no man, no *Monster*, it's all in your head. These voices in your head... they're telling you to kill, you need to *ignore* them, they can't harm you...' Sarah said this while looking into his eyes, he realized what she meant by *"ignore"* and he knew she could see them too, and that she was saying you can ignore these monsters and eventually they will disappear. He stopped shaking and nodded at her in silence, understanding what she meant. Sarah sat back down in her chair and Daniel Harriot remained calm, the monster got in his face trying to convince him of its existence, but he locked eyes with Sarah and the beast began to disappear. Once it was gone Sarah sat in silence thinking about the situation so far. Graham McDonald was not the Killer in town, he was just a lonely shell of a man who wanted to force himself upon another. Daniel Harriot however, it seemed like he had been haunted by this Demon, to go around killing teenagers in town, it became clear to Sarah that Daniel must have been the Killer in town, sure the murder of Jessica seemed rushed and unprofessional but he had just been spotted by that Richard Page, with a bit of time, perhaps Daniel was skilled enough to hide his tracks.

'Daniel, what I'm going to say next may come to you as a bit of a shock but... I believe that you killed Tiffany Wright, Kyle Cross and Jessica McKenzie...' she admitted, he sat back in his chair, tears rolling down his cheek.

'It was only Jessica...' he told her.

'The... voices... in my head were telling me to kill her. *It* wouldn't leave me alone, the stench of *it*, the way *it* snickered...' as Daniel explained what the monster was, it began to reappear behind him again like rising smoke, Sarah could see it's hideous face emerge from thin air and lick it's lips menacingly, she lay her hand upon Daniel's and mimed the words "stop" and darted her eyes behind him, he nodded in understanding. After a while it disappeared again. Sarah continued.

'That may be what you think, Daniel. But there's an unfortunate truth. Tiffany Wright was found dead in a similar spot to where you killed Jessica and Kyle Cross went missing that night too and was later found dead. I believe that may have forgotten what you have done and created a fictional story in your head that you now believe as truth...' She said this to him and he sat back in silence, awestruck at the possibility. He had heard of that happening to other people after all, but could it be?

'I'm sorry, Daniel, but you need to remember... sometimes our minds can play tricks on us, we believe things that aren't true because our minds can't accept the truth or face the guilt.' She wrapped her hand around his on the table, he squirmed it away and sat in silence.

'Maybe it is true... yeah... I think I... remember...' he cried, he buried his head into his free hand and confessed.

'I done it, I killed them all. The Voices, that *thing* I saw, it wouldn't stop calling, I only remember killing Jess, but other images pop up... it's me, I know it is...' he looked up at Sarah, his eyes red and full of tears.

'Please... you've got to believe me, I never wanted to hurt anybody. *It* just kept calling...'

'I know... this isn't your fault, you didn't do it out of spite or hatred, you're just... suffering from a mental illness. But we can get you help, you'll be committed to an Asylum, there Doctors will be able to help you, to help you recover. You just need to let us help you.' Sarah reassured him.

'Ok...' Daniel wiped away the tears from his eyes with his free hand. 'I'll do as you ask, what should I do now?' he asked her,

'We'll keep you in here for now, I'll have a word with the Chief.' She told him before standing up and approaching the exit. As Sarah was about to exit the room, he called to her,

'Sarah...' he called.

She turned around to face him.

'Thanks...' he smiled slightly, she nodded back with a look of understanding before opening the door and leaving the room.

Sarah White then proceeded to enter Chief Spencer's office again, she caught up with him as he was about to enter his office. He noticed her coming in as he entered, he held the door for her without smiling and she sat down on the guest chair before he sat down behind his desk to face her.

'Good job, White. It is hard to believe that you got a confession out of them so quickly. I watched your progress in the Monitoring Rooms, you got a confession out of Graham and another out of Daniel... so Daniel was hallucinating and hearing voices that told him to go around killing and Graham a Kidnapper. This wasn't what I was expecting, no sinister motivation, just a nut job and a loner. I shouldn't be surprised, most of the time murder is a senseless crime and often acted out without much thought.' The Chief said while scratching the back of his head.

'You don't think I got the truth out of them, Chief Spencer?' Sarah asked, puzzled.

'No of course not, they both confessed, and the Evidence suggests that what you believe is the truth, but... it just seems strange to me. The Murders seemed planned. Perhaps Daniel has a split personality? Like the other side of him knew what he was doing, I noticed you played into his insanity. That was a good idea, you led him right into confessing, I believe he's putting on an act though, like he's not really that upset about the Murders, or maybe it is his other personality that can't remember. That would explain a lot actually; the second personality was behind the Murders... he took control, but the Voices still had him kill, which is why the last seemed so... rushed. I don't know, the mind is a funny thing... anyway, Daniel will be sent to an Asylum and we'll see what the Courts say about Graham. Hopefully we've got this right and the killings will stop. We'll keep these two here, they're both insidious and dangerous individuals.' Chief Spencer sighed, then he lent his hand out towards Sarah, and she shook it.

'Thank you for coming in today, Sarah, your efforts in this

investigation have aided greatly in solving the Case, we couldn't have done it without you. Due to your outstanding work these last couple of years, I am pleased to announce that you have been promoted to the Rank of Police Sergeant. Officers will now refer to you as Sergeant White instead of Officer White and your new responsibilities will be taught to you by our Inspector, Miranda Carlton. Your new training starts next week on Monday, you have until then to prepare and continue your work on patrol with Officer Carr.' The Chief explained, Sarah smiled, he returned the gesture.

'What about Officer Carr, Chief? Will he be promoted, he aided greatly in the Investigation.' Sarah asked, the Chief tightened his lips and gave her a strange look.

'Officer Carr has done an excellent job on this case too, but he's only just started and has a lot more to do before he can reach a promotion, do not worry though, I will be giving him my thanks and he'll be set up with another partner once you have taken on your new role, your pay will also be raised once you begin on Monday. As for now you are free to leave, come back tomorrow, normal time, you'll be on patrol with Officer Carr until Monday. You'll be paid for the whole day today and I'll make sure everyone knows what you and Michael have done during this investigation.' The Chief thanked her one more time before letting her leave, she smiled on the way out and entered her car.

It seemed all was right again and although the lives of certain residents would never be the same, at least the killings would stop and eventually the town would find peace like it once did before. These thoughts comforted Sarah on her way back home from the station. However, she still had this feeling deep down inside that maybe this wasn't over yet.

Chapter 35:
Lindsay's Return

Lindsay hadn't been the same since her return, she was taken to Runcorn Hospital after her car accident on Thursday, before having her injuries photographed by Police Investigators. Once she awoke from her surgeries, she was met by a doctor. Stacy Evans and her mother, Kate Evans came in once the doctor called them, she was relieved to see them, and they shared an emotional moment, hugging each other and crying about how they missed her, she missed them too and for Lindsay, it felt like heaven, just to see them again. This bliss was shortly lived however as she had to give in a Police Interview with cameras on her, telling them what happened while she was kept prisoner inside of Graham's house. She gave short one worded answers and the Police were understanding and let her go, they were satisfied with her answers and she was then led out of the hospital by her mother, sister, an officer and a doctor. There were a few News Reporters waiting outside with cameras trying to ask her questions, the officer shoved them out of the way and led her to a Police vehicle, Lindsay kept her head down the whole time.

Once she arrived at her mother's house, she found it difficult to settle back into her old life, something just didn't feel right. It was like she had been away for a very long time and coming back felt like revisiting some long distant memory, almost like it wasn't real, like this whole house only existed in her mind like some wild fantasy that wasn't true. She had grown used to the horrors that Graham had put her through and this return to normality seemed strange, unreal even. (Stacy Evans had moved out of her old flat and back into her mother's in order to support her family.) Lindsay seemed to jump and often scream at every loud noise in their house, she seemed threatened by everyone, even her own sister and mother. Graham really must have messed her up, she was quiet, shy and became somewhat of a shut in.

It had been 3 days since she was found on Thursday by Officers Carr, White and Detective John Prescott. The date is the 28th of August 2001. Lindsay hasn't left the house in fear that she may get abducted again and she only leaves her room for food and drink, she doesn't say much to her mother or sister and refuses to talk about her time at Graham's, in fact, she would either get upset or yell at her family, the most they ever got out of her was "Shut up!" or "I don't want to talk about it!" Lindsay barely eats and she is already losing weight. Kate cries when she's downstairs away from Lindsay and Stacy is also depressed.

One day Lindsay was sat in her room watching TV and Stacy decided to check up on her, she knocked on the door.
'Yes?' Lindsay asked, with a small fright detected in her voice.
'Don't worry, it's just me, Stacy.' she said through the door as she opened it slightly.
'Oh...' Lindsay spoke.
'May I come in?' Stacy asked.
'Sure...' Lindsay sighed.
Stacy opened the door, the bed room sat in darkness, the curtains were closed and the only light that lit the room came from the bluish glows on the TV. Lindsay sat in silence, cornered up in her bed with the quilt over her body, she grabbed the remote and switched it to mute and looked at her older sister with big bulging eyes. The silence in the room felt heavy and anxious as Lindsay stared at her sister.
'What do you want?' Lindsay asked with hostility.
'I just want to talk...' Stacy said as she sat down on Lindsay's bed,

Lindsay groaned, uncomfortably. The two of them sat in silence for a while then Stacy turned around and looked at the TV, it was BBN News talking about the Incident in Runcorn. Stacy sighed and smiled worrisomely at Lindsay.

'You sure you want to watch this?'

'They've caught the Killer...' Lindsay said, Stacy looked back at the TV. A photograph of Daniel Harriot was shown while a News Reporter announced that he had come out with a confession, they both watched the News Coverage together until it focused on Graham McDonald, his face shown up on screen and Lindsay shut the TV off immediately and whimpered a little.

'It's ok...' Stacy said as she approached her little sister, Lindsay jumped out of her quilt and hit Stacy in the chin, hard. She didn't do it on purpose, seeing her kidnapper on screen brought back some distressing memories and with Stacy approaching, it brought her back to that horrific bedroom he kept her in, for a split second she thought Stacy was Graham and she hit her in defense. Lindsay sat back in shock as blood spilled from her sister's mouth.

'I'm... sorry, I, I...' Lindsay almost cried but Stacy hugged her.

'It's alright, sis, it's alright! You're safe now and nobody is ever going to hurt you, not again, for as long as I live, I will always be here for you! We'll get through this, we always have, you and me... we're family...' Stacy cried and the siblings held each other tightly.

In time Lindsay would learn to live again, she would learn to socialize and fit in, but the horrors that Graham McDonald had put her through, those days that she had been imprisoned. Those memories would never leave her and the things he done, they would haunt her forever. Lindsay Evans would never be the same girl again, Stacy knew it, but she didn't care, she loved her all the same. They were sisters after all.

Chapter 36:
One Last Patrol

```
The 29th of August 2001,
11:46am, Monday.
```

'You're getting promoted!' Officer Carr gasped while they were driving, Carr was in the passenger seat while Officer White drove through Castlefields.
'Yeah... they're making me a Sergeant, you seem annoyed.' White snarled a little, Carr sighed.
'I'm not annoyed, no I think you deserve it, but... we've been working together, I've helped solve this case just as much as you have, why are they only promoting you?' he asked, clearly frustrated.
'Chief Spencer told me it is because you're new, he knows your efforts have aided greatly but you've got to remember Michael... *I've* been on the Force a long time, you have to do a lot of work to get promoted, I'm afraid.' Sarah explained, Carr nodded and looked outside the window with a disappointed frown.
'I understand... I guess I'll miss working with you. You've been kind and I've learnt a lot from you. I know it's not like your leaving, but I'll have a new partner and I'll hardly see you.' Carr chuckled.
'I have a bad feeling my next partner won't respect me, you know I've made mistakes...'
'Look Carr, the Force knows what you've done while investigating with me, you're highly respected by the others and you're on the Chief's good side. I'll be in charge of several patrols and I'll make sure yours is one of them, your next partner will know that you helped stop Graham with me and he or she will appreciate you, I can tell you that much.' Officer White told him.

'You really think so?' he asked.
'I know so.' she smiled.
The two of them sat in silence for a while as they drove through Castlefields and into Halton village, White then turned at the roundabout heading towards the Runcorn Shopping City, Carr wondered what they were doing out here.
'Where are we going?' Carr asked her, Officer White smirked.
'Let's take a break... we'll get coffee, it's on me.' White winked, Carr chuckled as they approached a local Café. They parked up the Police Cruiser. As White exited the vehicle she told Carr to stay behind, he offered to pay but she insisted it was free, he smiled and thanked her.

White returned shortly after with a paper bag and two paper cups inside of a cup holder. Officer Carr opened the driver side door for White to enter, she chuckled and thanked him, he nodded with a slight smile. Once White got inside the vehicle she closed her door and gave him his coffee and lay the paper bag on her knees, Carr took a peak at her legs before looking at the bag, it was a brown paper bag with the Café's logo on it, which was of a cartoon man smiling at a cup of coffee with the name of the Café on it.
'What's in the bag, Sarah?' he asked, sounding a little flirtatious.
Officer White gave him an amused "seriously?" look, he snickered.
Officer White put her hand in the paper bag,
'Donuts!' she cheered as she pulled out two chocolate donuts from the bag.
'Seriously!' Carr laughed loudly. Officer White laughed too.
'What's wrong with donuts?' she asked sarcastically.
'A bit cliché don't you think?' he rose his right eye brow with a grin, she chuckled.
'I have no idea what you're on about...' Officer White joked.
'Well... you know what they say about Coppers, right?'

'What do they say, Michael?' She teased.

Carr rolled his eyes jokingly.

'Don't make me say it...' Carr sighed lightly.

'Say what?' Officer White asked with a huge grin on her face, almost bursting out into laughter.

'That Cops drink coffee and eat donuts all the ti-'

White burst out laughing, interrupting Officer Carr, Carr rolled his eyes and turned away to look outside the window, hiding his smile from Officer White.

'Oh come on Michael... you've got to have a bit of fun!' she chuckled.

Officer Carr turned back around and faced her, he had an amused smile on his face.

'Yeah I guess so... did you put two sugars in my coffee?' he asked, Officer White nodded in an over-exaggerated manner. Officer Carr sipped his coffee and picked up his donut and took a bite out of it, White followed shortly after. They both sat in silence for a while, listening to the radio and not the Police Radio either but the local station, and the show was being hosted by a familiar name, Joshua Riley. He seemed happier here than he did during Police Interviews, the two of them found this amusing.

'You looking forward to becoming a Police Sergeant tomorrow, Sarah?' Officer Carr asked, Officer White took a deep breath and sighed.

'I don't know... the pay is better and it is a higher rank, but... I'm going to miss being on patrol. I've been doing this for a long time and I don't know if I'd be a good Sergeant, it's a lot of responsibility and you can't slack off as much.' Officer White chuckled quietly before taking another sip of her coffee.

'You think...' Officer Carr paused.

'Think what?' White asked, she stopped drinking and looked at Carr, he looked away, biting his bottom lip as if wanting to say something but didn't have the courage to say so.

'Never mind... it doesn't matter...' Carr sighed.

'Come on, Michael. You can trust me, we're partners, remember?' she told him, he sighed again then looked at her.

'Alright... how can I say this without sounding mushy... would you miss... working with me?' he smiled shyly at her, White fought back a smile and blushed slightly, choking on her donut a little.

'Yeah... I'll miss you, Officer Carr.' she nudged his shoulder flirtatiously, his eyes lit up and a large smile grew on his face. The two officers finished their donuts and coffee shortly after and continued their last patrol together.

Chapter 37:
Reconnect

```
The 29th of August 2001,
5:32pm, Monday.
```

Erin Cross lay on her sofa in silence, inside the living room with the curtains closed over, she lay there staring at the muted TV. She couldn't cope with the loss of her son and she was completely alone, wondering what on earth she had to live for, with no goals or desires, her previous life left in ruins and almost forgotten. The only audible sound came from the rain dropping on her windows, the small rustle of wind calmed her slightly but the greyness outside only drove her more insane as the ugly sights of grey skies and darkened tarmac from the day's rain only made things seem more depressing, so she had every curtain closed to keep out the grey. She had tried watching happier movies with the lights on, but it felt empty and un-fulfilling without her son there to watch them with her, sure he had spent less time with her once he reached his late teens but she still expected him to come home after college or return late at night from a round of drinks with friends. But the sad truth was that he would never return and then she'd remember, he really was gone after all. She found it hard to believe at first, like it was just some sort of horrid nightmare, she knew the truth, but it was a hard pill to swallow. Now it really dawned on her and she seemed to cry every day. At first it was wallowing, then whimpering, now it's just a few tears a day, but still, there's this empty feeling that won't go away, imagine feeling hungry, starved even, but no matter how much you ate, that feeling in your stomach, it won't go away, won't stop *hurting*. This is how she felt, every day. Without her son, life seemed pointless and unforgiving, gone were the days of raising a family, the innocence and happiness that overwhelmed her 20 years ago when she first met Kevin and moved into her new house, pregnant with a son named Kyle who was on his way. She was only 22 at the time and she finally moved out of her parents', she had grown sick of her mum and dad like Kyle had, and back in 1981, Runcorn was also a very different place. Back then a lot of people from Liverpool were moving away and into smaller towns around the north west of Britain, Runcorn was one of those towns that had a sudden population growth. Because of this, new buildings were built, and it was a confusing time to say the least, some people were happy with the new changes, others not so much, Erin couldn't remember if she liked this or not, but if it wasn't for this change, she would've never met Kevin at the age of 19. She had met him in the nightclub, which was known as a disco back then and it wasn't called The Dungeons back then either, it was called something else, (Erin couldn't remember what it used to be called as the place has had that many owners it's gone through a ton of different names, it was only a couple of years ago The Dungeons was called The Neon Light or something like that, now it was owned by some new company who often played American Punk there, a genre that was popular among the youth of the early Noughties.) Back in 1981 the music they played there was vastly different from the Rap and Punk of 2001, it was much more Funk, rather than Punk. However, bands like The Crash came into the scene introducing Punk Rock for the first time, but it had yet to grow into mainstream popularity, meaning only rarer clubs in London, Manchester and Liverpool were playing those sorts of arrangements. She remembered old friends wearing Drainpipe Jeans and long hair, some with Afros and long collared shirts, *the kids of today would've laughed if they saw us* Erin chuckled to herself remembering her older days, her youth. In all honesty she found modern day fashion to be equally ridiculous, teenage boys walk around with their boxers showing and some have their hair all spiked up and dyed different colours, while girls wear crop tops and glittery jackets. Erin missed the 80s and a part of her wished she could go back, to a time where she was young, popular and everyone loved her.

Erin met Kevin dancing one night back in 1979, there were a lot of new guys from Liverpool who all seemed so cool and different at the time, Kevin was one of them. Erin was dressed in white skinny jeans, red high heels and a demin jacket, her hair curled up into a high side pony tail with a glittery bobble holding it in place, her eyes shone a sparkling blue and her hair was a bright blonde, she had a cute smile and a killer figure that caught the attention of everyone, even other girls had jealous eyes upon her. She was popular too and everyone knew her name, everyone but Kevin and a few others from Liverpool who were strangers to the town. This mysterious persona that Kevin possessed only fueled Erin's curiosity all the more as he approached her at the bar, he was dressed a little differently from the rest as every other guy at this disco seemed to have a preppy look to them while it was clear, Kevin liked Punk with his black leather jacket, Mohawk haircut and dark blue Jeans. He winked at her and she found his strong, almost arrogant confidence a little... charming. She smiled and the two of them started talking, they surprisingly had a lot in common, but their music tastes were vastly different, however Kevin didn't care, and Erin found this new type of "Punk" music fascinating. The two of them got each other's numbers and met up with each other daily, once 1980 came around they were serious and he had a good job making the money as a bartender, while she worked equally hard at the Shopping City that had only recently opened in the late 70's, she worked as a waitress in a small diner that never got too busy so it was easy work for the both of them. They both moved together in late 1980 and she was pregnant by 22 and gave birth at 23. The two of them raised Kyle for 15 years before the couple finally divorced in 1997. The relationship had soured over the years and with Kyle being an only child, it was hard keeping him happy, another child would have been stressful but Kyle would've had a sibling to play with and there was no doubt in Erin's mind that her son would have been happier, but Kevin refused, he didn't want the responsibility of another and this was the main reason the relationship never lasted.

It had been 4 years since Erin was with Kevin and although he drove her crazy while they were together, (because he always disagreed with her and their tastes in fashion, music and culture eventually grew too far a part to the point where they hated each other's ways.) She missed seeing him around, even if he was in an angry mood, at least she had someone to vent her frustrations out on. He would often listen to her side of the story before the arguing commenced, but sometimes she wouldn't want to argue and he was just good to have around when she felt low, even if his advice wasn't helpful, she was glad of the company, their petty arguments seemed pointless now and she often remembered the good times, the old times when they first met, the love she felt for him and the way he cared for her when they met back in 1979. It was such a long time ago, a memory so distant it felt like a dream, fading away with every waking moment, a fantasy so far, so unreachable that it **hurt**. Erin smiled slightly and could feel a single tear roll down her cheek as the memories brought a small glimmer of hope back into her heart. Kyle was gone, but Kevin was still around, he had crusted over time into a grump of a man in his mid-forties, but he was still Kevin, he was still the guy she loved, the one from her youth, the one that made everything seem so perfect, calm and beautiful back in 1979. Erin wiped the tears away from her eyes and took a sip of the cola that she had left out on the coffee table just beside her. Erin sat up on the couch and threw the quilt she had brought down from her room to the side. She took a deep breath and walked over towards where the phone was, in the kitchen where she had called Josh the night of Kyle's disappearance. Before dialing any numbers, she brought up a chair from behind the dinner table and placed it in the kitchen beside the phone. Erin sat on the chair and picked up the phone in front of her and held it near her ear, she sighed deeply before dialing Kevin's mobile number. The phone rang for an excruciatingly long time before Kevin finally picked up.

'...Erin...' he spoke through the phone, sounding a little shaken and distant. Erin held back a tear as his voice brought back memories.

'Yes... it's me...' she breathed heavily, Kevin sighed deeply, tension could be felt, even over the phone.

'I... I'm sorry I wasn't there for Kyle, I'm sorry I wasn't there for *you*...' Kevin choked on his words, like he was struggling keeping things together.

'It's... it's been rough, Kev...' she sighed.

'Yeah...' He sniffed and let out a long, hard, emotional breath that caused Erin to tear up. Kevin could hear her whimper over the phone as he held his breath, waiting for her to calm.

'...I miss you, you know? Kyle's gone, I can't cope but I'm still here, holding on... because of you Kev... I know we had our arguments but...' Erin cried quietly into the phone, Kevin breathed heavier.

'I miss you too, Erin. These four years, they've been rough, living on my own... it isn't what I thought it would be.' he chuckled slightly over his cries, he was both crying and laughing at the same time, remembering his time with her, with Kyle and their little house in Stenhills. The two of them talked for hours, about their life together, they talked about Kyle, how he was such a good kid with a lot of friends and a lot of talent. They talked about the dreams and hopes they had for their son, they cried together and laughed together. Both of them had stopped working due to the shock and had been feeling the same way about his death, alone, scared and deeply depressed. Erin found it so relieving hearing Kevin say the same things, suddenly she didn't feel so alone, and it was a huge weight off her shoulders to let it all out and tell somebody what was going through her mind. Kevin found the same satisfaction telling her his feelings too and eventually the two of them came to an agreement, they would see each other more often and try and reconnect, their son may have gone, but they still had each other. The two of them eventually ended the call, Erin hung up and put the phone back into its place, she then sat back in her chair and thought about Kevin some more, she chuckled slightly remembering his old mannerisms and the way he used to call her name. She missed Kyle every day and there was nothing she could do to bring him back, and although nothing could ease the pain she felt after losing her son, she had some small glimmer of hope, that at the very least, Kevin Cross would be there to give her some comfort and maybe just maybe, she could one day learn to enjoy the life she once had with her ex-husband all over again. She wasn't 100% sure things would work out, but for the first time in a long time, she actually felt like her life was finally getting back on track.

Chapter 38:
The Verdict

Once Graham and Daniel were put into custody the murders stopped, they were soon sent to two separate Court Hearings. The Families of Kyle Cross, Tiffany Wright, Lindsay Evans and Jessica McKenzie were present at both juries. Lindsay Evans herself however, she was not present, she could not stand to suffer the sight of Graham again, she was not needed however as there was enough evidence to put him away for years.

Graham was charged with Abduction and Sexual Abuse, he got a prison sentence of up to 18 years, many thought it wasn't enough and it wasn't just Lindsay's Family who thought he didn't deserve mercy. Graham cried during his Court Hearing and apologized multiple times to the Families and Friends that were affected by his actions, they didn't dare care however, in fact, nobody felt pity or sorrow for such a man of despicable acts. There are people out there who still believe to this day, that Graham was behind the murders in Runcorn, however it was the Evidence and Confessions provided by Daniel Harriot that sold the Case to the Jury.

On Daniel's Court Hearing, everyone noticed that the man seemed to keep whispering to himself, often freaking out and yelling every so often, security had to restrain and calm him down multiple times and it became clear to everyone that there was something severely wrong with the man. Richard Page was there as a witness to Jessica's death and

Daniel openly admitted to the Murder and confessed that he was behind the others as voices were telling him to commit hideous crimes around the town. He had trouble explaining how he murdered Kyle and Tiffany however as he could only remember small visions of their screams and deaths. But it was enough for the Jury and Judges to decide that he was guilty of the murders of Tiffany Wright, Kyle Cross and Jessica McKenzie. He was not given a Life Sentence however as Daniel's mental health was clearly unstable, he was sent to a Mental Asylum (located in West London) for the Criminally Insane. Here he would undergo distressing mental treatment and would be cared for on a weekly basis by highly trained Psychiatrists while constantly under strict and constant surveillance of highly trained Security Officers at the Asylum, he would never be able to leave this place and would always be known as a highly dangerous and unpredictable individual.

With both Culprits behind bars it seemed that this strange little case in the north west of England was finally at a close. However, the case was about to take an even stranger turn as what happened next in the small town of Runcorn, was something not even the greatest of Detectives could figure. The next events that will unfold may seem unbelievable, fictional even, but this case has been well documented and studied by professionals a countless amount of times. Many believe that the Skinners Incident never took place and that this whole documentation is an elaborate hoax, Myth or Legend that has simply spiraled out of control and leaked into the media, however the people that are involved in this story, living or dead, they do exist and this is a documentation describing the events that took place back in 2001. Whether or not you believe these events is irrelevant, if it is true, it is a hard pill to swallow, but if it isn't? Then perhaps the reality is buried somewhere within these events. This is why YOU have been specifically selected to read these documents, if you are not a part of THE SELECT FEW this is your **FINAL WARNING**, if you are found with these documents outside of Hallington Palace, you will be prosecuted for your actions and anyone outside of THE SELECT FEW who read this may be subject to lobotomy as these events MUST be kept under strict and confidential evaluation by the Great British Government. With that said, take in these next events with an open mind, they may seem unbelievable, impossible or even un-explainable, but as this document has already stated above, that is why you are here.

Chapter 39:
Night Terror

You awake in a small area, it appears to be a hut of some kind, the walls are made of oak and you can hear the whirls of the night's wind against the confines of this small space. You stand up and find that you were lying on top of a straw bed with a wooden frame, it reminds you of something out of a medieval story, or a fairy tale perhaps? In fact, this place seems rather enchanted. You exit the small hut, the door creaks open on the way outside and you look around, you're in a wooded area and the moon stands tall in the sky, you notice it has a yellow glow to it that oddly seems to light up the night's sky in a dark purple, however as the your eyes drift from the focus of the moon you find the chills and darkness of midnight somewhat unsettling as the trees waver to the left and right due to the windy breeze. You also notice that there are no leaves to be seen, as every tree in your view is barren, their rickety branches stick out awkwardly into sharp, threatening points. You look to your left and notice that the trees lean towards you, their branches twisting un-naturally away from their roots making a strange sort of O shape in the center, like a cave made of Oak. You look to your right and the trees stand naturally in line, you want to walk to your right because it appears to be the safest root, but, for some reason, you find yourself walking to the left. It's strange, you feel your feet hitting the ground and you feel your lungs take in the breaths of clean air and you can feel the wind brush against you and feel the cold as it crawls up your skin, yet you are hopeless and you cannot walk away as it feels like something else has possessed your body, making you walk into the pit of the Oak Cave that stands before you. As you enter the Oak Cave, you begin to notice that the branches crawl towards you blocking the path you came in from, trapping you inside of its wooden core, and as you look up, you see the branches cave inwards onto you, they move more like fingers, slowly creeping in and blocking out the night's sky. Eventually you find yourself in complete darkness, but there's a small glimpse of light at the end of this wooden tunnel, so you walk onwards, and the trip seems to last forever. Now you're beginning to notice that you're almost out, as the light at the end of the tunnel widens, strangely, you don't feel tired yet but the walk is making you anxious as you keep on hearing something skirt around in the darkness behind you, you're not sure what it is, but the last time you checked, you seen something yellow in the distance, a small dot or two that quickly vanished and reappeared again like some eye blinking, the eyes of the trees? You wonder. You eventually make it outside and find yourself in an area that at first glance, appears to be the same place you started. You see another hut that looks eerily similar to the one you exited before, however as you look on further you notice that there is a swamp nearby with wooden logs on the water's surface and you may not be able to see them due to the darkness but you are sure there are a few frogs and other such critters around the water's edge as you can hear frogs croak and splashes in the water ahead, there are even a few dragon flies that can be seen buzzing around. You feel strange, what is this place? You wonder, "Why am I here?" Your curiosity runs wild and before you even realize it, you're walking over to the pond and looking inside. You see some beautiful sights such as fish you have never seen before, ones with sliver fins and pinkish bodies twirl around hypnotically, dancing almost, inside of the water. Your attention is taken by something even weirder as you hear the distant whimpers of somebody, or something, call out to you. You look up and see a huge log on top of a muddy surface and sitting just on top of that log is an un-naturally large toad with human features, it's skin a familiar pinkish colour to that of the fish below you and the creature's hands look human, but with the webbing of a toad, however it's the toad's face that looks the most un-natural. This toad has reptile like eyes, but the mouth looks human, with human teeth and red lips, including a human looking tongue that is the length of a dog's. It licks it's lips nervously in front of you and sighs. You then look at the rest of the toad's body, this toad is almost the same size as you, but this is where the human features stop as the rest of its body looks like that of a normal toad, expect human sized, it looks creepily unsettling and wrong. Yet, despite this unsettling sight, you don't run away in fear or even scream, in fact, you look at the Human-Toad with genuine curiosity as it begins to speak to you.

'It... it still lurks here, you better hide, ribbit!' The Human-Toad cries, tears fall from the reptile eyes, the tears stain it's skin blue and the tears seems to shine in a glittery fashion against the night's sky. Before you even ask what the Human-Toad is on about, it replies.

'The... I don't know what it is. It's black... dark, something else entirely, not of this dimension, not of your realm... or mine for that matter, ribbit!' The Human-Toad blinked, then it sneezed, it was a human sounding sneeze and the snot came out red, then it cried again, you think that sneeze hurt the poor critter and you're almost certain, that so called snot was actually blood. An echoed laughter escapes the Oak Cave you just came out of, the laugh does not sound human, no it sounds prickly and artificial, like something intimidating a human, expect it wasn't a human, it was something else, something else entirely, just like the Human-Toad had said. You look behind and see giant dark hands crawl out of the Oak Cave slowly, they are boney and skeletal looking with extraordinary long fingers that end in sharp points, you're scared enough and don't want a full look of this beast.

'Hide now, quickly! Get behind this log and don't come out until I say it is safe, ribbit!' The Human-Toad yells, you nod and lay down behind the log, you can feel the muddy surface below as it covers your body and face, the coldness of it only making your situation seem all the more terrifying. You hear the Human-Toad jump off the log and try to run away from the Beast from the Oak Cave, you hear Human-Toad call out for help, but you keep your eyes focused on the ground below you, trying not to make too much noise. You hear flesh pounding against flesh and blood squirting out of the Human-Toad as it squeals again, this time louder as you can hear the distorted laughter of the Beast beating the Human-Toad senselessly. You feel

a big thump against the log you are hiding behind and then you feel something crawl beside you, you think it is the Beast, you're horrified, but you can't help but look. You see the Human-Toad, it's upper body ripped in half, you can see it has a very human looking skeleton inside that is covered in guts and gore, some parts human, other parts toad. It flaps it's arms around pathetically and looks at you square in the eyes, a look of absolute horror, pain and desperation emits from within, and the creature's tongue has been ripped apart with greenish goo emitting from the wounds, it then begins to puke blood all over the place, the blood pouring out like a full bottle of red wine that has just been spilt. It cries as a long dark arm that reminds you of a Spider's leg reaches out from the other side of the log, with piercing fingers in a fearsome death grip, it digs into the dying creature and snatches it up in the air, you can hear the Human-Toad's neck break with a loud CRUNCH as it screams one last time before being thrown into the air, back towards where the Beast was standing on the other side of the log just out of your sight. You breathe heavily as you hear this beast dig into the creature you were just talking to, you can hear it rip open the Human-Toad and chew on the muscles and cartilage, bones cracking with every bite and you can hear the slither of flesh go down this beast's throat. You can only imagine what the Beast looks like as it devours the creature you just met. You wait for what seems like an eternity as you sob quietly, ducking your head further into the muddy surface below trying to hide the sounds of your breathing from the Beast that eats your friend beside you, on the other side of the log. Eventually when it seems like the coast is clear you peak over the log and notice that the Beast is no longer in sight, yet you see the Human-Toad's skeleton on the floor, broken in pieces, with skin thrown around the area with blood covering the ground all around you. You sigh as it is still midnight and you look over to the hut just in front of you, you wonder what is inside, so you approach. You open the door slowly, terrified that the Beast may be inside, but what you witness is much more horrifying. You see your own body on the bed, but your skin has been peeled off around your skull and there are huge chunks of your body that are simply missing with ugly stumps that lay in their place, both your legs are missing and two uneven stubs lay in their place with your right hand missing and the left severely cut up and peeled like your face, you want to cry, but before you can do so, you see the dead body of yourself rise up, get in your face and scream!

Daniel Harriot wakes up screaming, his eyes bulging with absolute terror, he tries to get up but he can't as he finds himself tied to a bed inside of a Straight Jacket. Then he remembers that he's in a Mental Asylum and the reality is far worse than the nightmare, then he sees it, *that* Monster. The one who made him kill Jessica and the others, standing silently in the back of the room snarling, blood drooling down from his disfigured and deformed face, somehow looking even more terrifying in the darkness, it's head spinning around slowly with the agonizing sound of bones clicking and breaking. It flies over on top of Daniel and he screams again, but nobody comes in to restrain or calm him (hell, he'd even be glad if they just turned on the lights) But there's nothing Daniel can do as the Monster that ruined his life, crawls on top of him and digs it's fingers into his eyes. Blood gushes out of Daniel's eyes as he shakes violently in his Straight Jacket, screaming so loud and painfully that it finally brings the attention of the Asylum Security, but by this point it is already too late. The last thing Daniel ever saw was the ghost of Jacob Kennedy on top of him, his deformed face in a fearsome snarl as it screamed; "Why am I still here! I made you kill Jessica, yet I am still here, Why!?"

The Security Officers opened the cell room door that Daniel was kept inside of, they turned on the lights and were quickly greeted with the sight of Daniel Harriot laying on top of his hospital bed with blood slushing out of his eye sockets, gore and pieces of his eyes laid out on top of the white Straight Jacket that was now stained red with the man's blood, Daniel was not dead however, in fact quite the opposite, he was screaming in absolute agony as he was still alive while all of this was happening.

Daniel Harriot survived the whole ordeal as Medical Staff came to his room and fixed him up, saving his life in the process, however they couldn't save his eyes, and he was left permanently blind. The Staff at the Asylum soon came to the conclusion that another patient somehow broke into his room and done this to Daniel, they did have another mental patient in custody that ripped the eyes out of his wife one night after a heavy argument. The blame was soon pointed towards that patient, however Daniel knew the truth. He tried to tell them it was the Monster, but of course nobody believed that, they all thought he was insane after all.

Part three
The Return of Kyle Cross

Chapter 40:
Trick or Treat?

```
31st of October 2001,
Friday, 9:30pm,
Halloween Night.
```

Erin Cross sat on her sofa, watching TV next to her divorced husband, Kevin. It had been just under two months since the murders that struck Runcorn, there had been a few fights and even one death since then, but they were not related, the fights came from drunks in bars and pubs, and it was Richard Page who died one night after he was involved in another car accident on the Sliver Jubilee Bridge connecting Widnes to Runcorn. His truck crashed into one of the side banisters and it fell over the edge and into the River Mersey below, Police found the vehicle, but his body was nowhere to be found as it appeared to them that he tried to escape. Although his body was never recovered, everyone presumed that he was dead, the Police searched the whole area thoroughly for 6 weeks, but they had no luck finding him. The murders two months ago affected lots of people in town, but eventually everyone moved on, even Erin had been living with her ex-husband after Kyle's death and they had moved in together at her house and he kept her company. She wasn't the same woman, but she was beginning to feel normal again and Kevin felt good about himself looking after her. They heard about Lindsay Evans and her family, Lindsay was beginning to socialize again too, Erin and Kevin would often bump into Lindsay and Kyle's old friends and they seemed to be doing alright as well. Everyone thought that whole nightmare two months ago was finally over and they tried their best to move on and live normal lives. Erin started working again and Kevin worked longer to save more money, the old couple were tired but luckily Erin had Friday night off and Kevin took the night off work too to spend time with her, even though it was Halloween night, they didn't fancy watching a horror, films about murderers and monsters only reminded them of their recent tragedy. They sat together on their new bright red sofa watching a romantic comedy on the TV about a young couple in the 1980's, the film was even set in England and it reminded them of their youth. They had one light on in the corner of the living room and they had a fire burning inside the fire place, the lighting was just as romantic as the movie they were watching. The comedy aspects of the film kept them happy and they laughed together, drinking red wine and sharing a packet of nachos together with salsa sauce tubs on the coffee table in front of them. Erin was a little drunk while Kevin seemed sober (he was a heavy drinker and it took a lot for him to get wasted.) She chuckled and started playing with his collar, he smiled, she was acting like they used to twenty years ago and he loved it. He smiled at her passionately and gave her a small cuddle, she snuggled into his arms and he took a sip of his wine while leaning back and smiling at the TV. For a small amount time the couple had forgotten about the mental torture they went through in August, it was only then, at this perfect moment, that they got a knock on the door. Erin's eyes widened with surprise then she remembered it was Halloween and smiled. (However, it did seem odd that kids would be out, there was a storm outside, it rained heavily and there was thunder & lightening.)

'I'll get it!' Erin smiled and kissed Kevin on the cheek, she wrestled out of his arms and walked into the hallway where their front door was, she had a small white bowl of sweets on the window shill that stood next to the front door. (She didn't see who was knocking through the window as they had the curtains closed over) she opened the door expecting to see some cute kids standing below her in childish Halloween costumes with trick or treat bags opened wide for sweets, but what actually stood at the door? It horrified her, she couldn't believe it, but at the same time she was so relieved to see it, no not it, him, her son, Kyle Cross! He was standing outside with a huge smile on his face, that was the first thing she noticed and she screamed, her emotions were haywire and Kevin thought somebody attacked her. Kevin shouted her name with panic in his voice, he ran around the corner with a distressed look that quickly turned into disbelief as he seen him too, his son, Kyle Cross stood there with this strange wide eyed smile that unsettled him deeply. Both Erin and Kevin had no idea what to think, Officers Carr and White said he was dead, yet here he was, smiling, with his head nodding forward, his eyes looking up at them creepily. Once they got over the shock, they both hugged him tightly, crying, telling him how much they missed him, he smiled and chuckled as they held onto him. They found his behavior odd, but they didn't care, here he was, alive and well again and the events that happened last August felt like a literal nightmare now, like they both had the same, horrifying dream about their son dying. They were just glad it was all over now, and they didn't even notice how different Kyle looked, he had the same face and height, but his clothes were completely different, Kyle went missing wearing a smart set of clothes, ready for a night out on the town. But now he was dressed like a homeless person, baggy clothes with holes in them, a large brown leather jacket that was far too big for him and it was Kyle's hair that looked different too, he now had a clean cut skin head and there were even a few scars around his neck and forehead. It wasn't until later that they noticed these things, they asked him about it, but he explained that he only just woke up and that he found himself buried under some debris near Wig Island. He told them that he had no recollection of that night out in town and he acted shocked when his parents told him he had been missing for two months and everyone thought that he was dead. They had to prove to Kyle that he had been missing, they showed him missing posters of him and newspapers, they even had a few recordings on video tape of his Funeral and News Reports describing his death. He thought they were joking but he noticed how much older they both looked, Erin looked thinner, his dad had a beard now and when they showed him a mirror, he didn't even know how much he had changed himself. Erin and Kevin were just as confused as he was. What really happened to Kyle? Why did he have all these scars around his neck and body? Why was his hair cut? What's with the rough looking clothes? Where has he been this whole time and why couldn't he remember anything?

Kyle's parents still had his old bedroom intact, all of his old clothes were still there, so were the posters, TV and gaming consoles. They had left everything just the way he left it as a memorial, but they had no idea he would be sleeping in that bed again, wearing the old clothes and playing his games. Both Kevin and Erin thought they were both going insane, but they didn't care, even if this was some sort of fucked up hallucination or dream, they relished in it, holding onto Kyle anytime they could. They both led Kyle into his room and gave him some space as he changed clothes. Erin choked and held Kevin's arm.

'This... this is a dream, right? I- I- I'm going to wake up any moment now and... Kyle. He-he-he he's going to be dead again tomorrow an- an- and!' Erin broke out into tears, falling onto the floor, holding her husband's legs. Kevin kneeled down on the floor in front of her and held her tightly.

'I don't know what's going on, Erin. I really don't, maybe it's me who is dreaming, I don't know what's going on. Perhaps this won't last, but... I don't know...' he told her, Kevin wasn't crying but he was clearly emotional, he was just too confused to even cry. Kyle exited his bedroom and seen his parents crying, he stood there in the doorway of his bedroom and looked at his mother, she looked up at him with tear filled eyes, she wiped them away and waited for Kyle to speak.

'I have no idea what's going on, Mother. But I am here, you're not dreaming, either of you, this is real, I can't explain how this all happened but... believe me... I'm here.' He nodded at them with little emotion, Erin smiled through her tears and held Kevin tighter, Kevin turned his head to look at Kyle, a tear rolling down his cheek, his eyes flushed red, yet Kyle just stood there stiffly with this stern look on his face. *Perhaps he's hiding his emotions?* Kevin thought. In fact, that was just like Kyle, he never liked to show emotion around his parents. But this whole situation, it was so emotional, confusing and bizarre, how on earth could anybody and I mean *anybody*, not get emotional over this. *Maybe he's just too confused to cry, like I was?* Kevin thought to himself again. Kevin kept on telling himself that Kyle was just in shock or that he's holding his emotions in. But seeing Kyle stand there, it was unbelievable, in fact if this was a dream that would explain it. But this whole situation felt far too real to be some sort of fantasy, Kyle was indeed standing there right in front of him, but Kevin just couldn't shake this unsettling feeling. He didn't know what it was, but he felt like something truly dark and insidious was at a foot. Something proceeding in a gradual, subtle way, but with very harmful effects.

Chapter 41:
A Call In At The Station

```
November the 1st 2001,
10:11am, Saturday.
1 day after Kyle's return.
```

The Receptionist at Runcorn's Police Station sat behind her desk with nothing to do but wait for officers or pedestrians to enter the building. Her name was Rebecca Charlesworth and she was a young woman of 23, with long chestnut coloured hair and a pretty face with a slim figure. She started working for the Police two weeks ago and this was the end of her second week and she couldn't wait for tomorrow as that would be her day off before returning on Monday. She enjoyed the job, although a little distressing at times, all she had to do was allow officers and pedestrians (with good reason) to enter the premises. She was digging little pieces of dirt out of her nails, waiting for something to happen or for someone to come in. She sighed and proceeded to look outside the window from where she was sitting, the sunny weather of August, long gone now, replaced with thick clouds and foggy weather, it was particularly foggy today as it had been raining heavily the night before. Water dripped down every surface outside and it reminded her of a certain Japanese horror game she used to play in her youth, she smiled at the thought of coming home, turning on her game console and plugging that beauty back on for a good session of interactive horror. She looked at her watch in the hopes that her shift was almost over but was disappointed to see that she had another 3 hours left, she groaned loudly and rubbed her forehead in frustration. Her mind wondered, she thought about the night out she was about to embark on later tonight after getting some rest from work. She was going to

Frodsham for a night out, the events that took place in August still freaked her out and she preferred Frodsham anyway, it has much better nightlife overall regardless. *Besides... there aren't any Serial Killers in Frodsham.* She chuckled to herself then immediately felt guilty for doing so. *Come on now Rebecca, that was tasteless...* She sighed to herself, embarrassed even though nobody was around. She looked around again, nobody in sight. Rebecca shook her head and sighed, 'This job is easy, but its sure as hell boring.'

Rebecca heard a knock on the glass doors in front of her, she awoke from her day dreams and looked up to see an angry looking woman in her mid-forties with a much younger man standing beside her, the woman looked rough but the man looked a wreck, he had a bunch of small scars on his neck and a couple on the top of his shaved scalp. The woman knocked again on the glass door, yelling something that Rebecca could not comprehend from her side. Rebecca pushed and held the buzzer that connected to an intercom outside.
'Miss, please calm down, what's the problem?' Rebecca spoke through the speaker.
'I need to speak to the Chief of Police!' The middle aged woman groaned through the intercom, Rebecca could hear the woman's voice pixelate through the out dated speakers on her end. Rebecca was about to reply but was shaken by the looks that the young man gave her, the lad stared at her with an emotionless blank stare. Rebecca also noticed the man's clothes were a little strange too, he dressed far older than his age suggested; he wore a medium sized jacket made of what appeared to be silk, it was grey with black horizontal stripes on it and he also wore a light brown buttoned up shirt tucked into his black trousers with brown formal shoes on. Rebecca found herself staring at him, his eyes were somewhat hypnotic and not because she fancied him, but because there was something wrong with this man,

she couldn't put her finger on it but something wasn't right and as she stared his face seemed to morph into a slight yet creepy smile.

'Hey, are you going to let us in or *what?*' Rebecca heard a woman's voice through the speaker, she blinked rapidly, shaking her head then she looked outside again and remembered the woman outside who wanted to get in. She looked back at the lad again, but his creepy smile had vanished and he still had that blank expression on his face, except he wasn't looking at Rebecca anymore, he was looking straight ahead, at nothing. Rebecca held down the buzzer again to speak with the woman outside.

'If you can just tell me why you want to see the Chief, I may let you in... depending on the answer.' Rebecca told the woman through the microphone, the woman nodded.

'My name is Erin Cross, you may have heard about me, I'm the mother of Kyle Cross, the boy who *"died"*. Well I just need to speak to the Chief personally, I need to inform him of something involving the Case.' The woman outside explained. Rebecca gasped, she remembered the woman's face from the News Papers and Reports.

'I'm sorry Miss, forgive me, I had no idea who you were. Come on in.' Rebecca told the woman before cutting off the microphone and pressing the enter button that lay on top of her desk. A buzzing sound could be heard outside near the door and the door's locking mechanism made an audible click. The woman opened the door slowly as it was heavy, she then held it open for the creepy young man behind her to enter, he entered the room and looked at Rebecca again with that unsettlingly blank expression. Rebecca looked away from the man and looked at the woman who was now standing directly in front of her.

'I just need to let the Chief know that you are here and then he'll send out an Officer who will lead you to his office.' Rebecca forced a smile and nodded before pressing a button on her desk that connected to the Chief's Office.

'What's the matter, Charlesworth?' he asked, sounding a little annoyed, but patient. (He probably thought she needed help with the operating systems again.)

'There is a woman here that you may know, her name is Erin Cross. She's here with a young man. She wants to speak with you about the Murder Case two months ago in August.' Rebecca spoke through the speaker, there was a pause on the other end.

'Ok... I'll send someone out to get her over here. Who's the lad?' The Chief asked. Rebecca looked at Erin.

'Just a friend...' Erin spoke with a stern, angered expression, Rebecca nodded and looked down at her microphone.

'She says he's just a friend.' Rebecca told the Chief.

'Alright, what's his name?' The Chief asked, sounding impatient. Rebecca looked at the woman again.

'His name's Robin, a close friend of mine, he knew Kyle...' The woman said to Rebecca, Rebecca looked at the young man, he looked at her and nodded without saying a word. Rebecca was about to tell the Chief what she said but he interrupted her.

'It's alright, I heard what she said. An officer is on his way out now, please wait.' the Chief spoke through the speakers before cutting off to silence. Eventually the door leading into the station opened and a tall Police Man in his late fifties stood in the doorway, he looked at Erin and the lad, giving them a nod.

'Alright come on in, follow me.' The officer said to the two guests and they followed the man into the next room. Once the door behind them closed over, Rebecca sighed.

'What a weird lad...' Rebecca said to herself before checking her watch again only to be disappointed.

Mark Spencer, the Chief of Police, sat behind his desk waiting for Erin

Cross, a young man and Officer Truman to enter his office. He sat up straight with his hands laid out on the top of his desk, tapping the surface with his fingers, waiting impatiently. Eventually the door opened with Truman holding the door open, he told the people behind him to wait and then he turned to face the Chief.

'Erin and her friend are here, Chief.' Officer Truman told him, Chief Spencer nodded in response and waved his hand towards himself, Truman nodded and told the people behind him to come in. It was then that the familiar face of Erin Cross came walking through the door with a furious snarl, it had only been two months but she had changed a lot, she looked healthier and a little chubby even, but not in a bad way, it made her look younger. The Chief wondered why she was angry, he thought that boy behind her had something to do with her mood, he did look like Kyle Cross, of course there was no way it was actually **him**. This must have been his brother or possibly his twin, but this boy's hair was shaven and he dressed a lot older than Kyle too. Before the Chief could open his mouth, Erin Cross beat him to it.

'You said my son... was dead.' Erin snarled, the Chief gave her a puzzled look, which slowly transformed into a look of remorse.

'Look, Erin... I couldn't possibly imagine how... I don't even know... painful, it must have been losing your son like you did. I have a son of my own and it would kill me if anything happened to him but... you've got to move on, the tr-'

'Shut up, Mark!' Erin interrupted the Chief, his face screwed up and it looked like he was about to explode, but he held back and took a deep breath. Before he could speak, she talked over him again.

'Don't you recognize who this is?' she asked him, pointing at the boy behind her, the Chief looked at the boy and shook his head in response.

'Who is it?' he asked.

'It's him, Mark. Kyle Cross... my son. Alive and well, standing right here...'

The boy walked in front of Erin. The Chief sighed heavily and looked at the boy again, he looked like Kyle, but it couldn't have been. But just as he was about to speak, he was interrupted again. This time by the boy.

'Here I am, Chief.' The boy spoke and the Chief sat back in shock as the voice sounded all too familiar to that of the recording found on the mobile phone beside that dead body found skinned near Hallwood Park back in August.

'I've lived here, in this town all my life and this... is my Mother. My Father is named Kevin and I have several friends... Josh, Steven, Jordan and I know Lindsay Evans as well...' Kyle spoke, with a small barely visible smile forming upon his lips, however his eyes remained unsettlingly still and blank.

'I... I'm sorry... Christ... we must have made a mistake, I can't begin to explain how... terrible I feel. But we tested the blood, it was a match... Do you have any other relatives, Erin Cross?' The Chief asked her, Erin groaned slightly in response.

'Of course I do, Mark. But... nobody in my family has died recently. Unless you suggest that somebody dug up the body of my Great Grandfather, the blood you tested... it wasn't mine, or my son's for that matter as he is still here. You know what I think, Chief? You made a mistake and tested the wrong blood...' She told him, the Chief grew suspicious.

'If this is Kyle... then why didn't you tell us that he was alive earlier? Why is it only now that you have brought him here...' He asked Erin, but before she could speak, the Chief directed his questions to Kyle.

'Where have you been this whole time?' He asked Kyle, Kyle paused, staring blankly at the walls in front of him, then he turned his head to face the Chief. The boy's eyes locked onto his unsettlingly and it was only then that Kyle began to speak.

'I do not know, Chief... I think, maybe I was asleep... I awoke sometime yesterday and found myself dressed in strange clothes, those a man of lesser fortunes would wear, in fact, I would say... that I dressed similarly to that of a homeless person. I found myself on Wig Island, sleeping on top of a pile of blankets inside of a bush somewhere out of sight, out of mind. Maybe I had forgotten who I was, and it was only until recently that I remembered, I am Kyle Cross, son of Erin and Kevin Cross. I believe that I may have suffered from a case of Amnesia, my dear friend.' He told the Chief. The Chief scratched the back of his head in dis-belief. Kyle's mannerisms were incredibly sophisticated and old fashioned even, he seemed to be speaking more akin to that of an older gentlemen of high stature, rather than that of a teenager who lived in Runcorn. It was strange, abnormal even, something was off here, but the Chief couldn't put his finger on it.

'Well... Mister Cross. Can you prove that such a thing happened?' The Chief asked Kyle, a little sarcastically. Kyle nodded in response and spoke again.

'Of course I can, dear friend. My mother still has the *disgusting* coat I was found in and other such wares. I can show you where I awoke too, it should be enough evidence to provide that I am speaking the truth, Chief Spencer.' Kyle smiled again, but only very slight with a humble but small, respectable bow of the head. The Chief nodded back and paused for a second.

'I see... well it appears our Coroner must have made a mistake and the body we found... it obviously isn't you. The test tubes must have gotten mixed up, it's the only reasonable explanation.... again, I am sorry about the misunderstanding. Perhaps we could check the body again but... that would meaning digging up the remains inside of that coffin you had during the Funeral. I have no idea what to do in a situation like this... this will look bad on both mine and our Coroner's behalf... I will inform my superiors of our mistake. You may go now, I will need some privacy before making my call to the Commissioner of Police stationed in Warrington. Officer Truman will see you out.' The two of them nodded at the Chief and Officer Truman, who was standing by the door the whole time, led them outside of the station.

Truman returned to the Chief's office, Mark Spencer sat in his chair behind his desk with his face buried into his hands screaming into them, which made a muffled yelping sound, then he looked up at Truman, his eyes red with tears.
'What will happen to you and Stacy, Chief?' Truman asked, the Chief shook his head in response.
'I have no idea, Truman... there's a chance we'll both be charged with a felony and my job as Police Chief? Well, that's certainly over, I can tell you that much.' He sighed.
'I can't know for sure until I call the Commissioner in Warrington... I better do it soon, Truman. Please... give me some privacy.' The Chief pleaded with his Officer, Truman nodded and left the office respectively.

Chapter 42:
The New Chief

```
November the 2nd 2001,
2:45pm, Sunday.
2 days after Kyle's return.
```

Mark Spencer sat behind the table inside Interrogation Room Number 1, Stacy Evans sat beside him on his end. They both waited nervously as the Commissioner from Warrington was here with a new officer and the Substitute Coroner, David Cartmen (who also worked on the Case in the past). The door opened and the Commissioner looked furious, his hair was short and bolding slightly, it was all grey and his face was severely wrinkled making him look sixty odd, the two other officers that were with him had stern, professional expressions on their faces, David's hair had grown since Mark had last seen him and the other officer standing beside David was a little over weight and he had a shaven head with a face that was only slightly wrinkled. The Commissioner sat down on the chair opposite to Mark, while David and the new officer stood by the back wall, facing Mark and Stacy. The Commissioner crunched his knuckles and gave them both the evil eye. Stacy looked down in shame, while Mark held his breath and kept eye contact, the Commissioner coughed, then he began to speak.
'So... let me get this straight. You thought the body you found in Hallwood Park back in August of this year was that of Kyle Cross. But **two months** after confirming this, he arrives at your station with his Mother by his side?' The Commissioner asked in a serious, stern and authoritative tone. Stacy nodded her head shyly in response.
'Yes that is right...' Mark told him, the Commissioner bit his bottom lip and his right hand formed into a fist against the table.
'Do you have **any** idea how bad this looks on our Reputation, Mister

Spencer?' He asked Mark with anger growing in his voice.
'Yes, I do Commissioner. We found the body and Stacy here did some tests and we came to the conclusion that the body we found was Kyle's as it was the same blood type of his mother's. We also found his mobile phone near the body with videos and photos proving that it was his.' Mark explained, the Commissioner rubbed his thumb against the fingers on his right hand, then he looked at Stacy.
'Well, Stacy Evans. I guess you must have gotten the blood mixed up with Erin's while testing, as it cannot be Kyle Cross if he is alive, however there is a chance that there may be another relative of the Cross Family... this may be your fault, Stacy, but it is the responsibility of your Chief that mistakes like this do not make it into Official Police Business.' The Commissioner explained, then he looked at Mark.
'Haven't you trained this young woman how to do Forensics, Mister Spencer!?' He asked rhetorically.
'Yes of course, Stacy has been with us for years. She hasn't made a mistake in ages, I... I thought she didn't need further training.' Mark winced.
'You thought wrong, Mark... the actions you have taken has left our Reputation in ruins, we are the Police, Mister Spencer. Mistakes like this cannot be tolerated, not under **any** circumstances! Now The Kyle Cross Case will have to be re-evaluated and studied further again and Daniel Harriot... don't even get me started on that. As you may have already guessed Mister Spencer and Miss Evans... we cannot allow you two to carry on this investigation, in fact, you're **both** terminated from the Force completely!' The Commissioner yelled, and both Mark and Stacy nodded their heads in silence and accepted their punishment, they had a feeling this was going to happen.
'David Cartmen will be taking over the Forensics side of this investigation and this officer here behind me is Greggory Henderson,

he will be taking over your Position of Chief, Mister Spencer.'

Stacy and Mark left the station sometime later with their things in cardboard boxes, Mark was oddly calm about the whole situation. Stacy however, she was clearly distressed, she had tears in her eyes and sat on the steps outside the station staring into the box that held her belongings.

'I'm sorry this ended the way it did, Stacy. We all make mistakes, but some are more… costly than others. No point getting angry about it now, I'm not your Chief anymore, I'm not anybody's Boss now, damn…' Mark looked up at the sky, he then took out a cigarette and lit it.

'…I spent years getting to this position, Mark… I can't believe that I made such an obvious mistake. But I thought I done it right, I took a syringe and took his blood and it was a match to Erin's, I don't know… who will even hire me now?' Stacy asked, genuinely.

'I don't know, Stacy… look jobs come and go, I'm sure we'll both find something else to do.' He told her as he began to smoke, there wasn't much pity in Mark's voice, secretly he blamed her for what happened. Stacy sat in silence while Mark smoked, the Nicotine calmed him further, he then pulled it away and yawned as the smoke escaped his lungs and into the air. Stacy picked up her box and unlocked her car that was parked up nearby, she put the box in her boot and entered the car and drove off. She didn't wave at Mark as she left, neither did Mark he ignored her car passing and continued to smoke on. Once he had finished, he threw it on the ground, his other cigarette buds lay on the floor from days before. Mark smoked a lot and he smiled at the burnt up cigs that lay in front of him, *I'll miss smoking out here* he thought, then he walked towards his car and as he opened his car's front door he took another long hard look at the Runcorn Police Station, **his** Police Station.

'See you later...' Mark gave the station a sad smile before getting into his car and driving off.

Chapter 43:
Hello Old Friend

```
November the 3rd 2001,
Monday, 5:32pm.
3 days after Kyle's return.
```

Joshua Riley sat on the sofa in his living room watching TV. It was a sitcom about a couple of friends who lived together in New York, he wasn't the biggest fan of it but there was nothing else on at the time. He had a glass of cola standing nearby on the coffee table in front of him and he was digging into a packet of ready salted crisps that he had bought several days ago in a big pack. He was still shook up about the incident that happened back in August, but he was beginning to settle back into normality now and it was fading from his mind. The show, although not great, took the events off of his mind for a while and it was a nice break from reality, perhaps he would invite Jordan or Steven out to come to the cinema later on as it was only 5:30pm, there was a late night showing on for the latest Superhero flick, there was also a new Horror but he didn't fancy it. Josh used to love watching Horrors but after the recent events that took place, watching a Horror about some crazed serial killer or monster seemed somewhat distasteful and upsetting. He was about to take another sip from his cola when he suddenly heard a knock on his front door, he was shaken by this as he would normally get a ring on the buzzer. He switched the TV off immediately and suddenly the room fell into darkness as the curtains were shut closed and a feeling of insidious uncertainly overwhelmed him and it only escalated as he approached the door to open it, only then when it was opened that his fears were rewarded. Kyle Cross, his deceased friend stood in the doorway smiling with a shaven head and formal attire. Josh gasped, his eyes wide open and jaw dropped. He first felt confusion, then fear, then relief and then a mixture of all the above.

'Surprised to see me, old friend?' Kyle asked with a raise of the eyebrow. A simple "yes" is all that Josh could muster. Kyle let out an airy chuckle and patted the right side of Josh's shoulder. Josh stepped to the side in revolt, like Kyle was a Spider or bug that he wanted to avoid. Josh then looked at his old friend and noticed the scars, but those were the last thing on his mind.

'How- How are you still here, the Police found your body, I was told it was ski-'

'Skinned and unrecognizable' Kyle interrupted him and smiled weakly.

'Yes... I guess, they must have made a mistake my dear old friend. As it could not be me, if I stand here before you.' Kyle explained, Josh nodded his head in silence.

'Yeah... that makes sense. So, that body they found, if it wasn't *you*, then... who was it?' Josh asked, Kyle shook his head in response.

'I haven't the faintest clue my old friend. But the Police are investigating and I am sure they will discover the identity of the young man that was found near Hallwood, it's just a matter of time.' Kyle smiled again, this time it was more apparent than the last. The smile put Josh at ease and he smiled a little himself.

'I'm glad you're alive, mate. It's been rough, but I'm sure everyone is going to be thrilled to hear the good news.' Josh nodded and shook Kyle's hand, Kyle smiled again with a nod.

'It's good to be back old friend, back again... after all this time...'

Josh invited Kyle into his apartment, Kyle sat down on the arm chair that faced the sofa, while Josh wandered into his kitchen to get Kyle a beer.

'Here you go mate, enjoy.' Josh said as he handed Kyle a can of larger,

Kyle looked at it a bit snobbishly then smiled at Josh and thanked him.

'Thank you, friend.' Kyle said. Josh then sat down on the sofa and took a sip from his now half-full glass of cola, he placed it back down on the coffee table in front of him and let out a satisfied sigh as he leant back into the cushions of the sofa, Josh then looked at Kyle and noticed that he was staring at him a little creepily.

'So...' Josh broke the silence.

'Where have you been this whole time, Kyle?' Josh asked him, and Kyle paused for a second before responding.

'...Honestly... I have no idea friend, it is strange. I awoke near Wig Island, surrounded by trees in a wooded area, I lay on an old worn out mattress, it was *disgusting*. My clothes were just as bad, I wore an old leather jacket with holes in it and trousers that looked equally improper. I had no idea how or why I was even there in the first place. All I knew, is that I had to get home, out of the cold and see my Mother. So, I did just that and apparently, I have been away for quite some time, two months in fact, unbelievable!' Kyle exclaimed. Josh sat in silence, listening in dis-belief and curiosity, Kyle seen this and continued.

'It is a strange tale indeed, I must admit, but it is the truth my friend... I have no memory of the night out we had back in August, but my Mother told me I disappeared with some girl... who was later found dead. I heard that the Police interrogated my Mother, thinking she was behind the murder and that I was hiding somewhere. I do not know what happened that night, but my best guess... I was attacked by the same Culprit who killed Tiffany Wright, the Killer must have hit me in the head which gave me severe head trauma, then I forgotten who I was and I've been wandering around with Amnesia this whole time, it would explain the scars upon my forehead, wouldn't it?' Kyle asked his friend, Josh paused and thought about the possibility.

'Yeah... that does make sense, so you think the Killer attacked you, then you got Amnesia?' Josh replied.

'Exactly!' Kyle exclaimed with a smile.

'Well... that seems strange. Everyone has been looking for you Kyle. It is odd that nobody came across you.' Josh said while scratching the back of his head.

'Hmm... that is strange, I must say. I guess I hid well, I must have been scared my dear friend, hiding away in Wig Island this whole time.' Kyle explained with a saddened smile.

'Besides it does not matter now, we've all been affected by this in some way or another. The last two months of my life have simply vanished and I can't remember a thing... Mother and Father must have been so worried and I am sure this has affected you and the others just as much.' Kyle explained with a saddened sigh. Josh took another sip of his cola, it was almost bad timing. He put the glass down and began to speak.

'Hey... well it's all over now, Kyle. That Daniel confessed to the killings and we know he's behind bars. Even though this is so hard to believe I'm glad you're back, me and the lads have missed you mate. Say... why don't we all go on a night out again, I know that's how this all started but it's been two months since he was put away and there hasn't even been a fight since. It will be a good way to see all of your friends again and let everyone know you're alive and well, and that the Police made a mistake. We won't drink too much and we'll all keep an eye on you to make sure you don't go missing.' Josh suggested the idea and Kyle paused, thinking about the offer.

'I doubt my mother would approve, *Mister Riley*. But, I am 19 and I can make my own decisions, so... yes, I think I will go out with you and the **lads**. When do you suggest that we throw such an event?' Kyle asked and Josh thought about it, then he clicked his fingers and chuckled.

'I know... how about this Thursday? You see it's not too busy then as it's only a weekday plus the town should be quiet because it'll be the day after Bonfire Night. We can all just hang out in The Kings Bar after work as it will be dead in there. It will just be a little catch up with the lads, that's all, that sound good?' Josh asked.

'That sounds superb!' Kyle smiled and brought his can of larger up for a toast, Josh cheered and tapped his glass of cola against his can. Josh did find Kyle's posh manner of speaking strange but he didn't question it as he thought that maybe it was a side effect of his Amnesia. However, there were a few things that still didn't make sense. If Kyle really had Amnesia and was living like a homeless person, why was his hair cut so short? Who would have shaven it and not inform anyone of his whereabouts? What happened to the smart clothes he was wearing on the night that he disappeared? Why was Kyle's phone found near the dead body in Hallwood? Why did the Police think it was Kyle's? These were all thoughts that popped into Josh's head, but he ignored them, he wanted to believe that his friend was innocent and that the crimes that were committed had nothing to do with him. Josh just wanted his old social life back, he didn't care about the technicalities or paradoxes of the Investigation, so he did not question them. He just ignored them and pretended that everything was alright. Even though, deep down inside, he knew that something was wrong.

Chapter 44:
Catching Up With Old Friends

```
November the 6th 2001,
Thursday, 6:12pm.
6 days after Kyle's return.
```

So here it was the night that Kyle, Jordan, Josh and Steve were all to reunite. The others had heard that Kyle was alive and would be joining them in The Kings Bar. Everyone except Josh and Kyle were sat by the entrance of the empty pub with only a few customers drinking near the back watching the football on TV while a bored Barmaid leant against the bar's counter, occasionally eyeing up the lads and looking at the TV, sighing audibly every now and again, Jordan thought she was kind of cute. The woman had ginger hair and appeared to be in her early twenties and she had a slim, slender figure. Eventually the woman left her position and entered the utility room behind the bar. Steve was watching the muted TV from where he was sitting as he was a huge fan of Football, but he didn't support any of the teams playing and they were lower league, so he didn't find it that interesting.
'You nervous about seeing Kyle again?' Jordan asked, finally breaking the silence. Steve looked at his friend and paused.
'I suppose so, yeah... I mean, I had gotten used to the idea of him being... you know.' Steve sighed then took a sip from his pint.
'I know what you mean mate, I think it's a good thing we're meeting him in here instead of that other bar, *The Harley*. That place is busy. Even during the weekdays...' Jordan replied.
'Aye aye...' Steve agreed, then they sat in silence again, waiting. They didn't feel so chatty as this whole ordeal seemed strange and unreal, almost like a dream. Their dead friend was on his way, they had been

to his Funeral, cried over the coffin, said their goodbyes and accepted that he was gone. Yet here they were, waiting for him arrive. They almost thought this was some kind of sick joke, but they knew that Josh was no Sadist and would never make such lies.

Eventually at 6:58pm the front door entering The Kings Bar opened and Josh walked into the building with a familiar face behind him, Kyle Cross. The lads were shocked to see that Kyle was dressed differently. Kyle normally wore jeans, a polo or Football shirt and trainers, you know? The clothes an ordinary teenager would wear. But Kyle dressed more like an old man now with suit trousers that were tucked into a brown buttoned up shirt with a grey blazer and brown formal shoes. It was only the face of the man himself that gave away the fact that he was still young, but even then, you would not suspect that he was a teenager as it was uncommon for one to dress as such, especially in a town like Runcorn. They also found the shaven head and small scars upon it unsettling. Even the Barmaid found herself looking at him in genuine awe. Josh seen Steve and Jordan, he approached them with a smile and Kyle followed swiftly behind without saying a word. Josh began to speak with the two while Kyle stood behind him staring at them both unsettlingly. Steve couldn't keep his eyes off Kyle, he knew there was something off about him, he just didn't seem like himself. Jordan didn't really notice Kyle's odd behavior as he was busy chatting to Josh. Steve noticed that the Barmaid was still watching them all with concerned curiosity. Josh pulled out one of the bar stools that was tucked under the table that the lads were sitting behind, he then sat down on the stool and Kyle did the same, Kyle looked at Steve and Jordan, he smiled a little stiffly.

'It is good to see you all again, my old friends.' Kyle spoke, Steve sat back in confused shock, while Jordan smiled and lay his hand out to shake his.

'Good to see you... I can't believe you're here, but... I bet you're hearing that a lot now, huh?' Jordan chuckled.

'More times than I can count, more times than I can count, old friend...' Kyle smirked and chuckled slightly.

'How're you Steven?' Kyle asked, staring directly into his eyes. For some reason this terrified him, but he held his breath and replied.

'I'm... great, thanks!' Steve rose his voice accidentally. The others chuckled, everyone apart from Kyle. Kyle looked at Steve with a look that unsettled him further, Steve looked away and down at his pint. Nobody seemed to notice this silent confrontation between the two of them. Jordan ignored Kyle's strange mannerisms and accepted that perhaps his personality had changed after waking from his Amnesia. It was like both Josh and Jordan did not want to admit that Kyle's return was strange, or how the way he acted was bizarre. If Kyle could remember everything about his life, how come he spoke, dressed and acted differently? Steve didn't know what is was, but he had this strange feeling that Kyle was not the same person that he knew two months ago.

'Say... it is rather *dead* in here isn't it?' Kyle announced mid conversation. The others looked at him and Jordan rose his right eyebrow.

'Well... we figured after what happened, you'd prefer drinking somewhere a little less busy.' Josh told him, Kyle sighed and took a deep gulp from the glass of red wine that he had bought from the bar earlier. The lads thought it was a strange choice, even the ginger haired Barmaid found it odd, but she didn't refuse of course, that would be unprofessional.

'You know... what happened that night back in August, it was a fluke, dear friends. A **Killer** was on the prowl and he may have assaulted me, yes. But he is locked away now, chaps. We can go somewhere a

little more... *populated.*' Kyle chuckled, again, Steve found that little pause at the end a little creepy while the others seemed to ignore it.
'Ok then. The Harley has Karaoke on tonight and it can be busy even on Thursday.' Jordan suggested the idea, Steve and Josh looked concerned but both for two completely different reasons; Josh was worried that Kyle may go missing again, while Steve feared that if they did what Kyle asked, something horrible would happen again in Runcorn. Jordan however seemed a lot more enthusiastic about going to The Harley and Kyle actively encouraged him by smiling and nodding his head.
'You sure that's a good idea, Kyle?' Josh asked him.
'Yeah, Kyle... don't you think it's a bit too soon, what's wrong with just catching up and talking here?' Steve joined in, trying to persuade Kyle to stay.
'Listen friends... I understand completely, I realize that you may be worried about me as it was only two months ago. But, as I have stated before, it was a **Killer** that got to me, a **Killer** that is now locked away behind bars! There has not been another Murder in town since then, if anything, I am more vigilant than before and will avoid certain danger. That I can promise.' Kyle explained, Josh chewed the bottom of his lip.
'Ok... we'll go to The Harley. We won't get too drunk and we'll keep an eye out for each other.' Josh said, Jordan and Kyle agreed, while Steve sighed but accepted the agreement, *if I stay with them, I can keep an eye on Kyle, make sure he doesn't do anything... out of the ordinary.* Steve thought.

The four of them exited The Kings Bar shortly after and walked through the town towards The Harley which stood on the opposite side a good 5 - 10 minute walk away. It was dark outside and raining moderately, cars drove by and could be seen a good distance away as

the wet surfaces of the roads, pathways and buildings shined brightly against cars' head beams as they approached, the beams often blinding the four of them as cars would drive directly towards them on the roads that stood just beside the paths they walked on. This happened less often as they approached the more populated part of town that The Harley was in, around here you had a long row of chippies, kebab houses, restaurants, shops and small bars. Some of these establishments were closed like the majority of shops, even some of the smaller bars were out of business, a fair amount of buildings lay abandoned as nobody wanted to buy them. The Runcorn Old Town was dying, but it still had a lot of residents and there were a few drunks heading home from The Harley that stood in the distance just in front of them. The street lights that surrounded this area lit the place up in an eerily orange glow that faded into darkness towards the end of the Strip. Kyle looked up at the sky and noticed how obscured it was by the thick black clouds that stood over them high above. As they approached The Harley, Jordan began to speak.
'Haven't been here in quite some time... even before you went- well... sorry.'
'I know what you mean, dear friend, no need to pardon. It's quite alright, I think it was last year we came here last.' Kyle smiled at Jordan, Jordan and Josh returned the gesture. Steve looked away, when he looked back, he noticed Kyle was giving him another unsettling stare. *Better just smile and pretend everything is "fine" like the others, he might stop then.* Steve thought to himself then forced a smile that Kyle acknowledged. After this they walked towards the entrance of The Harley, two bouncers stood by the door, they nodded at the lads and gestured that it was alright to enter as they recognized them from The Kings Bar, one of them was Connor O'Brien, the one who stopped Steve from fighting that lad back in August. As they were

about to enter, Connor made a remark towards Steve.
'Don't be starting any fights now, lads...' Connor warned with a cocky smile.
'We won't...' Steve replied without humor, Connor looked embarrassed, he did not mean to offend. Steve knew this, but he had other things on his mind and wasn't in the mood for jokes. The four lads passed the Bouncers and walked up the short stairway that led into the bar, the door was already pulled open from the outside and was kept there by a short chain that was attached to the wall. Once inside they could hear loud pop music playing and a woman singing horribly along to the lyrics, they turned the corner that led into the Disco Room, strobe lights flashed everywhere and the room was lit in a dark red. A fair amount of people stood by the bar, a lesbian couple danced together at the back of the room near the pool table and dart board, they were holding each other closely and it appeared as though they were flirting with each other, they were both young with short hair and slim figures, one blonde the other had her hair dyed red. Josh noticed this right away and snickered in amused excitement. Steve and Jordan looked around for a free table, while Kyle approached the bar to order another glass of wine. Two Barmaids and a male Bartender ran around behind the bar serving as many people as they could while a younger boy walked around with a cloth cleaning the services (he must have been too young to serve alcohol) Kyle looked around while he was waiting and noticed the woman singing with a microphone on the small stage that stood on the south west side of the club. She looked rough and was clearly intoxicated, swaying from left to right. Kyle found this amusing and as he watched he suddenly heard a quiet yell behind him under the sounds of her voice, he turned around and faced the bar, a chubby Barmaid with blonde hair held out a glass of red wine for Kyle to take, he thanked the woman politely and took the glass from her hands, she

smiled forcefully and returned to her duties. The lads were sitting at a table near the stage that had the DJ and singing woman, he sat down and joined them.

About ten minutes later, they were all sitting around drinking, Steve and Josh were taking things slow while Jordan and Kyle were drinking quite often. Kyle however only seemed to get a little tipsy while Jordan was getting wasted. Josh was having a good time, so was Jordan and Kyle, while Steve kept his eyes on Kyle and was only halfway through his first pint of larger. They applauded as the DJ announced that the current person singing was over, it was a blonde haired man with greying hair who appeared to be in his late forties, the man had been singing a song from the seventies that Steve found cringey, but the others didn't seem to care. As the drunk walked off stage Kyle came up with an idea.
'Say... Jordan, you like Death Metal, don't you?' Kyle asked with an odd smile.
'Hells yeah! Man, wh- why you ask... mate?' Jordan laughed and slouched in his chair with his pint in hand, a bit of it spilt over. Josh had a concerned expression on his face.
'Well... why don't we give it ago, aye?' Kyle asked while pointing at the stage.
'You- you want to do... Karaoke?' Jordan asked, with a puzzled expression.
'Unlike you, Kyle.' Josh remarked, Steve then leaned into Josh's ear and whispered, "Everything *HE* has done, has been unlike Kyle..." Josh sighed and nodded his head in response, Kyle didn't hear the exchange but knew Steve was talking about him. He gave him another glare that Steve didn't like.
'So... what do you say, old chap?' Kyle asked Jordan again, Jordan took another large gulp from his pint.

'You're on!' he laughed, Kyle smiled and stood up from his seat and approached the balding DJ who was behind the stage, the DJ leaned over his equipment to hear what Kyle had to say.

'You alright mate, what do you want to sing?' The DJ asked him, Kyle stared into his eyes.

'Play Dead Evil by The Army of Dark.' Kyle told him blankly, the DJ rose his greying eyebrows.

'Ah a classic rock song, eh? Might be a bit odd for this crowd, but...' The DJ looked around at the people in the bar, he noticed the lesbian couple were Rocker types and there were a couple of men in Rockstar attire, he also noticed Kyle's mate who also appeared to be into Rock.

'Yeah... I'm sure some of these folks would like it, hell I'd like the change! It's from my era you see, you singing this one alone?' The DJ asked.

'No, I'll be singing with him!' Kyle smirked and pointed at Jordan.

'Ah I thought so, I bet he requested this didn't he?' The DJ chuckled over the music.

Kyle shook his head with only a slight smile.

'Oh so it was you... alright no problem lad, I'll put it on after this song is over.' The DJ smiled, Kyle smiled back and sat down with his "friends". As they waited for the current song to end a girl caught Josh's eye, he smiled at her, but the girl had her eyes upon Kyle.

'I think that girl likes you Kyle!' Josh yelled over the music, Kyle turned around and spotted a girl standing in front of him, she was young with black hair and was dressed in a red stylish dress like that of Tiffany Wright's, in fact she looked rather similar to her, but of course it wasn't her. It couldn't have been.

'Hey aren't you that guy who... *died?*' The girl asked, genuinely confused. Kyle chuckled softly.

'No of course not dear, If I died, how could I be standing here before you?' he asked with a serious expression.

'Oh right, yes of course... It's just that, I thought you looked like that guy who- you know?' the woman asked, trying to avoid embarrassing herself further.

'Ah never mind... sorry to bother you.' she said one last time before turning away.

'Wait a minute, dear!' Kyle grabbed her right shoulder, Steve didn't like where this was going, Josh had a worried look and even the DJ looked over.

'You must be referring to the Kyle Cross Case, is that correct?' Kyle asked, the girl nodded.

'Yes... I heard that the Police found his body, it's just that you... I'm sorry, I meant no offense...' The girl said, shying away.

'Oh no dear, it's quite alright. I am Kyle, the Police made a mistake, that body they found was somebody else.' Kyle explained to her, Josh sat back in relief while Steve was still suspicious and watched on carefully, Jordan was too drunk to care, he kept drinking and nodding his head to the music that was playing, he was also staring into the strobe lights. The girl stroked her hair and blushed slightly.

'Oh I see... I guess you've only recently returned then?' She asked with a smile, nodding to the music.

'Yes I have dear, that is why the News has not spread.' Kyle smiled and walked in closer toward her, she didn't retreat, in fact she put her chest out flirtatiously, giving him *"the fuck me"* eye while biting her bottom lip. *Nice pair...* Kyle thought, biting his lips looking at her cleavage. Josh and Steve looked on in panic, Josh had a bad feeling this was a trap because he knew that not even drunk girls were this easy and the fact that she wore a red dress gave him flashbacks to the last night out they had. Steve was worried for another reason, he was beginning to suspect that maybe it was Kyle who killed Tiffany and this was possibly his second victim. It was only then as Steve was about to get up and confront Kyle that the song ended, and the DJ picked up his microphone.

'Next up is... damn... I didn't get your name son!' The DJ laughed, so did everyone else, Kyle turned around and looked up at the DJ who was now standing up on the stage.

'Yes, you lad! You're singing Dead Evil by The Army of Dark with your friend...' The DJ announced while pointing at Kyle and then Jordan and Kyle smiled while Jordan got up and onto the stage, Kyle turned to face the girl and asked her to wait with his friends, she looked annoyed but agreed and sat down next to Josh and Steve while Kyle followed his drunk friend onto the stage. The DJ then gave Kyle the microphone and sat behind his DJ equipment. Before the song started, Kyle looked at the area where his friends were, the girl was chatting to Josh, and Steve starred at Kyle like he had been doing all night. *He knows what I am...* Kyle thought and snarled at his so called "friend" *nobodies taking this away from me, I've waited too long.* Kyle's thoughts were soon interrupted when the song began to play. Kyle sung the song well while Jordan slurred every word and laughed far too often, he was hammered but at least he was having a good time. However, it was when the song came to the Screamo bit that everyone started to stare. Kyle screamed down the mic in this deep and truly demonic voice when it came to this part of the song, Jordan had a surprised yet excited look on his face while everyone else looked on in complete and utter bewilderment.

'TONIGHT IS THE NIGHT, THAT YOU WILL SEE THE DEAD RISE AGAIN, THEY'RE DEAD EVIL, DEAD EVIL! THEY ARE THE DARK, THEY ARE THE DARK, OH YEAH! YOUR DARKEST FEARS AWAIT, IN THE DARKNESS OF NIGHT. THE DEAD, THEY'RE DEAD EVIL!' Kyle shook his head around violently screaming the lyrics to this song, the majority of people were freaked, while the minority kind of loved it. That girl in red especially seemed to be enjoying it, moaning and stroking her face rapidly and hard,

Josh had a confused yet amazed smile upon his face, it was a bizarre sight to witness! Steve looked terrified, he knew there was something un-natural going on here and the loudness of Kyle's voice pixelated the sounds coming out of the speakers and it rang through his ears like a bee sting.

'Jesus fucking Christ!' Steve screamed, covering his ears. There were a lot of people hanging out in the quieter area peeping their heads around the corner into the Disco Room to see what was making that insanely loud noise, even the Bouncers came in. The DJ was having an amazing time while all this was going on but noticed that the Bouncers looked displeased including the Bar Staff, so he turned the song off quickly. However Kyle kept screaming and it was still loud as hell, becoming more of a chant now.

'YOU WILL SEE THE DEAD RISE AGAIN, THEY'RE DEAD EVIL, DE-...' Kyle stopped, he looked up from the ground and noticed everyone looking at him awkwardly in silence, he didn't smile as he handed the microphone over to the confused DJ.

'I guess you're not ready for that yet...' Kyle said out loud to everyone. He and Jordan then sat down with their friends. The girl in red immediately jumped over Josh and on top of Kyle, she then started kissing him everywhere like a wild animal attacking another.

'Give it up for... that guy...' The DJ smiled awkwardly, a couple of people clapped while the majority just looked confused. The DJ then put regular music back on, but it now had this broken pixelated sound to it. Kyle sung so loudly it actually broke the speakers.

'That was totally awesome man!' Jordan laughed out loud.

'Kyle, that some very interesting music.' The girl giggled while playing with her hair, she then leaned into him again, kissing him harder, holding onto him tightly. Josh shook his head in dis-belief, he didn't know how Kyle did it, girls loved him. Steve knew there something off about this girl though, she just appeared out of nowhere and looked eerily similar to Tiffany Wright, red dress included. Steve's attention strayed from the red dressed girl and onto the DJ who was standing up from behind his equipment with a frustrated snarl on his face. He gave Kyle's group an evil look as he walked passed. Steve watched as the DJ walked outside, Steve then leaned over to get a good look outside of the window, he could see the DJ arguing with Connor the Bouncer, Connor nodded his head and entered The Harley with the DJ behind him. The two Bar Staff approached Steve and his group, the DJ coughed loudly and it caught the attention of the girl that sat on top of Kyle, she turned her head around slowly to get a look at the Bouncer and the DJ, they both had frustrated frowns upon their faces, she laughed and got off of him, Kyle was chuckling too but Steve and Josh were both concerned. After this, Connor approached Steve as he sat closest to him, Connor leaned into his ear and began to yell.

'Alright, tell your mates to get out of here, now! I've been nice to you Steve, but now you lot have finally pushed my limits. You've broken the DJ's speakers and *you* especially have caused several arguments and nearly fights in this town. You're all banned, now get out!' Connor screamed over the music while flinging his right finger towards the exit behind him. Josh, Jordan and Steve nodded their heads in agreement and began to stand up, even the girl in the red dress looked concerned, but Kyle simply sat there staring at the Bouncer menacingly. Steve, Josh and Jordan (Jordan was stumbling behind due to being so drunk) were about to head outside when they heard the Bouncer yell behind them, even over the loud, pixelated music. They turned around and noticed that Kyle was standing in front of the Bouncer now, smiling right at him, refusing to leave, Connor looked furious. The girl Kyle had been snogging rushed passed Steve and Josh, bumping into their shoulders on the way out, her makeup had smudged and black eyeliner had rolled down into tears upon her delicate, soft cheeks. She cried loudly on the way out, covering her face in shame. They could hear her cries more clearly once she got outside, they shortly faded into the ambience of night as they heard her footsteps distance away. Steve looked out the window and seen her walking away and towards the strip of shops, a concerned couple approached her but she pushed them away with the one hand that wasn't covering her face.

'Get out of here, NOW!' Connor yelled again, this alerted Steve's attention from the girl outside and back onto Kyle Cross who was now standing still, shaking his head with a cocky smile. Steve and Josh quickly approached Kyle's side.

'Come on Kyle, let it go!' Josh pleaded grabbing Kyle's shoulders trying to push him outside, yet Kyle remained still, like a tree rooted to ground. Steve didn't dare touch him, he knew this man was not right.

'I don't see why we should, friend...' Kyle said to the Bouncer that stood in front of him.

'First of all, I ain't your *"friend"*, alright!' Connor gripped his right hand onto Kyle's shoulder tightly, Kyle stopped smiling and gave Connor a sinister look with a hideous wide open snarl that seemed to stretch the very fabric of Kyle's skin, revealing an infinite vortex of black shark like teeth that spiraled deep into his endless looking throat (they hid under the whiter human teeth and gums.) Kyle's eyes also glowed a quick fiery yellow. Kyle did all of this within the course of just a couple of seconds and it was only from Connor's direct angle that he saw all this. He only saw this for a split-second but it was enough for even a well built and intimidating man like Connor to back off and head outside. Connor had a look of absolute fright and terror that caught the DJs and just like that, his fear latched onto him, like some disease that spread through air. Although the DJ did not witness the face of a demon, he knew it would be wise not to anger this strange man, so he approached Kyle slowly with a forced smile. 'Alright listen man... I don't know how- eh... never mind, you can stay, just... don't break anything, ok?' The DJ pleaded and Kyle smiled politely and promised he wouldn't in that posh mannerism that Steve found unsettling. Jordan, Steve and Josh didn't witness Kyle's face transformation, but they realized this Kyle was not "Kyle", Jordan however was far too drunk to notice what was going on and he had this funny confused expression upon his face while he slumped around from left to right.

'So, we staying then!?' Jordan exclaimed loudly, it would've made people look over if they weren't already watching. Kyle didn't even know, *they're in the best-selling show! Look at those cavemen go!* Those words sung through Steve's head as he looked around at the people around them watching on with silent, worried expressions. In fact, those lyrics were playing out loud on the speakers, he hadn't even noticed that the song changed. Kyle seemed to calm down and pull a much more genuine smile as he looked over towards Josh (now just like Steve, this terrified him as well.)

'With that out of the way, why don't we sit down and have a drink, a jolly good time like we planned, **shall we?**' Kyle suggested, Josh was about to shout "No!" when Jordan interrupted.

'Hell yeah! I still ain't finished, give me another one of them booze!' Jordan cheered as he walked over to where they last sat and fell over onto the cushioned chair that Steve was sitting on prior. Jordan's head was dangling over the seat of the chair now and a loud puking sound escaped as a large spray of vomit came hurdling out of his mouth, he held his hand against the chair's frame to stop himself from falling.

'I... don't think so, Kyle.' Josh said as he and Steve ran over to Jordan to help him up. Once Jordan was finished puking, the two of them held him up and led him outside and passed Kyle who was busy watching and sighing to himself, he followed his "friends" outside.

Connor (who was still working on the doors) stepped out of Kyle's way and avoided eye contact.

'Hey, friends! **Wait up!**' Kyle yelled in a voice that was becoming demonic as Josh and Steve ran with their limping friend. Josh looked behind him quickly and seen that Kyle was running after them, fiercely and faster than any human, fortunately they were half way through the Strip as he began to run, but Kyle was catching up.

'Come on, Jordan, run, *FOR FUCKS SAKE*, snap out of it!' Josh pleaded, screaming in absolute terror, Jordan didn't know why they were running but he snapped out of his silly mood and began to run like a sober person, he was still incredibly drunk however but not knowing what was going on and being in such a state of confusion only terrified him more. Even more so than Steve and Josh who both knew what was going on, their friend Kyle was now some kind of hideous monster in sheep's clothing! They ran far and with their combined effects they managed to run into the darkness that was not lit by the neon signs and street lights of Runcorn Old Town. They knew they couldn't out-run Kyle, but they could hide! They spotted a derelict building that stood unlit behind a darkened alleyway, they quickly jumped into an open window that had been smashed in and waited for Kyle to run passed. They waited patiently, Steve and Josh held their breath with their hands held over their mouths, but Jordan didn't do the same.

'What the hell's going on?!' Jordan yelled in fear, he was too stupid due to the liquor to realize saying that was a fatal mistake. They then heard the footsteps of Kyle Cross approach them slowly in the darkness of mid-night.

'Shut up!' Steve whispered harshly as he forced his hand over Jordan's mouth, Jordan trusted his friends and allowed them to do so, he then understood the seriousness of the situation and kept quiet. They waited in silence, hoping Kyle would vanish. It was then that they heard a sinister chuckle come from the outside of the building nearby, they hid under the window's sill in response, Steve could feel Jordan's tears heat up over his right hand that was still covering his mouth. It was then that Josh noticed shadows reflecting against the building's ceiling above them, every time they heard a car whizz passed their head beams would shine against the ceiling and he would see the shadow of a man creep closer and closer towards them every time another car passed. Josh alerted his friends of the situation by pointing and they decided to move in closer towards the interior of the building, all the while crouching and taking light, careful steps. As their eyes adjusted to the darkness, they realized that they were now inside of an abandoned pub or restaurant of some sorts as broken chairs and dust ridden tables scattered all around the place, broken bottles, empty cans and debris also littered the floor all around them. They noticed a bar counter standing in the middle of this old establishment and as if by instinct they all gathered over there and behind the counter, it was then that they heard something climb into the building from the window that they had come in from. It made a scattering sound as it entered, like a Spider of some kind that had more legs than just eight. Josh looked up at the ceiling and could see shadows that resembled long spider-like thorns that reached out far and wide across the room, they twirled around unnaturally making creepy wavering patterns against the reflections that were passing by. It was then that they heard a whimper, an unsettling whimper that felt so wrong it made them feel ill and uneasy just hearing it.

'Guys... please, I sorry, please let me play, I be good...' it was the voice of Kyle Cross but not 19 year old Kyle Cross, no, it was his voice but with the vocals of a four year old. It continued to plead, almost crying.

'I-I-I Just want to be friends... can't we just be friends? And play? Like we used to... Joshua, Joshua, Joshua where are you, Joshua?' That beast pretending to be Kyle spoke, the voice was now fading back and to from sounding normal to uncanny, it would sound real then have this echo to it that would be followed by much deeper and static sounding growls deep within.

'**JOSHUA!**' it screamed, this time it's voice now a mix of the two, like a choir of the devil singing with children, it even sounded a bit feminine as it sobbed. Josh found this both disturbing and upsetting, Kyle hadn't called him "Joshua" since they were in secondary school and this beast sounded just like him, but he knew that Kyle was no more and the tears that were falling were no longer just from the fear. The monster skirted around the area, the lads could hear the thing's footsteps scurry around the surfaces as it approached them. Steve looked around frantically (by this point he had let go of Jordan's mouth as Jordan was covering his own) he noticed that there was a cupboard or cabinet of some kind standing behind them (he didn't care what it actually was!) all he knew was that there was two doors and a handle on both sides, he opened it and they all tried to crawl inside but there was only room for two people.

'Oh fuck, fuck, shit! What do we do!' Steve whispered frantically, it seemed to draw the monster's attention.

'I'll stay out here, I got us into this!' Josh cried, tears really falling from his eyes now.

'No, don't say that! I ain't leaving you out here!' Steve pleaded, but a look of rage and desperation took over Josh as he leaned into Steve and ordered.

'GET IN THERE NOW, BEFORE WE'RE ALL FUCKED!' Josh breathed aggressively, and Steve could see the monster's spider-like legs creep over the counter slowly, the legs flipping outwards and forwards. Steve nodded. Steve and Jordan got inside the furniture quickly, closing the doors just in time. Jordan cried silently in the fetal position while Steve dared to peek through the gap in-between the doors. All he could see was Josh's back and a black skeletal creature stand above him, Steve couldn't make out what it was as he could only see it's arms and upper torso. Steve was about to the look further but then he heard something so deeply upsetting and traumatizing that it almost caused him to faint right there and then.

Josh screamed, no I mean, he really fucking screamed, louder than you could possibly imagine. You could almost feel his throat burn as he let out this painfully loud and high-pitched wail! And it didn't stop there, no he begged and pleaded, and every scream grew louder than the next, (if that was even humanly possible!)

'NO GOD, FOR THE LOVE OF GOD, PLEASE, LET ME- LET ME- LET ME IN, PLEASE, YOU DON'T UNDERSTAND THIS THING IT- ITS -**ITS HIDEOUS!**' Josh looked into the gap of the cabinet, pleading with Steve inside, Josh's face had turned white and his eyes bulged so much he looked alien. His pupils were fully dilated, he looked like he was on Cocaine, Speed and Ecstasy all at the same time. Josh had never looked so alive, so animated and terrified before in all his life. Steve desperately wanted to open the doors, to let Josh in, to save his friend from whatever this *disgusting* thing was. But he knew he couldn't, he knew that if these doors opened, that beast would come in and kill him and Jordan too. He couldn't let that thing to get him, he hadn't even seen it, but he knew it had to be the most horrifying thing to ever walk this planet. Watching Josh plead, beg and cry like that outside killed Steve, but he had to let him die, he had no choice but to close his eyes and wait for his screams to stop. Josh started banging on the doors calling him a Cunt, a Bastard, a *Monster!* but Steve refused to help, he wanted to, he really did, he'd tell you how much Josh's screams still haunt him to this day and how many sleepless nights he had since that night, how he was never the same after that night. As Josh's cries and screams carried on, it seemed to last forever, and Steve just wanted it to STOP. He knew this was selfish, but he had no choice, all he could do now was close his eyes and let whatever that thing was finish him.

Then it happened. After what felt like an eternity, Josh vanished and a terrifying scurry followed behind with the sounds of something sucking. Steve and Jordan waited in the cabinet for what must have been thirty minutes before they heard another scream, this one much tamer and that of a female. Steve opened the cabinet doors slowly and peaked over, the girl from The Harley was cradling her legs on the floor in front of something both disturbing and equally upsetting. A dead body lay on the ground in front of her, but it's skin had been peeled off completely with chunks missing, leaving a bloody, pulsing red heap of a man behind. Steve found it hard to breathe, he knew this was Joshua Riley and the guilt for what he and Jordan had allowed to happen destroyed him and as if this sight wasn't depressing enough, the body that lay below them began to speak. 'Ste-Steve... yo-you let this- ha-HA-HAPPEN TO ME!' The skinned body of Josh screamed one last time before finally dropping dead. Forever.

Chapter 45:
There's Something Wrong With Kyle Cross

```
November the 7th 2001,
Friday, 1:06am.
7 days after Kyle's return.
```

It was just like August 12th all over again. Erin Cross sat wide awake staring at the little screen on her mobile phone in the darkness, waiting for either Josh, Jordan or Steve to reply. She couldn't contact Kyle as he did not buy a new phone after his return. *I should have bought Kyle a new phone when he returned, I can't believe I didn't think of that until now!* Erin thought as she threw her mobile on top of the mattress that stood behind her. Erin Cross was alone in her bedroom, in fact the whole house was free as Kevin Cross was out and about, driving around, looking for Kyle in the Runcorn Old Town. He told Erin to wait as he suggested that Kyle may return and that she should call him as soon as their son returns, she agreed with her ex-husband and has been waiting nervously all night for Kyle to return. They did not want him to go out drinking in the first place, but Kyle promised that he would be careful and would return before 11pm as it was only a Thursday and a quick little catch up with his old friends to let them know that "I am alive and well" as he put it. Erin groaned, she loved her son but the way he had been acting lately, it really got under her skin. He now came across as incredibly patronizing and a little sarcastic. Erin looked at the clock inside her bedroom that was barely visible due to the darkness of night, but she could just about make out the time and the clock fingers said that it was now 10 past 1 in the morning. Erin choked as she had no idea that it was that late and she was now even more upset about her son and the fact that none of his friends cared to reply to her texts or phone calls made things all the more worrisome. Erin sat down on the bed and picked up her phone again in the hopes that there would be a new message, she did not hear a ring tone (even though she set the volume to max) but she hoped that perhaps she had received one without it notifying her, she was disappointed to see that there were no new messages in her inbox. Erin Cross had done this a total of 13 times now and every time she checked, there were no new replies. She was getting desperate now, so she decided to call Kevin again, to see if he had any leads. She dialed his number and waited impatiently for him to pick up. The phone rang three times, then she heard Kevin's voice, he sounded distressed.

'Kevin... what-what's wrong?' Erin asked nervously, she knew the news was going to bad and a part of her wanted to hang up right there and then.

'Kyle's friend... Joshua Riley... he's... *dead...*' Kevin told her, she could hear fear in his voice.

'Oh my god... how... I... what happened?' Erin asked.

'Nobody knows, the Police have guarded off the premises from where his body was found. I spotted Steve talking to an officer outside near an ambulance, I sneaked around as I had a feeling this may have had something to do with our son. It was then that I heard him say that it was Josh who was murdered. I saw the body bag they put his body inside of, there are Police all over the place. It may be on the News, I think you should proba-'

It was then that Erin heard the door downstairs open, she hung up the phone immediately and ran downstairs to greet whoever had entered, she presumed that it would be her son. She approached the front door and seen that it had been opened inwards, the night's breeze came floating in with moths who were attracted by the light. Erin gently closed the door over and smiled slightly. She then turned around and entered the living room, but her glee was short lived as she soon noticed that Kyle's jacket lay on the sofa with patches of blood all over it.

'Kyle!' Erin screamed as she looked up and seen that the kitchen door had been left open with the lights turned off inside. Erin ran around the corner to get a look inside the kitchen, the lights were off so all she could see was the silhouette of a man cradling himself on the ground, his back facing her. The man cried but his cries seemed to echo like they were inside of a long, narrow, dark and empty tunnel. Erin figured this must have been a hallucination of some sorts due to the stress, so she brushed it off and flipped on the light switch that stood inside the doorway of the kitchen against the wall. The light flickered for a brief moment, then it cut out completely as the long beam fell to the floor smashing loudly against the hard black and white tiles. Erin let out a surprised whelp and caught the sight of the naked man's back within that short glimpse of light. It was covered in scars and there were patches of blood leaking out slowly, his skin was pale, and she could have sworn that she had seen black veins bulging out under the man's skin.

'Mother please... I do not want to be seen this way...' The man whimpered, it was Kyle's voice but somehow different, almost other worldly with a harmony of deep and high pitched voices, both Feminine and Masculine.

'Son... I'm here for you...' Erin said as she walked into the kitchen towards the man sitting in the darkness.

'DO NOT. Do not come closer, I do not want to hurt you, I don't want to hurt anybody, **I only want to live among you all**.' Kyle spoke, but his voice morphed into that of another, but not that of another man, no, she could only describe this voice as Alien. Something that was unfamiliar and disturbing. Erin Cross stepped away slightly and the man heard it and turned his head slightly in her direction, she could see the side of her son's face and it was now covered in more scars and bruised badly. In that moment Erin didn't care if her son was acting strange, she seen the harm that had been inflicted upon him and as a mother should, she immediately ran to his aid without thinking.

'Oh Kyle, what happened to you!' Erin cried as she ran over towards him.

'**ERIN STOP!**' The man growled as it turned around to face her, Erin screamed and fell onto her back, kicking away to retreat from this freak that sat in front of her.

'Wha-Wha- WHAT ARE YOU!' Erin screamed again as she neared the doorway into the living room.

'**I told you, didn't I? Do not come closer... but you didn't listen... and now** I can't let you live!' The Freak's voice morphed back into that of Kyle's, only he sounded a lot younger than before, in fact it was crying in her son's baby voice making unsettling wailing sounds that disturbed her deeply. The Freak cried like a baby with unbearable squirming and scattering sounds escaping from deep inside of it. Erin imagined millions of ugly cockroaches, maggots, flies and centipedes wiggling around inside of this beast crying out to her, a choir of disgusting insects that lived inside, trying to mimic human vocals. The Freak's black skeletal hand reached out and grabbed her foot, she seen it within the artificial light of the bulbs hanging in the living room. She could clearly see the hand's bones under all of the gore, blood and elasticated skin that had been peeled backwards revealing it's freakishly long fingers with razor sharp nails that cut deeply into her right calf, cutting through the fabric of her trousers. She could feel her blood rinsing out quickly and the wounds that it left behind stung more than you could imagine. As she kicked the hand away, she could feel the warmth of her blood pool under her feet as they slipped around haphazardly trying to get up from off the ground, it was then that the monster wrapped it's long fingers around her upper legs and pulled her along the floor and deeper into the dark kitchen, Erin's tear filled eyes obscured her vision as all she could see now was the blurred out form of the Freak that pretended to be her son. She could feel her head slide against the large puddle of blood that had formed along the kitchen floor as her vision faded into darkness the further it pulled her into the room's corner. It was then that she could make out a single large and boney hand reach out towards her with two bright yellow eyes that peered behind it within the darkness, she then felt the Freak's cold, dry and prickly fingers dig into her temples and forehead, eventually hovering over her eyes. Then the fingers drove straight under her eyelids, lifting up the skin that kept them together and Erin's cries shortly turned into screams as it stretched them out towards itself, eventually ripping the skin apart like rubber. Blood squirted out of the eyelid's veins like a busted fire hydrant and just like ripping apart a threaded jumper, the Freak followed onwards, pulling the skin out over her skull and snatching hard where her hair lay on the top of her scalp. The pain of her skin being removed like wet wallpaper was torturous and she shook around frantically trying to get away, all the while screaming so loud it felt like her lungs were about to explode. But there was nothing she could do as the Freak had impossible strength that held her tightly in place with its un-naturally long hands that somehow managed to wrap around her small waist like she was some small animal within the hands of a relentless Predator. Once the Freak had ripped her scalp off with ugly chunks of flesh and blood soaked hair strands still attached to it, it continued to pull apart the rest of her skin from behind her neck and spine and continue to peel it down her back, ripping the clothes she wore in the progress. She screamed more as her skin would often stick and refuse to fold over, the Freak would use it's sharp fingers to cut the flesh that refused to budge. Her body pulsed and bulged into ugly swellings that the Freak would often pop with individual fingers, a disgusting puke like liquid would explode outwards every time it did this to her. Erin couldn't even cry without her own tears stinging the exposed flesh of the now deformed and hideous remains that were once the face that many a man had loved before. She felt her body rise up as whatever this thing was, held her up in the air like a child picking up a rag doll. She could then feel it's right finger dig under the elastic of her trousers as it began to rip them off in a fast and horrifying motion, she was now fully naked with the upper half of her body skinned and the lower half was about to meet the same fate as it flipped Erin Cross over onto her back and continued to peel her skin downwards, she shook her head around violently and screamed all the same, forming her bloody skinless hands into fists trying to punch the Freak, but it's spiked structure only battered her hands more until they were merely pathetic slumps of battered flesh. As the Freak spun her around without care she could feel her own body parts loosen up and splatter against the hard tiled floor beneath with loud and unsettling squishing sounds. Once the whole ordeal was over, the Freak threw her body onto the ground and she could feel her own detached flesh squirm and slide beneath her, the hair stuck to her wet and exposed flesh and she could even feel her eyes (that had been removed by the Freak) pop and burst as she fell on top of them. She expected the Freak to continue, to finish her off, but it never. She lay there, unable to speak, unable to see, unable to hear, smell or even move. All she could do was suffer in a never ending state of agony, waiting for the sweet embrace of death.

Kevin Cross was driving back to Erin's like a maniac, he was in a panicked state due to what he had just witnessed in Runcorn Old Town. Luckily Stenhills was not too far from town so he arrived at her house rather quickly.

Chapter 46:
Into The Darkness

November the 7th 2001,
Friday, 1:13am.

Kevin Cross drove his taxi through Stenhills towards Erin's house, he was speeding but nobody was around to notice or care. He barely parked his car on the curb outside, opening the car door quickly without locking it behind him as he exited. Kevin ran towards Erin's house and the sight of her front door wide open sent chills through his whole body. He gasped, and his light run turned into a complete sprint as he approached the house screaming Erin's name. He looked into the doorway and there were no lights on inside the house and a cold, un-inviting stink hid within the darkness right in front of him, he held his breath and entered without caution. As soon as Kevin entered the house the front door slammed shut as if somebody from outside closed the door behind him, the sudden slam made Kevin jump and when he turned around to inspect it, there was nobody standing outside, or at least he could see no one standing behind the stained glass windows that were attached to the door. He turned around and looked in the doorway leading into the living room, all was dark inside, the only light coming from the street lights outside. The smell from outside smelt all the more foul, once sealed within the confines of Erin's house and Kevin almost gagged from the sudden stench that filled his nostrils, but he held his breath, covered his nose and mouth, then wandered further into the darkness. His eyes adjusted to his environment rather quickly and soon he could make out the sofa, TV and the small space that allowed him to walk passed the area and towards the kitchen, he turned to face the kitchen's interior and that hideous smell that assaulted his senses only grew stronger the more he ventured further. A part of him wanted to walk away due to how disgusting the stench was, but he knew this had something to do with his love, Erin Cross. He knew she must have been in a really bad state and he just had to know if she was alive or not, so he held his breath again, (deeper than before) and entered the kitchen. He felt his right foot slip under the blood that lay on the floor, he hadn't noticed this due to the darkness but there was a long trail of thick blood leading deeper into the darkness of the kitchen. He wanted to run towards it, but he knew to avoid slipping in it, he would have to tread carefully, a part of him wanted to return and call the Police from the living room's telephone but he had to know if Erin was alive or not, he just had to know. So, Kevin walked on further, the smell getting worse and more unbearable with every step (he even had to puke into the kitchen's sink along the way) until he made it to the end, only to see a big pile of gore, detached skin and hair that once belonged to Erin Cross mount up on the ground like some twisted mess of a molehill that should not exist. Kevin ran backwards and fell against the kitchen's wall, holding his hands steadily around the frame of the door.

'Oh my god... Erin... what happened to you!?' Kevin cried out loudly, while covering his face with his left hand, away from the horror that lay before him. He breathed heavily, short and raspy, he could feel his heart pounding intensely within his chest. It was then that he heard it, a sound so chilling and un-natural it raised every hair on the back of his neck. A cold sweat creeped down his neck as he heard the words: *"sorry daddy"* echo towards him from within the dark corner of the room that stood in front of him, it was then that he saw the glimpse of a face so hideous it almost caused him to faint, but he held his ground and as he seen this creature's limbs wave around and shake un-naturally, he knew immediately, that whatever this thing was. It was not human. Kevin screamed as he spun around quickly to get away from this thing, as he ran away his feet began to slip and slide against the trail of blood, but he kept his balance and made it out of the kitchen. He stumbled over the dining table in the living room and bumped his right foot against the sofa's legs on the way towards the front door (the bump stung his toe, but he was far too stressed to care) he finally approached the front door and tried to open it, but it did not budge. He heard the Freak follow behind him, it's spider-like feet scattering loudly against the living room's wooden floor. Kevin tried to pull it open again with all his might, yanking on the door knob with all of his weight, but it would not budge. So, Kevin began to bang against the front door's windows screaming for help.

'Help me! For the LOVE OF GOD! SOMEBODY HELP ME, HELP!' Kevin screamed, louder than he knew he could, banging against the glass, stronger than he knew he could. He kept on banging on the glass all the while that beast crawled closer and closer towards him, so close in fact, that Kevin could even smell it! Then he managed to smash the glass open and his hands were cut to bits as shards of glass cut deep into his skin, it stung like hell, but a smile of relief caught up with him as he knew he had a chance to finally escape. He grabbed the door knob from outside and before he even managed to open it, he imagined himself escaping and getting away in his car outside. But Kevin's luck had just run out as the door knob would not shut down, almost as if the door was locked from the inside. It was then that Kevin realized his mistake, the door was locked and he needed to unlock it! Two cold hands locked themselves around Kevin's head, pressing deep into his temples. Before Kevin even knew it, it was game over as the Freak pulled him back into the room aggressively for a second serving of human flesh.

A teenage boy was riding passed Erin's house on his black bicycle when he suddenly heard a loud scream, followed by somebody calling for help, he got off his bicycle and looked towards the front door, he noticed there was blood dripping down the door from outside and the glass from the door lay on the ground in front of it. The boy then heard a loud gurgling sound from deep inside and two large yellow eyes peeped out towards him from within the darkness. The eyes had a hunger so frightening that the boy ran away immediately, leaving his bicycle behind.

Chapter 47:
It Has Happened Again

```
November the 7th,2001
Friday, 1:18am.
```

Sergeant White arrived at the crime scene in Runcorn Old Town with Inspector Miranda Carlton. Officers Davidson, Carr and Truman were already at the scene guarding the Police Tape that stopped people from entering the building and surrounding area where the recent murder had taken place. Officer Carr smiled slightly seeing Sergeant White again as he had hardly seen her after being promoted, but he soon came to his senses and reverted back to a frown again as he remembered the seriousness of the situation. It was a cold night and it was raining heavily, the sounds of people murmuring mixed in with the harsh rainfall. Car beams constantly lit up the area as they drove passed. Blue and green LED lights from the parked Police vehicles flashed the area in neon coloured glows and Sarah could see Steven sitting inside the nearby Ambulance with a female Paramedic sitting next to him, comforting him with hot drinks and a warm blanket, the teenager was clearly in shock; he just sat there staring blankly, shaking back and forth without saying much. Officer Carr noticed Sarah and Miranda looking over towards the ambulance, he approached. Miranda turned to face him with a strict look.
'Tell us about the situation, Officer Carr.' Miranda ordered calmly. He nodded and motioned his hands towards the building surrounded by Police Tape.
'We got a call from a woman named Theresa Black about... two hours ago now. Me and Davidson were on patrol when we got the response, she was crying outside the building and apparently she was with Josh

and the others, moments before his death at The Harley.' Officer Carr explained. White noticed how professional and confident Michael had become with his role as Constable, gone was the unsure and somewhat shy rookie that she had met three months ago.

'Can you tell us anything about Theresa, Michael? How did she know Josh and his friends?' Sarah asked professionally, Miranda watched on carefully as if inspecting and studying her behavior.

'She told us that she started talking to Kyle at the bar, they hit it off and he invited her to sit with him and his mates. Later on, Kyle got in some argument with the staff and she said he had this... *"Sinister"* look in his eye...' Kyle paused with an awkward facial expression, Miranda looked at him strangely.

'Her words, not mine. This Theresa has been out drinking with them, so I imagine the alcohol in her system has altered her perception. We had a Patrol Officer bring her back to the station for drug tests, that's why she isn't here right now.' Carr smiled ever so slightly but Miranda coughed abruptly before it fully formed.

'...Sorry, Ma'am.' He apologized and forced a blank expression.

'No matter.' Miranda Carlton brushed her hand away in dismissal, intending on changing the subject. Sarah laughed silently in her head, Michael was still that clumsy rookie after all, but he was getting better at the job.

'What did Theresa say about the incident. Did she witness the murder, or did she arrive after this occurred?' Miranda asked.

'She told us she heard somebody scream inside this building behind me, when she came in to investigate, that's when she seen the body.' Michael explained.

'Have you seen the body?' Miranda asked.

'Yes... the body, it was a... depressing sight. I think we may have a Copy-cat Killer on our hands.' Michael sighed.

'What makes you say that, Officer Carr?' Sarah butted in. It was then

that he took a deep breath and looked her straight in the eye.
'You remember last August, don't you? The body of Kyle Cross?' Michael asked.
'Skinned...' Sarah gasped.
'Yeah...' Michael nodded while looking away towards the ground, there was sorrow within his voice. After gathering information from Officer Carr, both Inspector Carlton and Sergeant White were about to enter the crime scene when a call came through on Sarah's Radio, she answered and a concerned Officer spoke on the other line.
'Sergeant White come in, come in!' The Officer on the other line yelled, the words buzzed so loud that even Michael and Miranda could hear what he was saying.
'I'm here, I'm here! What's the situation!?' Sarah yelled back in panicked breaths.
'Come quick, there's been another murder, in Stenhills!' The three of them could hear the man's screams through the heavy rain.
'Another... in the same night? I can't believ-...' Michael trailed off and even Miranda had a concerned expression. Sarah darted her eyes between the two of them before responding.
'I understand, Constable Paulson... can you tell us the address?' Sarah asked.
Sarah listened intently and was disturbed to discover that the address was that of Erin's. Michael murmured the words *"Oh my god..."* under his breath as he had heard it too, Miranda turned her back against the two of them and sighed quietly with a mixed emotion of frustration and failure that could be heard within her voice. After a fairly brief moment, the Inspector turned around quickly to face Sarah.
'Listen, Sergeant White... you get in my undercover car and head on over to that address, I'll stay here and go over this crime scene with Michael. Make sure you call back up when you head out, the Killer may still be around!' Miranda Carlton ordered.

'Yes Ma'am!' Sarah replied before running off towards the undercover car. Miranda then turned to face Michael.
'Don't worry about her, Son. She's got this under control. As of right now, I'm going to need you to help me understand what happened here with Joshua Riley.' Miranda Reassured Michael and patted his shoulder gently, he took a big gulp and began to go over the Case Report.

1:27am:
Sergeant White arrived at the Cross Residence, Police Cruisers surrounded the area, (about 3 - 4 of them) with their LED lights flashing silently, two Officers exited the premises rather quickly and waved down Miranda's undercover black car. Sergeant White pulled over onto the sidewalk and exited the large vehicle, closing the door behind herself. She left the vehicle unlocked as she approached the two Officers, a male and a female. The woman seemed more focused and in control while the male looked younger and completely confused, with a spice of fright that was written upon his face. It was clear that she had been on the Force for a while, while he was a rookie, just like with herself and Carr two months ago, *funny how much can change within two months* Sarah thought before talking to the two officers.
'What's the situation, Officer Redfield?' Sarah asked the female officer.
'Sergeant White... you may have already heard, but there has been another murder and I do not mean Joshua Riley. The persons in question are Kevin and an unidentifiable female, who we suspect to be Erin Cross.' Redfield explained. Sarah sighed and paused for a moment. She couldn't believe it, two people she had known, had met and talked to, now dead. This wasn't a first, but such an event rarely happens, not on the same night, not in the same month, not in a little rural town like Runcorn! But there's something wrong in this town

isn't there? Ever since Tiffany Wright, Sarah knew that something dark was lurking within the shadows of this once (somewhat) peaceful town towards the north west of England. She thought she had it solved, but the ghost that haunted Daniel was not the Boogey Man of Old Town after all. Now whatever it was had returned for a second feast of human flesh.

'...Are they inside?' Sarah asked, holding back her tears.

'Yes Ma'am... we got a call for a disturbance in the local area. I arrived with my Partner, Officer Carr here an-'

'Officer Carr?' White interrupted Officer Redfield. Redfield nodded in response.

'...Oh yes, I'm sorry, you're Peter, aren't you? Michael's younger brother... sorry, this situation it is... difficult. Even for me.' White apologized, Peter smiled uncomfortably in response.

'It's fine, Ma'am. No need to apologize, my brother has talked about the Skinners Case. It's upsetting to hear...' Peter replied, Sarah noticed that Peter seemed to be a lot more aware and confident than his more clumsy and awkward counterpart, however still a rookie with a lot to learn. Peter Carr had his hair combed over neatly and somehow wore the uniform a lot tidier than his older brother, he looked cleaner too with a shaven face and clearer skin. *More handsome too, come to think of it.* Sarah blushed slightly at the thought. But this was no time for pleasantries, a murder had taken place, 3 in fact, in the same night mind you. Sergeant White had to be professional, but that blush caught onto the two officers, but they didn't dare to complain or even mention it, she was their superior after all and who were they to give her grief? So, the gesture was forgotten, but Peter was well chuffed. A purple firework sounded off in the far distance, breaking the silence of midnight. (Of course, it was early November and folks still had left over fireworks from the fifth, it seemed almost insulting, that despite the horrors that had taken place in town, life continued as normal for those that were un-effected.)

'Alright, I'm going to go into Erin's house now. You two, wait out here and make sure nobody enters the area. If anyone asks what happened, you know what to say, right?' Sarah asked the two Constables.

'We tell them, this is Police Business and that...?'

'There's nothing to see here, if you persist any further, we may have to legal action against you.' Officer Redfield finished Peter's sentence, with a slight reassuring nod of the head. Sarah nodded back in response and walked towards the door entering the Cross Residence, but before she entered the building, she remembered one last thing and turned to face the two officers again. They noticed her looking and glued their eyes upon her, waiting for further orders.

'Where are the other officers?' Sarah asked, pointing at the other Police Cruisers surrounding the area.

'Oh yeah... sorry about that, forgot to mention. They're already inside, going over the Evidence, making sure everything is guarded off and looking around for the culprit. But I get the feeling, whoever he or *she* was is long gone now, Boss.' Redfield explained, Sarah nodded before turning around to enter the building, ducking under the yellow Police Tape that had been placed over the smashed in front door. Once inside, Sarah noticed that there were already Police Officers, carefully tip toeing around the area, with plastic gloves on and disposable respirator masks. One officer, (a male who appeared to be in his early thirties) led Sarah into the kitchen where the female body (suspected to be Erin Cross) had been found.

'Be careful, Sergeant White. There's a lot of blood pooled around the floor.' The Officer explained as he opened the door into the kitchen. A bloodied corpse lay on the floor, skinned to the point where bone was visible and the flesh, dried up into an ugly brown as if left to decompose within the harsh sunlight of a Summers' day. The stench was foul, as you may imagine, but Sarah held her breath out of respect and dared not to complain. As she neared the body, the officer she was with handed her a respirator mask and she took it gladly (although not showing appreciation) and placed the mask on carefully over her mouth and nose before putting on a pair of blue plastic gloves. Sarah would not touch the body as she knew this was a job for Forensics, but she kneeled down nearby and inspected it with her eyes. Sarah noticed that not only had there been large chunks of this woman's body missing, but there were also small holes scattered around the body in major areas, such as the stomach, breasts and thighs. These were large areas of the body where a lot of blood would be stored, it was like the Killer had been drinking the blood from the corpse like a carton of juice through a straw. It was sick and disturbing, but it painted a picture in Sarah's mind that whatever this Demon was it had a Fly-like Proboscis that it used to suck the blood from its Victims. Imagine a Mosquito bite if you will, where the insect feasts on your blood, leaving a nasty pimple, except on a much larger scale. A scale where it is twice your size, feasting on an entire body until there is nothing left but an empty husk that was once a human. That is exactly what has happened to Erin and Sarah knew it. But if she said this to her superiors, she'd be off the Force in no time, in fact she'd probably end up in an Asylum like Daniel Harriot. Sarah would have to leave that part of the investigation up to the Forensics Team to figure out, it wouldn't be the truth, but, sometimes fact is stranger than fiction. Hiding her Psychic Abilities was often the hardest part of her job and sometimes there's no way around it and somebodies got to pay the price, even if they're innocent. Once Sarah was done inspecting the woman's body, she asked the Officer if they had found anything else.

'Yes Ma'am, behind this body, we found items of clothing belonging to Erin Cross... they're covered in blood and although we can't confirm the blood type, to me and the rest of us, it is quite clear that they belong to her.' The Officer explained. A look of fury took over Sarah White.

'Officer Harrison, you haven't moved the clothing off Erin Cross, have you?!' She snarled in a whispered tone.

'No Sergeant White. We found the clothes inside of the utility room just in front of you, some clothes have been stuffed inside of the washing machine. We suspect the culprit must have been trying to hide his tracks.' Officer Harrison explained. Sarah seemed to calm and give the man a look of apology that he silently accepted. He then led her into the utility room, and she witnessed the scene that he had just described with bloodied clothes hanging outside of the washer. But it was the back door that caught her attention the most as it had been slammed open, with the stain glass windows shattered apart like the ones on the front door. Blood stained the white surfaces of the door below the windows on the inside, indicating that something or someone had dragged something bloody outside on its way out. Of course, this struck Sarah's natural curiosity.

'What happened here then? Any ideas?' Sarah asked Officer Harrison, he sighed heavily with a look of despair.

'I think you're going to need to see this for yourself, we found Kevin's body outside in the back.' Officer Harrison explained as he led her outside the back door, a trail of blood became visible as the security lamps attached to the house lit up the walk way outside. Blood smeared the gravel leading towards the garden behind the house, the two of them followed without stepping in it. Behind the house lay a small footpath made of cobble stones that eventually ended in a straight line and beyond that line lay grass and a single tree that stood towards the end of the garden, the area was squared off by tall wooden fences. The tree stood relatively tall and the leaves were a dark red maroon colour while the bark had a dark brown that almost looked black within the darkness of night and heavy rainfall. Two Police Officers in Hi-vis Jackets surrounded the tree and Sarah wondered why, but she soon came to the conclusion that Kevin's body must have lay in front of them. Sarah approached the officers with Harrison following slowly behind. They noticed her coming and tightened their lips in an almost smile as she neared.

'It don't look pretty, Sergeant...' One of the officers, a young rookie just like Peter said to Sarah, she groaned slightly as she found that remark a little disrespectful.

'Have some respect boy, a man died tonight!' Sarah white moaned in a whispered tone.

'I... sorry Ma'am...' He apologized and stood up straight, Sarah pushed him out of the way, gently. Behind the young rookie lay the body of Kevin Cross, slumped up against the tree with a look of pure terror scarred upon his face. The other officer was kneeling beside it, looking at Sarah. On further inspection, Sarah could see that large scratches covered the body. Large holes were cut into Kevin's clothes, his skin revealed with flesh wounds underneath. Blood also soaked the clothing around the areas where he was cut, Sarah kneeled down and noticed that there was something wrong with his neck. She didn't touch the body (again a job for the Forensics) but she turned her head to get a look at the side of his neck, a deep small hole could be seen and it reminded her of the same holes found on the skinned body inside. She came to a conclusion; the same beast that killed Erin, also got to Kevin, but why didn't it skin him also? Sarah was glad he did not meet that same fate, but why only skin her and not him? Does this thing need skin to blend in? Perhaps. Truth is Sarah White didn't know for certain, she was just guessing, but she knew something Sinister and un-natural was in town she had seen it in her dreams. It was rare that she ever encountered a Demon, but this one was like no other and even she was dumbfounded. With nothing else to investigate, Sarah White told the lower ranking officers to wait outside with Officers Redfield and *Peter* Carr. Once they were all outside, she called the Forensics Team and when they arrived, she and the other officers left the area apart from Harrison who would keep guard in order to stop civilians from entering the premises. Sarah called her superior, Inspector Miranda Carlton, once she got back inside of the black undercover car. Miranda explained that the situation in Old Town was under control and all Sarah had to do now was drive back and leave the vehicle with her.

Once Sarah arrived in the Old Town, Miranda told her that she was no longer needed for the night and that she could go home and resume her duties tomorrow morning. Since Sarah lived in Runcorn Old Town anyway, she just walked home and when she entered her apartment building, she got undressed out of her uniform and fell asleep on her bed. She was so tired that she didn't even bother brushing her teeth or putting on any pajamas, it had been a long shift and all she wanted now was a long, peaceful rest. Being a Police Sergeant was exhausting.

Chapter 48:
Another Nightmare?

Sarah lay in bed, dreaming. But they weren't pleasant visions, they were ones of true horror. She didn't know if they were a by-product of the hideous sights see had seen of gruesome crime scenes and horrific ghosts, or if they were related to the Skinners Case. Were the Spirits giving her signs again? She did not know as she could not tell. This dream was not lucid like the others, this dream was scattered with no sense or reason, merely images and sights of a Demon with black scales and disturbing arachnid features. But also visions of a church scattered her mind, the Church was on fire with sounds of a woman screaming, except the voice was all too familiar, it was her own voice and then something truly unsettling crossed over. She saw herself with the Demon's claws around her! Then she had a vision of her face that had been exposed, skin removed, revealing pulping red flesh, grotesque muscle tissue and veins, with her blood dripping down onto the long black claws of the beast that disfigured her face. The sounds of her screams and fire burning blurred into a hideously tense rhythm. Her vision zoomed out to the sight of the Church set ablaze in the far distance standing on top of a cliff beside a ruined castle, it was a sight that she recognized. The castle and church stood near Castlefields, a small housing area that she and Carr had drove through countless times back in August. In her visions the sky was dark, but an orange glow grew from the flames.

Sarah awoke in a fit of terror as she threw herself around and screamed, when she opened her eyes, she noticed that she was on the floor, the quilt wrapped uncomfortably around her ankles on top of the bed's side. She kicked herself free and stood up, she was covered in sweat and needed a shower, the bedding was damp, and a ringing sound harmed her ear which was strange. But perhaps her own screams caused the pain (she did have a sore throat). She then heard a loud knock on her front door, Sarah threw her green dressing gown on, she opened her bedroom door and as she walked towards the front, she heard another knock followed by someone asking her if she was ok. Sarah then approached the front door and opened it slightly, leaving a small gap. A woman Sarah knew as Zoe stood behind the gap, she had a concerned expression upon her face. Zoe was a young woman with brown hair, in fact Sarah and Zoe looked very much alike.

'Yeah, I'm fine, Zoe... just having... nightmares is all.' Sarah cringed.
'Nightmares? Oh ok... I guess being a Copper is stressful what with all the crimes you have to deal with. I heard you screaming and thought... Well it looks like you're all right, I'll just be going then.' Zoe smiled slightly before walking back to her room, Sarah then smiled to herself before closing the door over. She then walked back into her bedroom and looked at her alarm clock, the time was 3:25am and she was back on duty at 6:30, she had three hours to kill and that nightmare put her off sleeping. So, Sarah White walked into her bedroom and picked up a clean pair of underwear, she undressed and got a shower and after that put on the new pair. She then dressed into her Police uniform and had something to eat with a cup of tea with one sugar and milk. By the time she had ate, washed and was ready for work the time was only 4am. But Sarah thought about the Visions. The Church was on flames and that Demon looked eerily similar, she had seen it before in the dream she shared with Andrew Bates, *the other Psychic in Runcorn.* The Church was a sign and she knew she needed to go there, Sarah had no idea what was waiting behind the walls of that old crooked and abandoned building, but she knew that the answers were hidden inside and that a hideous

monster lay beneath. She looked at the clock on the living room's wall one last time and the time was 4:05, she still had plenty of time before work and the Church stood nearby the station anyway. So, Sarah stood up and cleared the dining table, she grabbed her work gear, a Bible (that she kept inside of her bedside draw) and a salt shaker too. She left her apartment room and locked the door, entering the lobby. Once outside she got into her car and drove towards the Demon's Lair.
'This ends tonight.'

Part Four
A Date With The Demon

Chapter 49:
The Demon's Lair

```
November the 8th 2001,
Saturday, 4:22am.
```

Sarah parked her car outside the pub that was attached to the castle that stood nearby the Church. The place lay abandoned, it had been closed since 1:00am and nobody was around. It was still dark out and although the rain had stopped, it left its mark as puddles scattered around the area and a cold mist lay thick within the air as condensation rose from the ground like the stench of a decomposing corpse. A small ever so slight but clear scent lay within the thickness of it somewhere, mixing in with the dampness. It was a moist yet foul odor that reminded her of day old sweat, except much more rancid and sinister than that. The smell became even more present as she opened the car's door and exited the vehicle. (Yes, she could even smell it within the confines of her car). Once outside, Sarah began to look around. The castle, church and even the old Victorian style pub looked all the more ominous given the situation. From the thick, ghostly fog to the darkness of night and harsh bitterness of a winter's chill. Precise to say; the whole scene looked like something ripped straight out of supernatural thriller. A paradise for horror film enthusiasts perhaps, but for Sarah, it only confirmed one, hideous and disturbing fact; that her visions rung true and that something really was hiding within the depths of this once derelict and untouched church that now stood directly in front of her. It stood tall and hung over her the same way Cody used to when he lost his temper and just like when she was a child that same fear and uncertainty that crossed her mind countless times before, had suddenly came crawling back, like seeing an old bully from school years later, remembering memories of being pushed around and humiliated all come back and you fear that they may harm you again. But you know, if you look them straight in the eye and stand your ground, assert yourself and show them you're not afraid no more, you know they'll back away, *I ain't small no more, I ain't afraid, I'm confident and I know I can do this because I must and I **will**.* Sarah told herself as she took a deep breath and wandered over towards the Church.

The place looked abandoned, as if nobody had entered for years, with cobwebs hanging around the corners of windows and dust blocking out decals from the stained glass windows. The bricks almost black from years of grime had pieces and chunks missing from all the decaying and erosion that had taken place throughout the many years. Moss could be seen growing from the roof's damaged drainpipes as well and wet Autumn leaves stuck to the windows, flying off and breaking away with the harsh wind that blew against it, almost like the leaves themselves knew better than to stick around for too long. In fact, a whirlwind of discarded foliage breezed around the Church in a circle, rotating around the whole building rapidly, going faster and faster as Sarah walked closer and closer. But once Sarah lay her hands upon the building's doors, the leaves fell, the wind deceased and the door in front opened without force. Sarah gulped and equipped the salt shaker and Bible (that she had kept inside her jacket) before entering the Demon's Liar, ready to face whatever horrors awaited inside.

Once inside, Sarah found herself walking through a short but narrow and claustrophobic corridor. The echoed sounds of *something* crying unsettled her and the unnerving yet almost tragic sounds became louder and clearer the further she stepped into this crypt like room. At the end of this corridor lay a door that hung open slightly, Sarah could make out the shadows of something tall with slender limbs reflect from the flickering candle light inside. Sarah approached the wooden door and as she leaned in to peak through, the cries stopped with a quick *whip*! sound as she seen the shadow wisp up into the ceiling real quick. Sarah then held her breath for the second time and entered; in front of her stood the altar at the back of the building, all the benches leading towards the altar had been ruined with time, the cushions once a bright blue (or so Sarah imagined them to be) had stained into a grim, almost blackish blue and parts of the furniture had decayed harshly with time. Some of the floor boards were missing too and the ones that remained were smothered in a dust so thick it left footprints as Sarah approached the altar that had a Demon's touch to say the least. Christ's cross stood upside down against the church's wall and beneath that stood a single candle that lit the whole room in a darkened shade of amber with a Satanic Pentagram that was painted on the ground around it. Sarah approached the Ritual Site cautiously and on closer inspection she could see that the paint the Demon had used, it was no paint at all, no it was thicker than that, darker than that, it smelt worse than that, no it wasn't paint, it was blood, human blood. As the realization washed over her a single drop of the red stuff fell from the ceiling above and Sarah looked up instinctively. She almost screamed at the sight of it, there were three pairs of human skins, strung up against the ceiling's pillars and the most disturbing part of all, is that she recognized them. Kyle Cross, Erin Cross and those of a man she had met briefly a few times at the station, he was a witness to two crimes, but Sarah could not remember his name and thinking of it right now, that was the last thing on her mind. Their bodies had been pinned up against the pillars by what looked like wooden stakes and they were covered in scars and stitched together like knitted blankets. It was then that she heard a loud snap, Sarah's fear filled eyes then caught onto something much more fierce, the Demon itself, naked without its victims flesh to hide its shame. The creature, truly was, a hideous sight to behold. The Demon's skin was covered in harsh, intimidating spikes and scales, it had this oily texture to it and the face was that of a skull that she did not recognize. It looked human, but the bones had sharp pointed ends and the eye sockets were narrow with a much wider jaw and a large assortment of grotesque sharp teeth that seemed to go on forever. It did not have eyes, instead yellow glows seemed to stem from inside of the body. It was skinny, almost skeletal with a tall, lanky and unsettling figure, it had arms and legs, but it also had these monstrous arachnid limbs too that kept itself up against the building's ceiling like a disgusting insect. It looked dirty and sticky. As it starred down at Sarah, *it* began to shake and squirm, making the same choir sound of insects singing deep inside. It spun around onto its front and began to crawl along the ceiling at a tense speed, twisting it's head at a 360 degree angle, keeping it's eye sockets onto Sarah, she could even hear the Demon's bones turn and creak as it moved around like some starved Spider that was about to attack. It used it's limbs to leap from one pillar to the next as it neared Sarah, it was then that she came to her senses and broke out of her trance. With a swift yet terror filled motion she jumped off the altar and emptied the contents of the salt shaker onto the ground around her in a small circle. The Demon leaped across the room to reach her but repelled quickly as it's skin burned entering the Circle. It then stood outside her barrier, starring and pacing around her like some crazed animal, despite the Demon's ugly appearance, Sarah could not help but look at it. It was unlike anything she had ever seen before, somehow human, yet arachnid. Like some twisted monstrosity of a giant insect and human skeleton. It was here that the Demon began to whimper again with an aggressive growl.

'**Don't you stare at me!**' It roared at her.

Sarah looked away, but her fears were fading, and she knew what she had to do next, she needed to use the Bible, so she searched through her jacket for it, but it was nowhere to be found. She turned around and there it was, on the floor besides the altar. But she could not reach it as the Bible was outside of the Circle, way outside and if she dared venture out of the salt, the Demon would surely devour her like it did the rest. The Demon saw this and acted upon it, it scattered over towards the altar on all six limbs and quickly picked up the Bible, screaming with pain as steam escaped from the Demon's hand beneath the book, it then threw the book across the Church, hitting the entry door. Sarah almost cried as that was certainly her last and only hope of ending this all and getting out of here alive, but she still had her Circle and hoped that perhaps, maybe, somebody would hear her if she called for help (The Demon had avoided large groups of humans, perhaps it was not so strong after all?) So, Sarah did just that and the Demon roared, telling her to stop but she wouldn't stop, it was her only chance of getting out of here. But Sarah screamed for minutes on end, but nobody came. Eventually she gave up on that and got down on her knees, begging and praying to some God, *any God* who may be listening.

'Please for the love of God, save me! Somehow, please!' She screamed and cried over and over again, until she could no longer speak, eventually her throat became too sore and dry, then all she could muster was a small croak or cough. It was here that the Demon began to speak again.

'**All I wanted, was to be like you, to know what it is to be *human*. But human skin is too weak, and I needed more... for a while I fit into the skin of a man, I lived in that skin for so long I even gave him a name. You would have known him as *Richard Page*.**' The

Demon told her, Sarah looked at it again, its sight still frightening but the story it was telling intrigued her enough. The Demon noticed this and continued.

'**He's up on the ceiling...**' The Demon pointed. Sarah knew who it was on about, but she didn't need to see that body again. The one next to Erin and Kyle was that of Richard Page, she remembered his face now. An audience of insects inside the Demon applauded into laughter as it chuckled. A couple of Cockroaches and Maggots spat out of the Demon's jaw and crawled along the floor, stopping just shy of the salt.

'**But even his body began to wear and tear... I needed to find a new skin, so I killed that boy and girl by the canal and took his body somewhere *private*, so I could skin him and wear his skin. I didn't think it would get as much attention at it did, so a diversion is what I needed... I kept Richard's skin so I could crash into that other girl's car, I had seen her around before with that man of hers, Jacob Kennedy... I knew he was the vengeful type, so I set it up. I didn't know which one would die, but I knew either way, Jacob would not rest until he got revenge, I would have set up my own "murder" to get it done, but he got Daniel to kill her for him and then I knew the Cops would blame him for Kyle and Tiffany's murder too.**' With every word the Demon spoke, more and more insects escaped it's mouth and gathered around the Salt Circle.

'Wh- Why... are you... telling me this...' Sarah managed to choke out her words.

'**You may have noticed my *little friends* coming out... they're going to surround this circle and eventually, you're going to need to sleep. When that happens, they will feast. I was going to skin you too, but I think you deserve something far more *painful*... that circle ain't big enough for you to lie in.**' By now, the Demon had spoken a total of 213 words, meaning the same amount of insects were now gathering around the Salt Circle in queues, surrounding her completely. There were huge Spiders with hideously long legs and humongous Cockroaches that crawled all over and on top of each other, Maggots and Centipedes also joined into the mix and some were even devouring each other right in front of her, it was enough to make anybody feel sick and Sarah actually puked all over them. Digested Baked Beans, chunks of Toast, Milk and chewed up Eggs escaped her and then the insects began to eat it up and crawl around in it, their bodies covered in Sarah's puke. She felt like she was in hell with a hideous Demon starring right at her, laughing and vomiting hundreds of bugs out of the mouth like an endless waterfall.

'**Maybe you'll faint from how *disgusting* this all is!**' The Demon laughed again.

Chapter 50:
Sarah White Needs Your Help

```
November the 8th 2001,
Saturday, 4:54am.
```

Michael Carr was sleeping, he had the day off today and was intending on lying in until the early afternoon, but fate had other things in mind. He was dreaming, but this was like no other, he had lucid dreams before, but this felt too real. He could feel the air around him and ground beneath his feet. He could feel the rain and the thunder in the distance. He found himself walking through Castle Village, the sky an impossible black and the streets so empty it seemed un-natural, every building in sight had their lights shut off like a blackout without the panic. Street lights blended in with the night as they remained off and the streets lay suspiciously clean and untouched like they had just been built, there were no cars parked along the roads either. Michael Carr was completely alone in this strange interpretation of Runcorn and since the dream felt so real, he believed this was reality and he had no idea how to get out. Whatever this place was, it was somewhere that he did want to be, and he didn't even know that all he had to was wake up. But how can one do such, if they do not know they are sleeping? He began to run, his footsteps echoing madly around the empty streets. He ran until he came across Castle Hill, the place where the castle and church stood, towering over Runcorn like a Hawk. He stopped because a single boy stood a top of the steep hill leading up towards the small pub. The Boy was young and appeared to be holding a can in one hand and something else in the other (it was hard to tell through the blanket of rain that stood between them.) A lightning strike blew the sky up in a quick loud flash of blue and everything around him became clear for one split second before returning to darkness. Michael gulped and walked towards the Boy, who remained unsettlingly still. As Michael came closer the Boy's features became more and more apparent, he was wearing a school uniform and appeared to be in his seventh or eighth year of school, he looked around 11 - 12 years old. As Michael approached, the Boy looked up at him unblinking.

'Who are you and what am I doing here, what is this place?' Michael asked, the Boy stared without answer. Michael stared back, confused and even a little frightened.

'I am Andrew Bates...' The Boy replied, finally.

Michael nodded and stood back a few steps, *perhaps the Boy is shy?* He thought. He smiled at the Boy, but he did not return the gesture, instead he held out the items in his hands towards him. A spray can of deodorant lay in his right hand and a lighter in the other. Michael looked at them and collected them, holding them in his hands, then the Boy nodded and his arms fell to his sides, hanging in place.

'You will need these... the Demon awaits. Sarah White needs your help.' The Boy spoke again in that same blank and emotionless voice. It was then that Michael heard a long and horrifying roar over the heavy sounds of rainfall and thunder escape from the Church that stood nearby. He looked over towards it and it was then that he seen four long, monstrous spider-like legs break through the glass windows on the Church. They were gigantic and strong, strong enough to dig into the ground below it and lift the whole building up in the air like some kind of bug, then the doors slammed open and two yellow eyes could be seen peeping out towards him from within the darkness.

Michael then awoke from his slumber, he was relieved to find himself out of that "world" and back into the reality that he known. He looked

over towards the curtains and noticed that the sun was beginning to show, he could not see what was outside, but a small blue hint of light flared through the curtains that blocked his windows. He sat up in his bed and looked around his bedroom, the room was packed with video games and posters of bands that he liked. A large square shaped CRT Television stood on top of a desk in his room and his game console was hooked up to it. His room was untidy and despite the fact that he was a Police Officer, he still lived with his parents. His pay was good, but he wanted to save up a lot more before moving out. Michael was about to go back to sleep, but then he thought about the dream and he remembered what the Boy had said:
"You will need these" A can of deodorant and a lighter "Sarah White needs your help".

Once he thought about this, he remembered that Sarah was a Psychic and that she often had strange dreams and visions that gave her clues. *What if I'm experiencing those visions now?* He thought. A part of him wanted to believe it was just some crazed nightmare, but he knew it had to be more, that dream was no dream, it was too real to be false. It must have been a vison and he knew that the Boy's warnings must have had some merit. He told himself that he was crazy for thinking this, but this whole damn case has been crazy, nothing makes sense and the Evidence doesn't fit, yet somehow Sarah White was able to solve the Impossible using her Supernatural Abilities. He knew she wasn't crazy and just because HE couldn't see the dead, did not mean they weren't walking among us. So, in a hurried panic, Michael jumped out of bed and opened his wardrobe. His clothes came tumbling out onto the floor as they had been leaning against the doors inside. His uniform was hung up neatly onto the wardrobe's bar, along with a black business suit and a couple of smart shirts. Michael dug through the pile of clothes quickly and picked out a suitable outfit for the rainy morning. A pair of cargo trousers and a thick hoodie. Michael ran down the stairs and picked up his waterproof Police Jacket, he could hear his mum yelling, but he had no time to respond as he had this feeling that Sarah was in danger, serious danger! He was about to exit the house when he remembered what the Boy in the dream said. Michael then ran into the kitchen, switching on the lights as he entered. He began to look through all the draws and cabinets in a quick succession, looking for a lighter or possibly match. Eventually he did find a lighter, it was a yellow transparent one made of plastic, (his mother had bought it from the nearest corner shop a couple of weeks ago.) Michael then proceeded to run upstairs, disturbing his parents and younger brother further, but he did not care. As Michael approached his bedroom upstairs, he could see his brother, Peter, peeping outside of his doorway with a confused and tired expression drawn upon his face.

'What the hell are you doing up this early, bro?' He asked him, but Michael just groaned and entered his room. As Michael began searching through his wardrobe for a spray can of deodorant, he heard the footsteps of his younger brother follow in behind him. When Michael turned to face Peter, he had the lighter and spray can in both of his hands, precise to say Peter was spooked.

'What the hell are those for!?' He gasped aloud and Michael put his finger over his lips and hushed.

'Look... I know this looks bad, but you got to believe me... this isn't what you think it is.' Michael panicked.

'Well, it looks like you're about to commit Arson to me...' Peter stressed and pointed at the objects in his hands frantically. Michael hid them behind his back in a quick response.

'Look, bro... you won't understand, hell... I don't even understand. But... I'm not using these things for Arson. I was after all, involved in one of the biggest Murder Cases to hit Merseyside... you really think I would resort to such petty crimes?' Michael asked his brother in all seriousness.

'No, I guess not... so, I take it this has something to do with the Skinners Case though, right?' Peter asked, and Michael nodded, they both sighed and there was a short pause between the two of them.

'Listen bro, it sounds like whatever it is you're up to... it could be dangerous. Maybe I should go with yo-'

'No!' Michael butted in.

'...I don't know... maybe I shouldn't go alone. But if you do go, you must know that we may come face to face with something... *unusual.*' Michael admitted and Peter looked confused.

'What do you mean by "*unusual*" Brother?' Peter asked, and Michael paused.

'I can't say for certain, but I suspect that we may come face to face with the Killer tonight. I got a... lead from Sarah White. So, I'm bringing protection.' Michael lied, Peter bought it. Just then, Michael heard their parents' footsteps about to enter, so he quickly hid the items inside of his Police Jacket. Their father entered first, he was a large man with greying hair that was originally black and he had a beer belly that stuck out of his white t-shirt. Their aging mother (dressed in a pink dressing gown) followed in next, she had a look of concern while the father had a look of anger.

'Go to bed, both of you, it is five in the fucking morning, for god's sake. Why are you wearing your Police Jacket!' Their father yelled, but Michael held his ground while Peter cowered a little.

'I got a call from my superior. There is an emergency and they need me!' Michael lied and his parents gulped uncomfortably.

'Michael... you don't have to do as they say, not tonight, you've already been on duty today. We don't care if you get in trouble, we worry about you, what with this on-going Murder Investigation after all.' Their mother smiled with open arms.

'Sorry Mum, but I can't... they really need me... someone's hurt, in serious trouble!' Michael lied again and just like last time, everyone bought it.

'That's exactly why we can't have you getting involved Son... look I know its good money and all, but... they can't expect you to do everything now, come on.' Their father explained, his tone had changed now, from an angered man to a deeply concerned father.

'I can't let them down, Dad. That Sarah White is in trouble and I'm not afraid to admit that I have feelings for her. I'm not doing this because they've asked me to, but because I want to make sure *she* is safe.' Michael pleaded with them.

'...Fine then, but come back as soon as she's out of trouble. If other officers tell you to stay out, just go home. Don't worry too much about the job, there are always positions opening at the building site, son.' His father shook his finger at him.

'Cheers Dad, I won't be long. I promise.' Michael smiled before heading out of his room. On the way downstairs, Peter called him from upstairs.

'Bro, I'm coming with you!' he yelled as he ran downstairs to meet with Michael.

'No Pete, don't you go too!' Their mother begged, but their father held his hand against her chest, stopping her from going downstairs.

'Let him go, Molly. I'm sure they'll be fine, nothing will happen to them with the other officers around, I'm sure of it, they'll protect them.' He assured her, she held her silence as they wandered back to bed and the brothers exited the house.

'I just hope you're ready for this...' Michael said to his brother as they made their way to towards the Church by foot. Luckily for Sarah they only lived 2 - 3 minutes away, but was that enough time to save her?

Chapter 51:
Burn in Hell

```
November the 8th 2001,
Saturday, 5:06am.
```

The insects were stacking up higher now, they towered over the salted line, but never crossed, they seemed to be forming into a shape that almost stood as tall as Sarah now. She looked at the Demon, the monster that she thought would be the end of her, it seemed to smile beneath the endless waterfall of bugs that escaped it's jaw. The Spiders seemed to grow, and every bug seemed to squirm faster and faster than the one before it. The sights were making her feel faint and that was exactly what the Demon wanted her to do. Faint, so that its *Children* could devour her to the bone and then feast upon the remains until there was nothing of left of Sarah White at all. But Sarah held on, she kept herself alert in the hopes that somehow, in one way or another, somebody or *something* would eventually come to save her, she found herself thinking about Andrew Bates the other Psychic in town. Maybe just maybe, she could get through to him somehow, it was a stretch, but she needed all the help she could get at this point. The Demon appeared a lot smaller than it did before, almost as if all the little bugs were a part of it, like this Demon was some kind of "Mother" of some kind, a walking, talking hive that all the insects lived inside of. This Demon was like no other and that mere fact terrified her the most, Demons were scary, but at least she could understand them, why they existed within their realms and she knew what they were after and how to stop them, but this one was a loose cannon and not even she knew how to get out of this one. She was beginning to believe that this was it and that there was simply no escape. But she still waited, and she didn't really know why. Perhaps waiting like that would be more torturous than just giving in and letting it happen, but at the same time she couldn't even imagine how horrendous the pain would be. Having hundreds upon hundreds of hideous and disgusting insects dig into your flesh and eat you alive while you screamed was a fate that she obviously wanted to avoid. But waiting there only delayed her unfortunate destiny. *This is it,* she thought, *this is what I get for interfering with Death's Business. A fitting end for a nosy mortal, who couldn't appreciate the life she had.* A tear rolled down her cheek and then she looked up at the Demon.

'Father... Mother... Grandmother... everyone I used to love. I'll see you all very soon.' Sarah smiled, looking up at the ceiling, her face a mess of tears and sorrow. But it was only then, in that final moment of surrender, just before she lay face down onto the monsoon of insects that the door entering the Churches interior sprung open with a burst of light that came from the early morning. Sarah held her breath and for a brief moment or two she thought an Angel stood in the doorway, but instead what stood in the doorway was something far more precious to her than that, it was a friend. Michael Carr stood in the light and the Demon froze and turned to face him. Michael took a few steps back, he knew something monstrous awaited him and his brother, but he did not expect **this**. The Demon was almost skeletal in figure and it had these two bright glowing yellow orbs where the eye sockets should've been and it had six limbs, two legs and arms just like a human, but with two giant Spider-like limbs exceeding outwards from the ribs and upper back. A beard of insects crawled out of the Demon's mouth and every bone on the creature seemed to end in dangerously sharp and grotesque points.

'**YOU SHOULD NOT BE HERE!**' It roared, the voice was deep and melancholy, like that of a thousand enraged men. The Demon began to spit bugs at Michael and when his younger brother peaked around the corner, he screamed louder than he ever thought possible. The Demon then began to twitch and thrust itself towards Michael and in a quick motion the 19 year old Police Officer grabbed the lighter and spray can from his pocket and used them to light the motherfucker and all of its *"children"* on fire! The bugs burnt up along the ground like a flame against oil and before they all knew it, the Demon was set on flames, screeching and dancing around in complete and utter agony. Parts of the insect like creature popped and exploded and an unsettling sound of boiling escaped it as the thin skin that covered the body began to melt like a candle. The Demon's screams turned into cries as blood and yellowish gore squirted out of the wounds like bursting pimples. It screamed again, but this time the scream broke the glass windows around them and a tense ringing harmed the humans' ears. But despite all this, the Demon still walked on further towards Michael and Peter. Michael snarled and walked towards the Demon, still using his spray and lighter to set the Demon on flames. Eventually, it collapsed under its own weight and the upper body detached from it's human like legs, but it still carried on, dragging itself towards him with the insect limbs set ablaze. It was then that Sarah remembered the Bible that she had come with, it still stood by the doorway where Peter was watching on in absolute horror and disbelief.

'Peter!' Sarah yelled over towards him, she had to repeat herself a few times, but eventually she caught his attention.

'Use the Bible!' Sarah screamed again, pointing at the book on the floor. He grabbed it quick, not entirely sure what it was for, but he just did as she said, he was far too terrified and confused to question it. But he guessed that he had to hold it up to stop the Demon, so he did just that and the monster stopped right there and screamed at him and Michael again, this time with so much more hate. But none of them were afraid, not anymore, Michael had this beast, this monster, this *bug* that caused so much pain in Runcorn, under his flame like an ant under a magnifying glass. Michael roared and emptied the entire spray can of deodorant onto the Demon, scorching it to absolute pieces, he thought about all the pain THAT THING had caused to the people he knew and loved. He thought about that poor boy Kyle and his mother who did not deserve their fate. He thought about the teenage girl who was butchered by something that was simply just wrong, by something that should have never existed, and he fought to end it all for good, tonight! All the bugs that smothered the Church turned over and died as soon as the Demon stopped breathing and was nothing more than a disgusting stain of ash and guts upon the derelict church floor. Now that Sarah had the freedom to move, she dodged through all the flames and escaped through the smashed open windows. Michael and Peter exited the premises the same way they entered, and they met her outside.

The three of them walked down the road leading into Castle Village, with the Church burning wildly behind them. At long last, after so many months, the Skinners Incident was now finally over.

Epilogue:

Michael, Sarah and Peter went on to becoming well respected Police Officers. They have only spoken of the Incident with us and no one else. Peter still lives in Runcorn, but the whereabouts of Michael and Sarah are currently unknown.

Lindsay Evans has never been the same after her Abduction, but she has grown to live a normal life with Steve. They married in 2004 and moved out to Cornwall, they now have 3 kids and haven't had any trouble since. At least not on this scale.

Mark Spencer and Stacy Evans were eventually given their respected roles back to them. Many were upset with this decision and residents of Runcorn still have trouble trusting them to this very day.

John Prescott eventually resigned from his duties and went on to becoming a Journalist and Writer, he wrote about the Skinners Incident from his point of view. It involved no mention of Supernatural Activity of any kind. However, the book has since been removed from store shelves as we want to keep the details of this investigation hidden from the Public Eye.

Donald Parker joined the Runcorn Police Force sometime after the Skinners Incident as he wanted to set a good example for his Daughter. He and his family eventually moved out towards Beechwood, a much nicer and quieter area of Runcorn.

Jordan suffered from a Mental Breakdown after witnessing Joshua Riley's Murder by the Demon that haunted Runcorn. A year later in 2002, Jordan hung himself and he is still missed by many to this day.

Prisoners soon discovered the truth about Graham MacDonald. He was stabbed to death by a group of inmates who hated what he had to Lindsay Evans.

Daniel Harriot still remains in Asylum. He is blind, but he is much healthier nowadays without being able to see the Ghost of Jacob Kennedy, however he still hears his voice at night and has been known to have many Night Terrors regarding his appearance.

The Skinners Incident left many dead in its wake. Tiffany Wright, Kyle Cross, Erin Cross, Kevin Cross, Jessica McKenzie, Jacob Kennedy and Joshua Riley were all murdered during the Incident. The original identity of Richard Page still remains a mystery to this day.

In 2002, the 4th of December, a whole year after the Incident. We discovered the burnt carcass of a figure that Sarah had described as "The Demon" the skeleton was similar to that of a human's except the bones were entirely black and they all ended in sharp points. It also had long spine like bones exceeding from the ribs and upper back like she had described. The Body remains with us, buried under Hallington Palace inside of a secure vault for further study.

THIS CONCLUDES OUR DOCUMENTATION.

About the author

Joseph Roy Wright

I am an independent author, who has only published two self-published novels (this one and The New Order of Alexandria) I grew up reading a lot of horror novels from a lot of different authors and I am also a huge fan of horror in general. I've lived my entire life in Runcorn (although I do occasionally like to go abroad). Writing and creating stories has always been a big passion of mine as I've always had these crazy ideas that I've always wanted to express in creative ways. I do hope that you have enjoyed reading my book and thank you so much for making it all the way through. This book has been in development for over two years now. So, I hope you enjoyed reading it as much as I did writing it.

Acknowledgements

Although this book is self-published, I would not have had the inspiration to write another without the endless support and compassion that my friends and family have given me throughout the last two years. A HUGE thanks goes out to Josh, Bill and other Presenters for allowing me to promote my book on Runcorn's Community Radio Station. I always appreciate everyone's feedback whether that be good or bad as it helps me to become a better author. I have met a lot of different people through this passion including another indie author named CeDany on Instagram who has always gave me great advise and even edited The New Order of Alexandria for me. My uncle Ed has always given me great business advice, that I have used to promote my book and it has really helped. Again, I can't express how much I treasure my relationships with you all and I hope to continue this Journey with you all in the future.

Check out

The New Order Of Alexandria: The Island of Hella

by Joseph Roy Wright
Follow Joseph on Social Media

Facebook - New Order of Alexandria
Intsagram - Joe_noa
Youtube - New Order of Alexandria

Printed in Great Britain
by Amazon